"In the deceased's mouth," Dr. Latham said slowly, "is a fresh clove of unpeeled garlic."

He put the clove on the evidence tray. It seemed ridiculously out of place there, an incongruous bit of seasoning that belonged in a kitchen pantry, not a murder investigation. But garlic was also a manifestation of ancient superstition, a vestige of a time when people bolted doors and windows, lined sills with wolfsbane, and made the sign of the cross against the fall of night.

He realized abruptly that it was very quiet in the room, so quiet that his ears were buzzing—that vague white noise caused by blood coursing through the auditory canals, noticeable only when there were no other sounds to mask it. Even the susurrations of the various electrical units seemed to have ceased. The still air almost crackled with silence.

Latham hesitated, then reached up and turned off the microphone. He stared at the body on the table. It lay there, pale and composed, with that perfect stillness that only the dead can achieve.

Waiting…

Tor books by Michael Reaves

Night Hunter
Street Magic

NIGHT HUNTER

MICHAEL REAVES

A Tom Doherty Associates Book / New York

This is a work of fiction. All the characters and events portrayed in this novel are either fictitious or are used fictitiously.

NIGHT HUNTER

Cover art by Barry Apell

A Tor Book
Published by Tom Doherty Associates, Inc.
175 Fifth Avenue
New York, NY 10010

Tor Books on the World Wide Web:
http://www.tor.com

Tor® is a registered trademark of Tom Doherty Associates, Inc.

ISBN: 0-812-51994-9
Library of Congress Card Catalog Number: 95-15466

First edition: August 1995
First mass market edition: February 1997

Printed in the United States of America

0 9 8 7 6 5 4 3 2 1

For Brynne, my best critic in life as well as art;
And for the Bat Pack:
Alan Burnett, Paul Dini and Marty Pasko.

ACKNOWLEDGMENTS

The following people were kind enough to answer questions, offer suggestions, read over the manuscript, editorialize and in general be supportive: Brynne Chandler Reaves, Jenna McCaffrey, David Stager, Lydia Marano, Arthur Byron Cover, Steve Perry, Paul Bishop and Beth Meacham. To all of them and anyone else I may have forgotten, my thanks.

All truths are for me soaked in blood.

—Nietzsche

You can live a long time in Hollywood and never see the part they use in the movies.

—Raymond Chandler

PROLOGUE:

Monday, October 21

The man pulled the faded curtains closed over the front windows, blocking out the pulsing glow of the neon sign and the view of the boarded-up storefronts across the street. In the distance, sirens mourned. He turned to face the boy, who sat on the bed, looking at him with a gaze that was both apprehensive and jaded. The man smiled reassuringly at him and spoke a few soothing words. The boy shrugged slightly, affecting a protective armor of indifference. He pulled his tight-fitting cropped T-shirt, emblazoned with a faded Guns 'N' Roses album cover, over his head, revealing a well-muscled chest and washboard stomach. He was only nineteen, but his attitude indicated that, no matter what this particular date wanted of him, it could not possibly be anything he had not experienced before.

He was wrong.

The man set a small black bag, like a physician's satchel,

on the table beside the bed. The boy had assumed it contained bondage equipment, and the man had done nothing to discourage that impression. The boy watched, fascinated by the smooth precision of the man's movements as the latter opened the bag, reached in and took a firm grip on a thin black leather bulb filled with buckshot. He pulled the blackjack out of the bag and, in the same smooth, continuous motion, whipped it around and against the boy's head, just behind the left ear.

The boy dropped without a cry, sprawling on his back against the bed. The man moved quickly, opening the bag wider and lifting two more items out of it. The blow to the head had been carefully calculated to momentarily stun instead of kill. His movements swift and economical, he opened the small Rubbermaid container in the bag, removed the bulb of fresh garlic and pushed it between his victim's slack lips. Then he dropped the container back into the bag and pulled out the mallet and stake.

The stake was made of ash wood, hard and smooth, one end tapering to a lathe-sharpened point as fine as that of a pencil. The man placed the tip against the bare white skin of the boy's chest. He knew exactly where to strike: just left of the sternum, between the third and fourth ribs, the point angled slightly to the left.

He lifted the mallet and swung it down, a hard but precise blow, done with the ease of long practice. It was like trying to drive the wooden point through a sheet of thick rubber, but the man knew precisely how much force to apply, and only one blow was needed to puncture the tough skin. The stake's tip grated wetly against one of the ribs. Then another strong blow of the mallet drove through the cartilage connecting the ribs to the sternum, and there immediately followed a lessening of resistance as the point slid into the chest cavity.

The two blows needed to penetrate this far were accomplished in less than five seconds. His victim was yanked back into consciousness by them, but the man knew that the massive shock brought on by the attack would keep the boy momentarily paralyzed and give his attacker time to strike yet again, driving the stake deeper. The hand gripping the doweled wood felt it meet a solid mass deep within—the heart.

The man lifted the mallet high and brought it down once more with all his strength.

It was like trying to spear a slab of raw beef. The sound was different as well this time; a hollower tone as the vibrations of the impact echoed through the body. The point tore through the pericardial sac and plunged into the thick muscle fiber of the left ventricle. The victim, fully awake now, convulsed in agony, a bubbling scream tearing from his throat. Shock locked the muscles in tetanic spasm. There was no time for the brain to flood with endorphins to mask the pain; it filled every cell, raced like wildfire throughout the nervous system like the mother of all heart attacks.

The man concentrated on his work, knowing that the paralysis resulting from the pain would prevent interference.

He absently noticed a small amount of blood seeping from around the wooden shaft; the majority of the bleeding would be contained in the chest cavity, the dowel-shaped stake effectively sealing the wound. Once he was sure the first two inches or so of wood were firmly embedded in the heart muscle, he dropped the mallet and seized the wood with both hands.

Only then did he raise his head and lock his gaze with his victim's.

Already the brain was beginning to shut down, its nurturing bath of warm blood draining away. But the awareness of what had been done, though fading, was still there. The man drank that in, watching death fill the other's eyes with bottomless black depths. He could feel the boy's life fleeing his body like a static charge on a dry day, crackling, almost causing the air between them to tingle. He felt himself grow hard, the erection rising violently, straining within his pants. This was the moment, this instant of total communion, when hunter and hunted were one. The sensation rushing through his body was of orgasmic intensity.

All too soon it was over. The boy's body relaxed beneath his own, the eyes growing glassy, sightless in death. The man breathed in deep, ragged breaths, noticing the sharp tang of urine and feces that his prey had voided in a final atavistic reaction. His hands tingled from gripping the stake. He pushed himself to his knees and sat on the edge of the bed. Releasing the stake caused it to break its seal with the skin, and rivulets of blood trickled down both sides of the victim's chest, staining the torn shirt and the sheet beneath. He dipped his index finger in the red flow and rubbed the viscous liquid between thumb and finger, enjoying the heightened tactile sensation.

He stood and crossed to the window. Pushing the curtain aside slightly with the back of one hand, he looked out. The harsh glow of neon and halogen greeted him. Somewhere above that, hidden by the glare but no less real, were the stars. He felt renewed, strengthened, at peace.

The movies were right about one thing.

The blood was indeed the life. . . .

CHAPTER 1

Tuesday, October 22

Except for the constant sound of the city, a white-noise blur of traffic, helicopters, curses and sirens which he had long since learned to ignore, the only noise in the parking lot as he stepped out of his car was the sputtering of an unseen generator. The static hum was accompanied by the intermittent flickering of a neon pink bird poised on one foot over the words HOLLYWOOD FLAMINGO HOTEL.

As Detective Sergeant Jake Hull walked past the black-and-whites parked there, the units' party lights pulsing red and blue, he noticed another sound: the staccato murmur of police band radios. He had learned to ignore those over the years, too.

Jake made his way up the dirty white stairs toward one of the upstairs apartments, where a patrolman was stringing yellow plastic crime scene tape around the door. As he went inside, looking at the carpet and stepping carefully, he noticed a couple of Halloween decorations in the windows of one of the other units: paper cutouts of witches, black cats and pumpkins.

Inside, light from a cracked overhead lamp gave the room a greasy yellow look. The decor was K-Mart clearance table and the place looked like it hadn't been cleaned since Eisenhower was president. It was a room that usually rented by the hour.

Two more uniforms were inside, one snapping pictures with a Polaroid and the other jotting notes on a pad. Jake's gaze was immediately drawn to the bed. After ten years in Hollywood Division he had learned never to assume he had seen it all. Every time he started to think that way he was proved wrong.

Lying on the bed in a welter of blood-blackened sheets was a dead man with a wooden stake in his chest.

Jake pushed back his rumpled suit jacket and stuck his hands into his pockets. "Now there's something you don't see every day," he said.

"Little present for you, Jake," Dan Stratton said, looking up from his notes. He was a slightly balding man in his mid-thirties, with the inevitable cop mustache and the kind of body typical of someone who lives on doughnuts and coffee.

Jake sighed and glanced around the room, pulling his own notebook from his pocket as he did so. He knew that Stratton, as first officer on the scene, would be recording the myriad details that might have bearing on the case; still, it was second nature to him to notice them as well. The windows were all closed, the curtains drawn save for the front window, which showed a two-inch gap of glass. The bed was unmade and there was little evidence that anyone had been in the room for long; the ashtrays were empty, no clothes were strewn about and there was no sign of any food having been consumed.

The cop taking pictures put the camera aside, pulled out a sketch pad and began blocking the scene with a pencil, drawing an overhead view of the room. Jake turned his attention to the corpse. Upon closer inspection he realized it was a teenager—sixteen to eighteen, he guessed. Hardly more than a boy. The body was dressed like a street hustler: tight jeans, T-shirt, a do-rag peeking out from under the right buttock. Judging from the hue and gloss of the bloodstains, the murder hadn't occurred too long ago.

"Any idea who he is?" he asked Stratton.

"Aside from being a dead guy with a wooden stake in his heart?"

Jake gave Stratton his patented don't-fuck-with-me-it's-been-one-of-those-days look. He'd had occasion to use it practically every day on this job for as long as he cared to remember.

"He's Jimmy Ray Tate," Stratton said. "Street kid, hustler, small-time crack dealer."

"Who'd he piss off?"

Stratton shrugged. "That's your job, detective. I just find 'em, I don't explain 'em."

Jake stepped over to the window and peered through the narrow aperture between the grimy curtains. "Don't you love this town?" he said as he looked down at the side street a half block away from Hollywood Boulevard. On the sidewalk a small crowd of people had gathered—the usual panoply of leather and chains. Several drifted away as he watched; a police incident around here was hardly news. Jake pressed a hand to his stomach, massaging his gut and wincing.

"Witnesses?"

"You're kidding, right?"

Jake turned at the sound of footsteps entering the room. A woman a few years younger than his own forty-two came in, attractive but not overly pretty, her dark brown hair pulled back in a bun. She was wearing a white lab coat over her jeans and blouse and carried a medical bag. She nodded briefly at Jake and moved toward the corpse, stifling a yawn.

"Morning, Doctor Allen," Stratton said.

When Sarah Allen got her first clear look at the corpse she stopped rather abruptly. Jake glanced at Stratton and grinned slightly.

"So," he said to the medical examiner, "how do you think he died?"

Sarah started pulling medical gear from her bag. "Offhand, I'd say he had a cardiac arrest."

Jake glanced at Stratton; the latter raised his eyebrows, acknowledging the woman's comeback. Jake asked Stratton, "Who found the body?"

"Motel owner. Downstairs."

Jake watched Sarah take a pair of latex gloves from her case and pull them on. He had thought he was tired when he got here, but now he felt as though someone had suddenly turned up the gravity to about the level of Jupiter.

"Okay," he said to Stratton. "You stay for continuity. I'll talk to the manager."

He walked out into the crisp night air. A Santa Ana weather condition, not unusual for this time of year, had engulfed Los Angeles for the last week. The influx of clean, cold desert air was good for thinning out the smog but the dryness made tempers as inflammatory as the parched brown brush on the Hollywood Hills. Murders, family disturbances and ADWs all skyrocketed during this type of weather. Jake remembered a line by some mystery writer Stratton was fond of quoting, something about meek housewives, kitchen knives and husbands' necks. He shivered, pulling up his coat collar.

There were still several curious onlookers on the sidewalk and in the parking lot. The night people of Hollywood: streetwalkers, pimps, druggies and other assorted dirtbags. From behind him Stratton said, "You want me to round up the usual suspects after the post-mort?"

Jake looked down at the thinning crowd below. Several of

its members looked back up at him: gazes of challenge, con-fusion, beseeching, apathy. The faces changed from night to night, but the looks were always the same.

"Don't bother," he said as he started down the stairs. "They're already here."

CHAPTER 2

Tuesday, October 22

Jake made his way to his desk with a cup of coffee, pushing past the crowd of suspects, all there in a brief stopover from nowhere to nowhere. The air in the big room was hazy despite the anti-smoking regulations, and other smells permeated the air as well: fear, rage, desperation. He glanced at the clock on the urine-yellow wall as he sat down. Five-thirty. His day would soon end with the rising sun.

He reached his desk, the last in a series of nondescript metal rectangles under a dangling ceiling sign that read HOMICIDE, and sat down, shifting uncomfortably over the crack in the chair's Naugahyde. He shoved arrest reports aside and hunched over the computer's keyboard, two fingers laboriously hunting and pecking out the words on a phosphordot image of a Form 187—a murder report. The amber words on the screen flickered and he slapped the side of the monitor. The screen blinked, then steadied.

"You writing up the vampire?"

Jake glanced up to see Stratton, now wearing civilian clothes under a leather jacket, beside his desk. The cop had a grin on his face. "What are you babbling about?" Jake asked.

"What's the matter, you never saw a horror movie? A stake through the heart, that's how you kill vampires."

"Is it."

"Silver bullets are good, too."

Jake leaned back in his chair and took a sip of coffee. He made a face; it tasted like someone had used it to bathe a cat. "You've been out in the sun too long, Dan. You should go on nights."

"Not a chance," Stratton replied. "That's when they come out." He leaned closer to Jake, pulled his jacket across the lower half of his face and wiggled the fingers of his free hand at the detective. "I vant to sock your blood," he said in a melodramatic accent, rapidly raising and lowering his eyebrows as he spoke.

Jake laughed. Stratton was one of the few cops in this division who could still maintain a sense of humor, albeit a pretty black one at times. Every once in a while he could make the detective laugh. Jake was enormously grateful for this and Stratton knew it, though neither ever spoke of it.

"You sure that's all you want to suck?" he asked.

Stratton lowered his jacket from his face. "No doubt the dirtbags out on the street enjoy your whimsical sense of humor." He took a sip from Jake's coffee cup.

Jake took the cup out of Stratton's hand and set it on the opposite side of the desk. "Get your own fucking coffee."

"You don't want to deal with this, fine. I'll take a crack at it. Maybe I'll make detective if I solve this vampire case."

Jake took another drink of coffee and grimaced. "What'd you do, spit in it?"

Stratton sat down on the edge of Jake's desk. "You're in a good mood tonight. What's your problem?"

Jake sat down the coffee cup. "After fifteen years working

Vice and Homicide, I'd like to see how good you look." He glanced up at Stratton. "Look at my face. Is this the face of a man who smiles a lot?"

Stratton looked uncomfortable. He glanced at his watch. "I gotta go." He stood up, hesitated a moment, then said, "Hey, I'm sorry, Jake. I didn't mean to come on too hard."

Jake did not reply. Stratton left the room. Jake glanced out the window at the brightening horizon. Soon the first tour bus would come rolling down Hollywood Boulevard, full of fresh and eager meat from the country's heartland, families who had saved for years to take a vacation in Los Angeles. They would do all the rides at Disneyland and Knotts' and Universal, they would snap pictures of mansions in Beverly Hills and Bel Air, they would squeal with glee if they happened to catch a glance of a daytime soap star, and they would listen and look in awe as the tour guide pointed out the sights of fabulous, mystical Hollywood. The Wax Museum. The Chinese Theater. The bronze inlaid stars on the sidewalk. The tinsel. The glamor.

Hollywood is a state of mind, he thought. The tourists see what they want to see. They don't know that the soap star probably has no money in the bank because he's got a two hundred dollar a day coke habit; that many of those multimillion dollar mansions are owned by people who put more feet in cement than Sid Grauman ever did; that store owners have to hose vomit and shit off of the sidewalk stars every day when they open their shops. Kids barely old enough to shave or menstruate lived in abandoned buildings, spending their days Dumpster diving, doing drugs and selling themselves for a few bucks. Gangbangers like the Goblins or the Hollywood Rats cruised the Boulevard, looking for prey, their weapons of choice lead pipes, box cutters, sharpened screwdrivers. The city was a bubbling cauldron, boiling over constantly.

That was the Hollywood Jake Hull knew. For more nights than he cared to remember he had sat behind a gunmetal desk in a building that had been yellow-tagged in the Northridge quake and had gone downhill from there. He ate high-cholesterol specials from the pizza and burger joint a few blocks down and bullshitted with the other detectives and uniforms while waiting for the inexorable and frequent calls that sent him out on the streets to view a cooling human body and invited him to try to puzzle out the identity of whoever had snuffed this latest unfortunate's life. Because he was a member of an elite fraternity: the murder police. He was a homicide detective. His job was to seek out everything most base and ignoble in the human soul, to flense it with an intuition and a skill born of long hours in the dark, and to build a structure of those despicable facts strong enough that it would not crumble when the full weight of the law was dropped on it in court.

He shook his head. He felt a twinge in his gut: an ominous foreshadowing. He leaned back in his chair, breathing deeply, trying to relax while wincing in pain. He sat down the coffee cup, opened his desk drawer, took out a bottle of Maalox and swigged it, grimacing at the taste. The rumble within subsided, the ulcer settling back into uneasy sleep like a beast disturbed within its cage. Jake put the bottle back and continued his slow, tortuous typing.

"Unfinished business," he murmured, too soft for anyone nearby to hear; it was possible that he did not even hear it himself. The screen flickered and he slapped it again, hard enough to cause the coffee in the paper cup to slop over onto the desk.

CHAPTER 3

Tuesday, October 22

Doctor Todd Latham had been a forensic pathologist and coroner for the city of Los Angeles for the past eleven years. During that time, as he had said more than once, he figured he had seen death implemented by just about every means imaginable, including a woman stabbed through the eye with an electric carving knife, a man bludgeoned to death with a laptop computer and a small child smothered by having a rat's body rammed down his throat. He had long ago accepted it as a fact of life—or death—that there was no limit to man's ingenuity and depravity when it came to devising ways to dispose of his fellow man.

He had never before, however, seen someone killed by having a wooden stake driven through his heart.

Latham was a tall black man in his early forties, wearing, at the moment, a labcoat stained as if by heavy barbeque over his slacks and shirt. Surgical gloves covered his hands and a paper breathing mask protected his face. He stifled a yawn as he carefully removed the corpse's clothing. It had been quite a night, even for Hollywood: two knifings, three shootings and one woman beaten to death with, of all things, a frozen leg of lamb. It reminded him of the old story in which the killer had cooked and eaten the murder weapon. Fortunately for law and order, the man who had killed his wife this way had been too drunk to do anything more than sit crying on the floor and pound her brains into paste with the hunk of meat until the police arrived.

And now this one, to top off his shift. Lying on the autopsy table was the late Jimmy Ray Tate, the stake that had killed him still embedded in his chest. The wooden shaft now bore a dusty patina, having been checked for fingerprints back at the motel.

Latham shook his head wryly. A lot of negative things could be said about this job, but one thing was certain—it was never dull.

He tucked his gloved hands under his armpits to warm them. The examining room was always kept a bit on the chilly side, for obvious reasons. It was a long, narrow chamber, with sinks and disposals near one end and the body bins at the other. Currently there were no other bodies lying on gurneys along the walls, though there were times when the room was packed with corpses awaiting examination.

It was very quiet, save for the near-inaudible buzz of the fluorescents, the hum of the refrigeration units and the occasional crackling burst from the bug zappers hanging from the ceiling. The latter gave the cold white lights an eerie purple tinge. A skeleton hung from a suspension rack in one corner, and charts of organs and muscle groups decorated the walls. Not a place many would classify as homey, but it was as familiar to Latham as his own living room, if not more so.

He made sure the surgical instruments and organ buckets were close at hand, then adjusted the shotgun mike over the table and clicked it on. "Okay," he said, "let's see what Sarah has brought us this time, Susie." He cleared his throat. "The deceased is a well-developed, well-nourished white male, approximately twenty years old, who presents with a wooden rod—"

He paused, pulled a tape measure from his coat pocket and measured the stake's diameter.

"—approximately three-point-one-seven-five centimeters in diameter, firmly embedded in the center of the sternum."

Sweet Christ, he thought. And they say that all those gory horror movies have no effect on people. Sure, and heroin's good for you.

He seized the stake and, with some effort, yanked it free with a sound like a cow pulling her foot out of mud. He measured its length with the tape.

"The rod, which is cut flat across the exposed end, tapers to a point and measures sixty-point-nine-six centimeters in length." He looked at it closely. "It appears to be hardwood— ash, perhaps—and workmanship indicates that it has been turned on a lathe and sanded."

He deposited the stake in one of the buckets. "Put in the usual strict chain of evidence shit here, Susie," he instructed the microphone.

The really amazing part, Latham realized, was how calm he was about all this. You really can get used to anything. He had come to have almost a grudging admiration for the twisted minds who devised ways to kill their fellow human beings. Immolations, mutilations, molestations, all resulting in death, often of a most unpleasant and protracted variety. Occasionally he could still be surprised, even shocked, but not often anymore. Sometimes that knowledge, even more than all the horrors he encountered on a daily basis, made it hard to sleep nights.

"Sorry, Susie," he said to the mike. "Wool-gathering."

Latham turned his attention to the deceased's head. He

lifted the eyelids, noted the condition of the pupils, then shone a penlight up the nostrils and into the ears. No surprises in any of those orifices. He opened the dead man's mouth.

And was surprised.

"I'll be damned," he said softly. After a moment's thought he had to admit that what he had just found made a strange kind of sense. The murderer obviously was not the type to leave anything to chance.

He fished what he had found out of the mouth and held it up to the light. There was no doubt as to what it was.

"In the deceased's mouth," he said slowly, "is a fresh clove of unpeeled garlic."

Latham put the clove in the evidence tray. It seemed ridiculously out of place there, an incongruous bit of seasoning that belonged in a kitchen pantry, not a murder investigation. But that was only one way of looking at it, he knew. Garlic was also a manifestation of an ancient superstition, a vestige of a time when people bolted doors and windows, lined sills with wolfbane and made the sign of the cross against the fall of night.

He realized abruptly that it was very quiet in the room, so quiet that his ears were buzzing—that vague white noise caused by blood coursing through the veins of the auditory canals, noticeable only when there were no other sounds to mask it. Even the susurrations of the various electrical units seemed to have ceased. The still air almost crackled with silence.

Latham hesitated, then reached up and turned off the microphone. He stared at the body on the table. It lay there, pale and composed, with that perfect stillness that only the dead can achieve.

Waiting. . . .

Stop it, he told himself.

A scene from some movie seen long ago came unbidden to his mind: a coroner working late in a room very much like this one, absorbed in whatever task was at hand, unaware that behind him a sheeted corpse on one of the tables was slowly stirring, rising. . . .

Latham shook his head almost angrily, as if to dislodge thoughts he knew to be foolish. His uneasiness did not subside, however. His mouth felt dry. He was suddenly very aware of the faint scent of decay that always permeated the room, a gritty underlay to the pungent formaldehyde, no matter how many air fresheners and cans of Lysol were marshaled against it. It was omnipresent; sometimes at home, or even in the car, he could smell it, emanating from no conceivable source, tickling the back of his throat, dry and gritty. The smell of death.

This is ridiculous, he told himself. Nevertheless, he could not deny the fear he felt, rising and opening within him like some dark flower.

He knew what he had to do.

He drew in a deep breath, sucking the paper mask against his lips, shuddering slightly as the foul air entered his lungs. He leaned closer to the late Jimmy Ray's head, took the cold chin in his hand and turned the head slightly away from him. The neck muscles were stiff with rigor, and it felt at first as if the corpse was resisting Latham's effort to move it and get a good look at the carotid area.

One of the refrigerators behind him chose that moment to grind abruptly to life, and Latham spasmed, leaping back from the metal table and biting down on the cry that welled in his throat. He felt his heart thudding against his ribs, dancing on the edge of tachycardia.

"Oh, for God's sake," he said out loud. Quickly, before the fear could seize him again, he stepped back to the corpse and grasped the jaw firmly. He set his teeth against a sudden vivid mental image of the dead boy's eyes opening, shifting toward him, locking onto his own gaze with a terrifyingly hungry stare, the mouth opening in a smile revealing incisors mutated to wolfish fangs, a hand rising from the table, cold fingers gripping his arm with more than human strength. . . .

Latham blew out a whistling breath, bent close over the still form and turned Jimmy Ray's head first one way, then the other, looking closely at both sides of the neck.

There were no puncture wounds over either the carotid or the jugular.

Latham let go of the corpse, feeling simultaneously relieved and foolish. Satisfied? he asked himself.

The body on the table before him was that of a dead boy— no more or less than that. Jimmy Ray Tate had come to Hollywood, as so many other teenagers had, to live the life of a runaway, perhaps hoping vaguely of being discovered and given a career in pictures, more likely just to escape a family life that was even worse than the abuse he endured on the streets. And he had had the bad luck to encounter some sicko who, for God only knew what insane reason, had decided he was a vampire and had treated him accordingly. Exit Jimmy Ray Tate, no doubt wondering to the last why this was happening to him.

That was what had happened. That was all that had happened.

In a moment, Latham told himself, he would proceed with the autopsy. Soon Jimmy Ray would be reduced to a mound of dissected organs and dry statistics. But right now he needed a cup of coffee.

Hot coffee.

The room still seemed much colder than it had a moment ago.

CHAPTER 4

Wednesday, October 23

The phone rang. Jake fumbled around and knocked it off the night table one ring too late to avoid triggering the answering machine. His own voice, sounding tired, said, "You've reached 555-3549. If this is an emergency, I can be reached at—"

He rolled over, wincing as the phone's close proximity to the answering machine caused a howl of feedback before he could turn off the latter. Behind the message he could hear a female voice saying faintly, "Hello? Jake? You there?"

"I'm here." He sat up on the futon. There was a sour taste in his mouth; he'd awakened with it every day for years, no matter how extensively he brushed his teeth the night before. Darlene had said his morning breath could strip paint. "This better be good," he said to whoever was on the other end of the line.

"Jake, it's Sarah Allen. I'm sorry I woke you."

He yawned hard enough to squeeze out tears. "It's okay. I had to get up to answer the phone anyway."

"We need to talk about last night's DOA. How about we meet for dinner?"

Jake glanced at the digital clock radio on the night table: four-twelve P.M. "You mean breakfast."

"Whatever," Sarah said. "Six, okay? At Toby's. See you then." She hung up.

Jake rolled over on his back, staring up at the beamed ceiling. He knew he would not be able to fall asleep again. He got to his feet, made his way to the nearest window and pulled up the blinds, wincing at the light.

After he had shaved, brushed his teeth and was halfway through his second cup of coffee, he thought there might be some hope of survival. He folded up the futon and replaced the cushions. The place was easy to keep clean, thank God: one room, a kitchenette and a bathroom small enough that he could hit the toilet from outside the room. The only decorations on the walls were travel posters showing scenic views of the Pacific Northwest. They had been here when he rented the place.

He ran wet fingers through his graying hair and looked at himself critically in the mirror. He was probably the only one in the department who didn't have a mustache, though he hated to shave. There were three faint red scars visible along his left cheek, one just missing his eye, from when he had worked Vice and had arrested a hooker who had worn fragments of razor blades under her fingernails. There was also a small puckered scar on his right side, just below the ribs, from a homie's knife. Those were all he had gotten in the way of wounds during fourteen years of law enforcement, thank God.

Others hadn't been so lucky. . . .

He poked a finger gently at the puffy folds of flesh under his eyes. You could read a man's job in his face as easily as you can tell a tree's age from the rings in the trunk. Still, he wasn't doing too bad. He could still see faint hints of stomach muscles if he tightened them hard enough to risk rupturing himself. Not bad for forty-two, he supposed. He managed to get to the gym maybe once every two weeks. It was better than nothing.

Outside the air was already turning cold, even though the sun still hung low over the wooded hills. With a little paint and some major repairs, the converted garage Jake lived in at the end of the cul-de-sac could be picturesque. Still, coming out and looking at the pine trees always made it easier to pretend, however briefly, that he wasn't really in Los Angeles. Though he knew it was a delusion, living at the end of the twisting Laurel Canyon street made him feel safe and protected.

Jake sighed and got into his ancient Nissan. The city would let him go for a while, but it always pulled him relentlessly back.

Toby's Diner, on Western near Sunset, was a classic in the greasy spoon tradition, an Art Deco remnant of a time when English had been the primary language in Los Angeles. Jake and Sarah sat in a booth of red tuck-and-roll vinyl with several eight-by-ten morgue photos on the table between them. Through the window the horizon was beginning to redden in another glorious smog-tinted sunset.

Jake picked up the top picture and looked at it: a head-and-shoulders shot of the late Jimmy Ray Tate, lying on an examining table. "Latham did the work-up?"

"Right."

"You're not going to tell me Tate had bites on his neck, are you? I don't think I'm ready for that."

"No bites. But," she added, "Todd did find a clove of garlic in Tate's mouth."

"Garlic?"

"Yeah, you know . . . garlic's supposed to repel vampires."

Jake tossed the picture back on the pile. "Maybe he had an Italian for his last trick."

"In addition," Sarah said, ignoring that, "Jimmy Ray had just over four liters of blood in him."

Jake blinked. "That means he was—"

"About a quart low."

They were both quiet for a moment. Then Jake said, "Could the stake wound account for the blood loss?"

"We're not sure yet. It's possible."

"Any other marks on the body?"

She shrugged. "What you'd expect. Tracks on both arms. No sign of sexual encounter."

"No fangs?"

She answered that one with a look. Jake leaned back. "Well, fine. If he is a vampire, at least it'll be a change of pace."

"You guys got any leads?"

He shook his head. "Not a goddamned thing. This bad boy slipped in there with no trouble and didn't leave print one, not even latents on the stake. Nobody saw anything, which isn't surprising in a town where people wouldn't notice a chainsaw murder at high noon. Nothing in VI-CAP on this MO. Unless you know something else, we got zip."

Sarah shook her head. "I can't tell you much more. The stake was made of ash wood and turned on a lathe. Driven in by a wooden mallet with two or three blows."

"So we're not after a wimp here. Takes some muscle to punch a piece of wood through a chest wall."

"The murderer was probably right-handed. That's all I can remember right now. Check the sheet for anything else."

The waitress brought them their meals: shrimp salad for Sarah, eggs and hash browns for Jake. She paid no attention to the grisly photos of the dead man with the huge wound in his chest. Jake figured she had probably seen worse in her day.

He shoveled in bites, maneuvered forkfuls of hash browns into the bloodstain of ketchup. "Great," he mumbled around his food. "Just great. You realize this has all the makings of a fucking red ball. Just watch—everyone from the Mayor down is going to have their eye on this—and on me."

He glanced up at her, saw her looking at him. He stopped the fork halfway to his mouth and said, "What?"

She said, "How are you doing?"

The fork continued its journey. "Let's see," he mumbled, chewing. "I got a case load big enough to have its own zip code, I'm driving a deathtrap, alimony's overdue, my ulcer's eating me up from the inside and my ex is threatening to—"

"No, Jake," she said gently, "I said how are *you* doing?" She tapped her chest. "In here."

Jake swallowed, put the fork down, leaned back in the booth. At the other end of the diner a teenager in scruffy, over-sized clothes put a quarter in the Wurlitzer and a rapper began shouting hatred and contempt for everyone within earshot. "Fine."

Sarah rolled her eyes. "Darwin didn't have all the answers; nothing explains why men are an evolutionary success." She pushed her meal aside and leaned across the table. "Look, we don't know each other all that well, and maybe I'm out of line here. But I just had to say something. It's been five months; Stoughton says you never saw the department shrink, never really talked to him or anyone else about it. You think it doesn't show. It shows, Jake."

He was beginning to feel trapped. "What do you want me to say? Shit happens. Part of the job." He pushed the congealing egg around on his plate, his appetite having suddenly deserted him, his stomach feeling like someone had opened the floodgates on a deluge of lava. "Look, you want me to say I still think about it? Okay, I still think about it. I still dream about it, but not like at first."

"And you still feel it's your fault," she said. It wasn't a question.

Jake looked up from his plate and met her gaze. "It was my fault." He stared straight at her, challenging her to dispute him. She met his gaze for a few seconds, then dropped her eyes, pulled her plate back in front of her and took another bite.

"What can we learn from the stake?"

"Not much more than what I told you," she said with her mouth full. "I suppose it could have been professionally made, but it's just as likely the guy did it at home in his garage. In any event, I doubt you'll find many listings in the Yellow Pages under Vampire Hunter Supplies."

Jake nodded glumly. "This is a real shitcan. A fucking vampire killer, for God's sake. The press is gonna love it."

"They love it already. Seen today's papers?"

"I can imagine." Jake looked out of the window. The streetlights were coming on now. Hustlers of both sexes strolled casually or lounged against pawn shops, fast-food stands and adult bookstores. An old man, his filthy clothes padded with newspaper to keep the cold at bay, trundled a shopping cart loaded with his life's possessions past the window. As the hour grew later, the street people would get progressively weirder. Jake sometimes wondered if the ones who came out past midnight were even human.

"He's going to do it again," he said abruptly.

Sarah looked up from her last shrimp. "You think so?"

"I feel it. This motherfucker's a pattern." Jake looked at his mostly uneaten breakfast and pushed it away. "And he's just getting started."

CHAPTER 5

Wednesday, October 23

Dan Stratton cruised down Santa Monica in the one-man radio car, the scratchy mumblings of the dispatcher a constant part of the background noise. In his year on the force he'd learned to tune out all but the important calls. Most of the other traffic came under the heading of NMP—Not My Problem.

Though it was not the sort of thing he would readily admit to just anybody, Stratton still enjoyed being a cop. The past year had left him with no illusions as to how much of a difference he made on the streets—little to none, in most cases—but nonetheless he liked the job. It was the closest thing one could come in the real world to being a force for justice, and the part of him that was still a kid—the part that still read comic books and enjoyed watching the old *Adventures Of Superman* reruns on Nick At Nite—responded to that. Though most of the days were a boring routine filled with endless paperwork, there were still occasions—quite a few, actually, in L.A.—where he got to feel like a hero.

He had joined the force fresh out of the army, honestly believing he could make a difference. He was no longer sure if what he did really mattered to the hordes out there living their scared little lives, but it still made a difference to him. And he was the only person he had to please.

He turned north on one of the Hollywood side streets, moving slowly toward Fountain, passing buildings tattooed with gang graffiti, houses sporting barred windows and doors, decaying furniture piled next to the curb. It was evening; he'd been on shift for about two hours. He was doing a four-to-one: four P.M. to one A.M. He hoped there wouldn't be any heavy-duty problems tonight. He wasn't up to it.

Stratton wondered if he would look like Jake Hull after he'd been that long on the force. The man's face had the lived-in, rundown look of a projects tenement. Christ, he hoped he wouldn't wind up a burn-out case like that. Most cops seemed to think it was inevitable; that the longer you're out on the streets, the further down it brings you. Until you're so far down there's no way up.

His comrades in arms had told him, over drinks at the Blue Light, that the world was divided into two camps: cops and everybody else. He could feel that already, even in the short time he'd worn the uniform. The worst part was learning that to most people most of the time he wasn't a hero. The first time he'd walked into a restaurant for a bite to eat everyone had stopped talking and stared—cold, resentful stares that said as plain as words that he was unwelcome there. An outsider, a stranger with blue skin who had no right to be in there unless he was preventing a crime.

He hoped that would change as he rose in the ranks and was eventually able to make Detective and drop the uniform. But that would be years from now. Right now he was a lowly P-II, a grunt; the only ones below him were the rookies.

He drove slowly down one of the small back streets in the

Hollywood area. The avenue was lined on both sides with auto parts shops, burned-out and barred storefronts, and bungalow-style buildings housing independent film production companies. One of the richer ironies about Hollywood was that, while junkies were making love to needles and probably giving themselves AIDS in the buildings' recessed doorways, television shows that cost a million-and-a-half an hour to produce were being plotted behind those doors.

Only in this town would you find a case like the one he'd discovered last night. A fucking vampire killer, for Christ's sake—some crazy latter-day Van Helsing ditty-bopping around the city staking citizens who had the misfortune to look a little long in the tooth, so to speak. Did cops in other cities have problems like this? Dan wondered. Did uniforms in Detroit, say, or Minneapolis have to contend with fruitcakes ripping people apart every full moon like werewolves? Were cops in Salt Lake City right now barricaded in their precincts against waves of zombie Mormons? Not likely. But here, right here in River City, he had answered a call by a hysterical motel night manager and found that someone was trying to keep Los Angeles safe from being overrun by hordes of the undead. Un-fucking-believable.

Well, the good news is he won't last long, Dan told himself as he turned east on Hollywood Boulevard, passing the old Aztec Theater. Assuming it isn't a one-shot. Then it's going to be damned hard to nail the bastard. Every cop knew that a random murder still unsolved after seventy-two hours usually remains unsolved permanently. But if "Van Helsing" was a pattern killer, if he kept hammering people the same way, it was only a matter of time. Stakes through the chest weren't exactly low-profile killings, and anybody looney tunes enough to make a career out of it would probably say something to someone eventually. That was how nine-tenths of these assholes were caught. The worlds they live in are so far out of touch with reality that someone usually notices.

The down side was that it might take a dozen more citizens

whacked before they caught him. And the media were already pumping this. The *L.A. Sun-News*, which in Dan's opinion wasn't fit to wrap mutated fish from the Santa Monica Bay in, had already named him "The Night Hunter." Some of the tabloids had leaped on the bandwagon as well, claiming that L.A. was full of vampires. All it would take would be one more corpse you could play horseshoes on and the city would be even crazier than usual. He could see it now: people stocking up on garlic, wearing crosses, swigging holy water like Evian. . . .

Jesus, Dan thought. Only in L.A. Only in fucking L.A.

CHAPTER 6

Wednesday, October 23

Jake regarded the large bulletin board on the wall of the detectives' squad room. Three-by-five cards were stuck to it by pushpins in more-or-less orderly vertical rows, each row headed by a card bearing the name of the investigating detective. At the top of the board the name "Stoughton" was printed in large block letters on a card, Stoughton being the Detective Third Class in charge of Homicide.

There were other charts on other walls, bearing case listings for Robbery, Juvenile, Sex Crimes and other departments. But the Homicide board was the one Jake was interested in. On the cards under the detectives were written the names and brief descriptions of murder victims and their case numbers. The victims' names in the cleared cases were written in black felt-tip; those still unsolved were listed in red. There were far more red cards on the board than black ones. One of the latest to be posted was James Raymond Tate's, at the bottom of a line-up of six cards under Jake's name. Four of those cases were listed in red.

Stoughton came up to Jake, stirring powdered cream into a Styrofoam cup of coffee. "I suppose I don't need to tell you that McNamara's not happy with the ratio of red to black on this board," he said.

Jake turned his gaze from the board to his superior. Since getting the desk job, Stoughton had put on a good twenty pounds and a crop of gray hair. He had started wearing bifocals last month, a hardship he was still bitching about to anyone who would listen. "I know a lot of people I could arrest," Jake said. "They maybe didn't kill the vics up here, but they would have if they'd been there."

"Don't I wish we could do that. Don't I wish we could just shoot the cocksuckers on the street—save a lot of time, money and hassle all around." He pantomimed a gun firing with thumb and forefinger. "Boom! 'Why'd you shoot him, officer?' 'He was a dirtbag, your Honor.' 'Case closed.'" Stoughton leaned against the wall and regarded the board. "Unfortunately, street justice is not an option. Therefore, we must rely on actual detective work." He cocked an eyebrow at Jake. "That would be your area of expertise, I believe. Which is why the Captain asked me to ask you how the Tate case is coming."

"Jesus Christ, Stoughton, I haven't been on the case as long as it takes to take a piss. What does he want from me?"

"What he wants is what I want—for you and the rest of the crew to put down cases," Stoughton said reasonably. "Our job is to find killers and arrest them. He wants us to do our job."

"What is this 'our job' shit?" Jake asked sourly. "*Your* job, as far as I can see, is to sit on *your* ass behind *your* desk and give *me* a hard time." Before Stoughton could respond to that, Jake went on: "McNamara's got a hard-on for me—you know that. You know why. He wants me off the street, he's just looking for an excuse to kick my ass." Jake took a deep breath and tried for a more moderate tone. "Keep him off me,

Mick. Look—" he pointed at the board "—I'm two for four.
I cleared the Tripway shooting last week. That's a better solve
rate than Anders's or Kosinski's, and as good as Stillman's."

Stoughton listened with a neutral expression. "What have
you got?"

"Not much," Jake admitted. "This time. But he's going to
do it again, I'll put my badge on it. And next time he'll leave
me something."

"You're not giving me a lot of ammunition here, Jake."
Stoughton sipped his coffee. "What if you don't bring down
Stake Boy the next time out? Or the next? This is already a
hot case—it gets much more press, I'm going to have to put
the whole squad on it." He gestured at the board. "And that
will *really* cut back on the black."

Jake said nothing. After a moment Stoughton sighed. "I'll
tell McNamara you've got some leads. Don't make me a liar."
As Jake nodded and turned away, Stoughton put a restraining hand on his arm. "And if you need help—ask. Don't go
cowboy on me, Jake."

"C'mon. Do I look like Steve fucking McQueen?" Jake
tried to sound more confident than he felt as Stoughton left
the room. He poured himself a cup of the machine oil that
passed for coffee and downed half of it.

He stared at the board, at the mocking red ink on his four
cards. There were two basic types of homicides: whodunits
and slamdunks. He and Stoughton both knew that the Tripway shooting had been a dunker. Nelson Tripway had been
found sitting on a couch in his living room, still holding the
.45 with which he had shot his wife and his second cousin,
who had been in the bedroom enthusiastically giving each
other sheet burns. All Jake had to do was ask, "Did you shoot
them?" to which Tripway had replied, "Fuck yeah, and I'd *still*
be shootin' 'em, I hadn't run outta bullets!"

Bam, right through the hoop.

Slamdunks were easy. Whodunits were not. A whodunit—
officially known as a Category Three—might be a call to the

middle of an asphalt parking lot where the body of a name-
less black man lies facedown in a pool of his own blood and
nothing more. No identification, no spent casings, no foot-
prints or tire treads—nothing but the grim mockery of the
corpse, challenging you to name its killer. A whodunit might
be a six-month-old pile of decaying body parts found buried
in Hefty bags at the far end of some vacant lot. Or a twelve-
year-old girl raped, stabbed and stuffed beneath the refuse of
an overflowing Dumpster behind a fast-food outlet.

Or a young street strutter with an oversized tent peg through
his heart.

The irony was that, slamdunk or whodunit, they both
looked the same on the board. A case cleared was a case
cleared. The four red cards under his name were all whodunits
of the first order, and he'd made precious little progress on
any of them. The chopped-up body buried in the lot looked
to be a vagrant, judging by the remnants of clothes on him.
But why go to so much trouble to hide a vag's body? The yo
in the parking lot they'd finally managed to ID as Eriq Tupac
Joba, a twenty-year-old homeboy and crack entrepreneur
from Lincoln Heights who'd been missing for nearly a
month—but, as the line of people ready and willing to shoot,
stab or otherwise put an end to young Eriq's life would probably stretch around Parker Center, this case was still a long
way from closure. The girl in the Dumpster was still a Jane
Doe, with no leads at all.

And now Jimmy Ray, all staked out and no one to blow.

While it was true that a crime scene in a house or apartment was the best you could hope for in terms of finding clues,
this particular crime scene had been cleaner than the men's
room at the Beverly Hills Division. No sign of forced entry,
no evidence of a struggle, no prints anywhere. Not even skin
samples to be found under Jimmy's fingernails from where
he might have scratched his assailant.

It had been a pro job. Obviously the killer had posed as a

john—but why would a professional whack a nobody like Jimmy Ray?

No matter which way he came at it, it made no sense.

But it had to make sense, he knew, and soon. This had all the trappings of a red-ball case, which could mean around-the-clock shifts and continuous reporting to every fat-assed bureaucrat all the way up to the Chief Of Police, the Mayor and possibly even the Governor. It could, as Stoughton had ominously indicated, cause other cases to be put on indefinite back burners as detectives were pulled from rotation to take a crack at this one. It could become a shitstorm of hurricane proportions if it wasn't put down.

He took another swig of coffee and his ulcer kicked up again, making him feel like he had a gut full of razor blades. Jake grunted in pain and headed back to his desk and the Maalox in the top drawer. Before he left, he took a final look at the board. His case load looked like it was bleeding to death. So much crime, so little time, he thought.

So much unfinished business. . . .

CHAPTER 7

Wednesday, October 23

Sarah Allen entered the huge walk-in refrigerator in the morgue. She found the gurney with the sheeted form whose toe-tag identified him as all that remained of Jimmy Ray Tate and pulled the sheet back for one last look at the damage before the body was shipped to the crematorium.

The stake had long since been removed, of course. The gray-white flesh was puckered around the gaping bloodless hole in the chest. Jimmy Ray's face still seemed to wear a look of shock and disbelief.

A stupid, senseless death—God knows there are no shortage of them in the nineties, Sarah thought. And yet this one tugged at her particularly hard. Maybe because Tate had been so young. She had been struck, at the autopsy, by how fresh and new his organs had looked: colorful and identifiable, like the acetate overlays in her anatomy books. A sharp contrast to older victims she had seen whose viscera had been gray and indistinct, worn out by age and abuse.

Sarah stared at the dead boy for several minutes before she let the sheet drop. She wasn't sure why she had come to the morgue for a final look at the body before it was reduced to ashes, ashes that would be shipped back to grieving parents who would probably never face up to the fact that they were to a considerable degree responsible for their son's death. There was nothing further that autopsy and forensics could say about Jimmy Ray. The loss of blood, it had been decided, had been due to the outgushing when the sharp point of the stake punctured the pericardial sac and rapidly pumping heart muscle. There had certainly been nothing supernatural about his death, despite the stake in his chest and the garlic in his mouth.

So why had she felt the need for one more look at the corpse?

Sarah left the fridge, breathing shallowly until the huge steel door closed behind her with a hushed sound. She walked slowly along the corridor, reviewing the case in her mind, trying to find some clue she had overlooked.

"Sarah!"

She looked up to see Todd Latham striding briskly toward her down the corridor, his white coat streaming behind him, his teeth gleaming against the black skin of his face.

"Haven't I told you to stay out of the fridge?" he mock-scolded. She managed a somewhat wan smile in return, and his grin was instantly replaced by a look of concern. "You got something on your mind, that's obvious. Tell Doctor Latham."

"Just our latest mutual problem," she said as they walked on together toward the elevators. "Jimmy Ray Tate: his life story. Or rather, his death story."

"Damned creepy," Latham agreed as they entered the elevator. "Been working in this town nearly seventeen years, never seen anything like that. And I thought I'd seen just about every way man could come up with to off his neighbor.

I remember this case once, this guy had tried to give his girl-friend an enema with—"

"What gets me about it," Sarah said, "is that somebody died because the killer watched too many old horror flicks or something. Used Tate as a prop in his own sick little mind movie. That's no way for anyone to die. There's no dignity in it."

"Absolutely," Latham said, not seeming to mind that she had interrupted him. "You know, they say violence in movies and TV doesn't affect people, but I say that's bullshit. Every time one of those Schwarzenegger pictures comes out, people think they won't get killed jumping a motorcycle over a car or trying to swing through trees or some shit. There was this one fellow who saw that movie with the electric drill in the head, what was it, and he—"

"Tried to drill his brains out, I know," Sarah said as they came out of the bay door into the warm night air. "He'd put six holes in his head and hadn't hit a vital area, and wanted you to show him where to put the bit. Come up with something new next time."

Latham chuckled and headed in the opposite direction for his car. The sun had just set. Sarah waved good-bye and headed for her Cherokee, beeping the alarm off. As she pulled out of the parking lot she thumbed the air-conditioning on; it was one of those warm Santa Ana nights that sometimes occur in Los Angeles in the fall. Yesterday had been chill; tonight it was shirtsleeve weather as the coastal desert climate lurched reluctantly into autumn.

As she headed down the dark street, Sarah realized she was still mulling the case over in her head. Enough, she told herself firmly. With luck, she could look forward to an evening of relaxation unless her pager summoned her to another scene of violent death. She hoped that wouldn't happen. She had been on the go for the last forty-eight hours; she deserved a rest.

But it was hard not to think about the case. She was a classic obsessive-compulsive that way, she knew; a workaholic with definite co-dependent tendencies. The line of thought elicited a wry smile. *And don't forget you're a Taurus, with a penchant for over-analyzing.*

Of late Sarah Allen had been trying to engineer some sort of a life for herself outside of her work, and finding it much more difficult than she had thought it would be. At thirty-nine, with one failed marriage behind her and a couple of near-disastrous romances narrowly warded off in the past twelve months, she had come to the conclusion that she was not taking proper care of her inner child, not to mention the adult woman who encased said child. For most of her life since puberty she had been conditioned by her mother to believe that only marriage and a family would make her feel fulfilled and complete. She had gone that route, with less than laudatory results. Her seven-year-old son now lived with his father in Malibu and she got to see him every other weekend. This was an arrangement that Matt, her ex, considered far better than Sarah deserved, and was not shy about letting her know it. All in all, it had not been a very successful ten-year chunk of her life.

As she drove west on Sunset through the neon glory of the Strip, she turned the tape deck on and pushed a cassette in. Moments later the soft strains of the Grateful Dead's *Blues for Allah* album filled the car. Musical taste was just one of the many areas in which she and Matt had differed wildly; Sarah was an unregenerate and unrepentant Deadhead, had been since she was old enough to know what rock and roll was all about. Matt found the band at best mediocre, at worst jejune and soporific. He actually used words like that to describe things he didn't like. He was into what he thought was aggressively cutting-edge stuff like Philip Glass and Laurie Anderson. Why they ever got married in the first place was one of the great mysteries of the universe, Sarah thought, right up there with planarian flatworm genetic memory and finding a good, cheap and unknown restaurant on the West Side.

But they had been young and impulsive, and hadn't seen a lot of each other for the first few years of their marriage. The last seven they had stayed together largely because they thought it would be best for Brandon. With both of them in residency at different hospitals, there had hardly been time to say hello to each other before they collapsed, exhausted, in bed for a few hours sleep before the grind would begin again. It was a wonder they had ever found the energy to have sex.

Notice, Sarah thought as she turned south on Fairfax, that I said "have sex" instead of "make love." Important to stay aware of these occasional Freudian slips.

She had been working sometimes as much as a hundred hours a week back then, in a sink-or-swim situation made doubly hard by the fact that she was a woman and thus judged inferior until she proved herself equal. The long hours and hard work had paid off, but she still felt bitter sometimes about her training, particularly the condescending attitude of the male surgeons and specialists and the hazing from other residents and interns who were lucky enough to wear their sexual equipment outside their bodies. Law school, later, had not been any better. Her medical and legal training had single-handedly supported the coffee industry, not to mention, on some occasions, less legal drugs.

The main thing—the only thing, in retrospect—that she and Matt had in common back then had been a love of medicine. For her, forensics was always the chief fascination. It was a way of combining the jobs of the two people she admired most in her life—her father and her uncle Nathan—detective work and medicine. It had been quite an uphill battle to get where she was today, and it had cost her. She did not mind the wreckage of the marriage so much—it had become obvious to both of them fairly early on that they were not meant for each other—but her demotion from Mother First Class to Occasional Parent had really hurt.

By the time she pulled into the driveway of her condo building just off Olympic in Santa Monica a fog was coming in. As she waited for the gate to slide back, Sarah thought that if it weren't for the continuing presence of Brandon in her life, the time spent with Matt would seem like someone else's marriage. She did her best not to think about him except in connection with her son. And she hadn't given up on getting full-time custody back either. For the past two months she had been gathering statements from friends to support her re-petition. Though the laws no longer supposedly favored the woman in custody settlements, Sarah knew that many judges were still influenced by the idea that children were better off with their mothers. And she would take whatever advantage she could to get her son back under her roof on an ongoing basis.

Matt, surprise surprise, was vehemently opposed to this idea. He'd told her more than once that there was no way she could raise a child full-time with her workload. She was oft-times on call twenty-four hours a day, and what would she do with Brandon when the beeper sounded—drag him off at three A.M. to help Mommy work up some sorry crackhead wearing his guts for a necktie? As if he had any more time for the boy, Matt Fletcher with his pediatrics service to the stars and his regular appearances on *Southland Morning* with avuncular advice on skinned knees and bedwetting. He had time for every kid in Southern California except his own.

She turned the engine off and leaned back against the head-rest, savoring the relative coolness and quiet of the parking garage. Well, fuck Matt, she thought wearily. In a purely metaphorical sense, of course; at this point the idea of having sex with some disease-ridden derelict down on Sixth was more appealing. At any rate, there was nothing to be done about Brandon's situation tonight, and she would only make herself miserable for the rest of the evening if she kept on thinking about it. She grabbed her purse and briefcase and headed for the stairs, subliminally checking about her, as always, to make sure someone did not come lunging at her from the shadows.

Inside her small two-bedroom apartment she headed for the bathroom, yawning, to brush her teeth. She was still feeling the effects of last night's late hours. Normally she was not the M.E. responsible for investigating graveyard shift crimes, but the city had been short-staffed for months now and there was no sign of it getting better anytime soon.

That was one of the worst things about the medical profession in general that she had never been able to overcome. She was a wren, not an owl; a day person, body and soul. Even when she was a teenager, staying up past midnight or one left her a zombie at school the next day. When she was younger she had thought being a night person was romantic, had regretted being unable to function well in those soft dark hours that stretched like a black river from midnight to dawn. Now, however, knowing what went on during the night had her wishing her job did not take her out into those hours so often. What she wanted now more than anything else was at least six hours of uninterrupted sleep. Feeling vaguely guilty, she turned off her pager and disconnected the phone.

She glanced at the clock just before drifting off. It was a quarter to ten; early even for her. Her last coherent thought was, But it's late enough for vampires. And then she was asleep, and white faces with bloodstained fangs pursued her through nightmares.

CHAPTER 8

Wednesday, October 23

Working graveyard was always a bitch. The audience this night consisted mostly of drunks, a couple in the corner far more interested in each other than anything Tace had to say, and a few diehards who were determined to catch the last act, no matter how lame it might be. No doubt more than a few of them had stayed, she told herself, because of how she looked in the black jeans and motorcycle jacket. Hey, whatever works.

She could feel the tension in her back and across her neck. The hardest part, for her, was looking loose and relaxed when there was so much to concentrate on. She had to work just as hard for these few night owls at the tables down front as she would for a roomful of people.

She had gone through most of her set, and the responses had been disappointing. Part of that wasn't her fault—the room was a comic's nightmare, far short of the critical mass needed to ignite. The next thing to playing a morgue, she thought unhappily.

But how much of it *was* her fault?

She pushed that worry way down to the bottom of her mind and kept going. The bit about the Odd Couple sharing a cardboard box under the freeway didn't do as well as she'd hoped. The part of her brain that was constantly analyzing, even while she was onstage, started dissecting it . . . maybe she was taking it too far with Felix's dog casserole . . . ?

A waiter was upending chairs on tables in the back. She considered working it in—"Hey, want me to grab a broom, help you sweep up?"—but decided against it. It was a lousy night anyway; best not to accentuate it.

She hated working closing. Most of the audience had left after seeing Tony Benuta, the club's headliner tonight. She wasn't bombing, was getting a few laughs, but nothing to tell her diary about. It was one of those nights where you just had to keep slogging. Under circumstances like these twenty minutes of material can seem an eternity.

She swung into the bit about her mother's belief that her daughter had been conceived as a result of being raped by Satan. "Makes it hard to count on money from home. . . ."

That one scored the best so far. Tace let the laughter wash over her, nourish her. She thought, not for the first time, how holding an audience is such a tenuous thing; one moment they're with you, urging you on, willing you to do good—the next they're lighting torches and howling for your blood.

But when it was good, there was nothing better. Feeling the power of controlling a crowd, making them laugh, making them beg for more—no drug could compare to it. She had only really killed two or three times since she came to L.A., the last time two weeks ago at the Comedy Factory on Fairfax. It was a high Tace Daggett still vibrated from.

This was her fifth paying gig since she had started doing stand-up nearly eight months before. She had begun working amateur nights at the Improv and other clubs. Her first stint onstage had been in a dive down on Sixth Street where, halfway through her act, someone had gotten knifed. The manager had told her to keep going: "People can use a laugh after something like this."

The line about mistaking a taser for a vibrator went over well too; the ten or so people out there were finally starting to respond. But then, in the midst of the laughter, one of the drunks shouted, "Sit on my face, honey!"

Oh, God, no . . . she felt tremors of panic wash outward from her gut. Hecklers could turn a crowd against you faster than a televangelist could spend money. No way she could let it pass. She stepped to the edge of the stage, pointed down at him. "You!" she barked, sharp enough to startle him and a few others at surrounding tables. "Out of the gene pool—*now!*"

There was laughter and a few scattered cheers. Tace moved back to continue with her set, but the drunk was not so easily dismissed. "C'mon, honey," he slurred, standing unsteadily and knocking over his chair. "You want what I got," he continued, gesturing in the general direction of his fly.

"What, syphilis?" But the laughter wasn't as strong now. She could feel the subtle shift in the room—she now had to prove herself against this imbecile. She stepped forward again, leaned down, holding the mike close to her lips.

"You like sex, huh?" she asked with just a hint of huskiness to her voice. The drunk, weaving slightly, leaned forward on the table and blew an alcoholic gust Tace's way. "Oh, yeah. . . ." All the carnal attraction of a traffic accident, she thought.

"Like to travel?"

The drunk blinked, thrown off by this unexpected tack. "Huh? Sure, I guess. . . ."

"Good," Tace said, straightening and stepping back as she jerked a thumb toward the exit doors. "Then *take a fucking hike!*"

The other patrons erupted in cheers and claps. The drunk looked confused and angry. Tace continued: "There's a live sex show down the street. Go pass out in your own vomit there, Bluto."

There were shouts of support from the other tables now. "Yeah, shut the fuck up!" "Get out!" The drunk threw his drink on the floor and stormed out.

Triumphant, Tace went on with her set. Maybe the sense of exhilaration from her triumph intensified the rapport with the audience; whatever the reason, her last few lines got great responses. They were laughing so hard she cut it short, thanked them and got the hell out of the spotlight, almost forgetting to grab the small microcorder from the stool behind her. Always leave them wanting more.

The "green room" was hardly bigger than a walk-in closet, with a sprung couch and a broken coffee machine. Davis was waiting for her. He held a dead rose, its petals black and curled.

"Hey, lady," he said, "anybody ever tell you you've got a nice pair of wits?" He handed her the rose. "In honor of tonight's kill." Tace laughed, broke the stem off close to the blossom and stuck the latter in a buttonhole of her leather jacket.

"I ought to find that asshole and buy him a drink," she said. "They would've been feasting on my corpse if he hadn't gotten them back on my side." She sat down, let her long legs sprawl out before her. "Jesus, I'm still shaking."

Davis dug into a jeans pocket and pulled out a cloth-covered glass capsule. "Got just the thing for that."

Tace took it gracefully, snapping it between her thumb and forefinger under her nose. The strong chemical smell suffused her senses. She felt a jackhammering in her head that lasted only a few seconds, and then her body seemed to melt into a pool of warm oil. She sighed, blinking at the blue sparkles the exhalation produced before her eyes. "Ahh. Better. Mo' better."

Davis sat down beside her; she turned to him and they

kissed, the amyl nitrate rush producing an almost orgasmic intensity. "What time is it?" she asked dreamily.

"One-thirty."

"The night is still young and so are we." She stood, running fingers through her short spiked black hair. "Let's hit the clubs."

CHAPTER 9

Wednesday, October 23

Candy wanted some crystal meth in the worst way, but she was out of coin. The easiest way to make the bucks for a good hit of ice would be to hang out on some corner like Fountain and Highland and wait for an expensive German or Japanese car to stop. Five minutes with her face in some businessman's lap, and she could be flying for the rest of the night.

The problem was the hookers and their pimps who had staked out most of the Hollywood area frowned like hell on sweet little sixteens like her undercutting them. She'd narrowly escaped having her face slashed last week by this black guy who'd caught her strolling up Orchid near the Chinese looking a little too sultry. She'd gone easy on the makeup since then. Her usual street outfit of tight shorts and T-shirt had changed to a pair of old ripped jeans and a denim jacket, as much due to the cold weather as any fear of more attacks.

But this late—it was past two A.M.—she didn't think she'd have any grief.

After a half hour or so of watching traffic pass with no takers, Candy moved north, hoping to find more luck up on Sunset. A few sleek machines had slowed down, but none had stopped. She unbuttoned the denim jacket and tied her T-shirt in a knot that left her midriff bare and covered with gooseflesh in the cold wind. She knew she'd find some action if she headed west on Sunset into the Strip, but there she'd also find competition. Best to stay east of Highland, she decided.

The desert winds had died down and a fog was blowing in from the Pacific; the streetlights and car headlamps wore soft halos. The increasing mistiness blurred and softened the outlines of buildings, making the street look slightly out of focus.

She wished Ziplock or Angel were here. Zip always seemed to have some hustle going that kept bills and pills in his pocket, and he was always good about sharing the good times with her. Angel wasn't as much fun—his heavy usage of PCP had fucked up his head some, Candy felt—but he was okay to have around when he didn't have a snootful. The three of them had shared a room at the Blue Pacific over on Ivar for awhile, till they were tossed out for drugs. Now they all prowled the same area, along with dozens of other runaways: a grid on the map more or less bounded by La Brea on the west, Beverly on the south, Western on the east and Franklin on the north. They still hung out together, and Candy occasionally slept with one or the other or both. They shared beds more for companionship than sex, the latter not being something any of them really associated with closeness.

She passed Hampton's Burgers and, obeying a sudden impulse, turned east on De Longpre, leaving the street and store lights of Highland Avenue behind her. She knew it wasn't bright to stray off the main drags this late when she was by herself, but Zip had been crashing of late in a deserted apartment complex over on Gower; maybe she'd be lucky and catch him there. If she could score some meth without getting her tonsils sticky it was worth walking a few blocks in the dark.

The fog was growing rapidly thicker; already it was hard to see to the end of the block. Candy stepped up her pace; the cold sea air cut right through her thin layers of clothes, chilling her like the steam off a block of dry ice.

This area was mostly residential: bungalows and small apartment courts, most of them run-down, many with iron grillwork bolted over windows and doors. It used to be a pleasant neighborhood, Candy had heard, decades before her time, but looking at it now it was hard to believe it had ever been anything more than a step above a slum. Still, there were pleasant touches here and there. One window had ghosts crafted from white cotton balls taped to the glass, and another house sported a jack-o'-lantern on the porch, a glowstick providing orange backlighting for the pumpkin's eyes and gap-toothed grin. She passed De Longpre Park, a small expanse of patchy grass and graffiti-whorled benches. Several derelicts huddled there, sleeping, little more than lumps of grime in the hazy dark.

It was impossible now to see more than a dozen feet in front of her. The air she was sucking into her lungs felt clammy and damp; it beaded her hair and moistened her cheeks like tears. There was a strange scent to it, Candy noticed uneasily; a smell so distant and vague that it was almost more of an impression than an actual olfactory experience. It spoke of bottomless black oceanic depths and of things long dead and bloated, stirred to grim lifeless movement by dark currents. It was more than some faint taste of the sea carried inland by the fog; it felt unhealthy, unclean, like a drifting miasma from some underwater lair.

These images, like the tainted air that inspired them, swirled just below her level of awareness. She only knew that the thickening fog was spooking her big-time. And so she was already primed for panic when she heard the footsteps behind her.

They were just suddenly *there*—that was the worst thing about them. Maybe she hadn't noticed them approaching, but the street had been pretty quiet, almost as if the marine fog was capable of muffling sounds. Traffic on Highland, just a few blocks behind her, could not be heard. The only sound for the past ten minutes or so had been her ancient Nikes hitting the pavement and occasional muffled bits of TV conversation or radio music from the houses she passed.

And then, just like that, the footsteps, sharp and definite, like the soles of boots or some other serious footware striding purposefully along, and Jesus Christ they couldn't be more—

—*he* couldn't be more—

—than a dozen yards behind her.

Candy didn't turn. The suddenness, the surreal arrival of those footfalls so close on her heels somehow fostered a kind of desperate superstitious hope that, as long as she didn't look behind her, the rhythmic tap-tap-tap would remain not real, a trick of her hearing, perhaps, some weird acoustical anomaly caused by the fog or the lateness of the hour or maybe fucking sunspots or something. But to look, to even glance over her shoulder, would be to grant whatever it was behind her the presence, the reality, to be a danger.

It had been a long time since she had been really scared by anyone or anything. When you're raised in a state home and sexually molested by the administrators and members of the staff for almost as long as you can remember, and then shipped out to a series of foster homes that would make Dickens turn pale . . . when you eventually decide that living on your own couldn't possibly be as soul-crushingly hideous as living with the monsters in whose care you'd been placed, when sharing a lice-ridden mattress and pissing in a bucket and grubbing day-old take-out actually feels like a step up for you . . . well, after all that crammed into only sixteen years, you start feeling like life's rich pageant isn't quite all it's cracked up to be.

But then you start down a deserted back street in Hollywood, U.S.A., and all of a sudden someone's doing the Spahn Ranch shuffle so close behind you that you can practically feel hot breath on your neck; you can sense eyes, bright and burning with some fever that no amount of penicillin will cure, focused like twin lasers on your back; you can smell the kind of desperate need that's probably only satisfied by a freezer full of dead children, and that's when things get real practical and life, diamond-hard as it can be most of the time, isn't something you're ready to trade in just yet.

Candy walked, not daring to increase her pace or slow down. The footsteps matched her own, almost in lock-step. One block passed, then another. It was impossible for the fog to thicken still more, but somehow it did; now it seemed that she was walking through some timeless gray afterlife, only her and her stalker inhabiting this dead universe. A Halloween horror story turned all too real.

A bit of doggerel she had learned long ago in some dormitory surged through her mind: *Trick or treat, smell my feet, give me something good to eat. . . .*

A warped desire to laugh abruptly swept over her; she tightened her throat against it. Where the hell was she? Still on De Longpre, since she hadn't made any turns, but what was this cross street coming up? She could barely read the street sign, though she passed right by the pole. Seward . . . a few blocks ahead and to the north on Ivar was Phoenix House, a place where she and some of the other runaways could get a hot meal and a shower, as well as clean clothes and toiletries on occasion. There was relatively little bullshit to put up with in return for the services; the place was staffed mostly by volunteers.

Unfortunately, it wasn't a shelter—there were no beds or provisions for staying overnight. Its doors would be closed now; there would be no help for her there. Assuming she could get that far. . . .

Were the footsteps behind her closer now?

Trick or treat, fresh young meat, live and die out on the street. . . .

Candy took a deep breath; though the air was cold, it seared her lungs like a fire's hot backdraft. No doubt about it; he *was* closer. The cadence of his steps was speeding up.

He was overtaking her.

Suddenly, with no conscious intention of doing so, she stopped and spun about to face him.

The figure behind her stopped as well. Light, diffused and tinged with rainbow colors by the fog, welled up from behind him, making it impossible to see his features; he was nothing but a tall, angular silhouette momentarily frozen by surprise.

In that instant of tableau Candy realized that the brightening light behind him was the headlights of an approaching car.

She lunged into the street, waving her arms. The car—one of those small vans, a Mazda MPV—stopped quickly. Candy ran to the passenger's side and tried the door. It was locked, but then she heard a click and the latch button sank under the pressure of her thumb. She yanked the door open and scrambled inside.

The van started forward. Candy got a momentary glimpse of her stalker in the driver's side mirror, still standing there as if unable to believe how quickly and easily his prey had escaped him. She breathed a sigh of relief and turned to look at her savior.

His face was hidden in the shadows of the van's interior. It was impossible to tell how old he was, although something about the way he sat behind the wheel said he was young— late twenties or early thirties, Candy judged.

Her heart was still hammering at the nearness of her escape. There was no question in her mind now that her pursuer back there had been a modern-day Jack the Ripper, and if she hadn't flagged down this ride she would shortly have been a Rorschach blot of blood and organs in some nearby alley.

The van accelerated, turning a corner. The headlights illuminated nothing but a pearlescent aluminum-gray void in front of them, but the driver seemed to be guided by some sort of psychic radar, handling the car as if it were high noon on a deserted highway.

"I've been looking for you," he said in a calm, resonant voice.

And it was then that Candy realized, with a sickening burst of renewed fear, that he had shown no sign of surprise or resentment at her jumping into his car.

The van pulled to a stop by the curb.

Candy clawed for the inside door handle, grabbed it even as she heard the electric lock tabs snap again, felt the lever pull toward her with futile ease.

It never occurred to her to scream.

He left the van parked in the deserted shell of what had once been an auto repair shop over on Selma Avenue. Everything had gone even better than he had hoped for. He had had his eye on the girl since the day before, and had tracked her tonight. He had thought for a moment that he would have to deal with the street scum who was following her, but her fear of him had actually driven her right into his grasp. Even after all this time, the workings of fate could occasionally surprise him.

He would not make the same mistake with her that he had made with the last one. He had not expected the discovery of a young transient's body to cause such a stir, particularly not in this city. It was the first time in a long while that he had chosen his victims in an urban setting; previously he had kept to rural areas where disposal of the bodies had been a much easier matter. He had underestimated the reaction that the public would have to the manner of the killing. Even a man of his experience and proficiency could still make mistakes.

The fog was beginning to lift as he walked halfway down the block, then turned and aimed a device resembling a TV remote control back at the hidden vehicle. He pressed a button; the MPV and the stucco husk concealing it erupted in a plume of fire and smoke that torched the night sky.

The thermite burned fiercely, lighting the street with a ruddy orange glow. In a few moments both the girl's body and the stake that had transfixed her heart would be reduced to ashes. Let their scientists and investigators try to link this death to the mysterious "Night Hunter" killings.

He smiled and continued down the street, turning the corner and walking south toward Sunset as the faint wails of the sirens began to build.

CHAPTER 10

Wednesday, October 23

Club Dystopia in Echo Park was in an old movie house from the black-and-white days that had been gutted and given a look equal parts disco inferno and industrial funk. Tace liked the eighties-style retro-tech feel, and she liked the music, which was mostly acid jazz and techno.

Davis paid the twenty-dollar cover charge and they entered a tightly packed chaos of humanity that vibrated to the raw driving sound of a local band. Spotlights with colored gels swung wildly, lighting the high-ceilinged room in tones of green, purple and red and causing the fluorescent graffiti on the walls to pulse and throb. A screen behind the band pulsed with short loops of atrocity videos: the famous Viet Nam footage of a prisoner getting a bullet in the brain, South American nuns being cut down by machine-gun fire, and "ethnic cleansing" in Central Europe were among the incidents Tace recognized. Razor wire was strung along the edge of the stage.

Near one wall a gutted school bus, its original yellow almost completely obscured by more spray-painted scribbles in various neon shades, vibrated to the dancers within it. Where rows of theater seats had once been, tables covered with sheet metal now surrounded a dance floor.

Tace commandeered one of the tables while Davis went in search of drinks. The sound hammered at her like tsunami waves. The lead singer was a black man, hair cut in a high fade, wearing a baggy silver jumpsuit. A metal plate with blinking LEDs was glued onto his shaven right temple.

Tace leaned back, grinning. The music was loud enough to cause calcium loss in her bones, and she knew she'd pay for it in mid-range deafness over the next few decades, but she didn't care. It was worth it.

She fucking loved L.A. She knew that, other than Randy Newman, there were not too many people ready or willing to make that statement these days. Sure, the town had drawbacks—neighborhoods that made Beirut look safe, air worse than the atmosphere of Venus, a cost of living measured in astronomical units . . . but New York had all that and a winter that could freeze the fillings out of your teeth to boot. L.A. also had the Venice boardwalk, where she could get a sausage sandwich at Jody Moroni's, first-run movies, Eddie Brandt's Video Matinee in North Hollywood, great theater, the Farmer's Market, Tower Records on Sunset . . . the list was endless. And it was the place to be, no question, if you were young and determined to make it in stand-up. Which was a fair description of Anastasia "Tace" Daggett, twenty-three years old and an L.A. native for all of eight months. Baltimore, her mother's house, the two years of city college, all seemed a universe away.

Her plan was simple: work the clubs, get noticed, score some appearances on that mecca for comics, the *Tonight Show,* and after that her own special on Showtime or HBO. Followed, she hoped, by movie roles and maybe a sitcom. It had worked for others—it could work for her.

If she was funny enough.

That, of course, was the Big Question: was she in the same league with the men and women who could make her laugh herself into spasms, who had inspired her to get up on stage that first time for five minutes in a local comedy club back in Baltimore? Five agonizing minutes—there had been a few scattered laughs, but basically she had bombed big time. You could have heard a pin drop in the room. You could have heard a pin drop in *Detroit*.

Even now the memory made Tace wince.

But she had gone back the following week. And bombed again, but not before getting a few more laughs. She had made notes of the jokes that had played and pondered long into the night how to fix the ones that hadn't. She had played comedy tapes over and over, breaking each comedian's set down line by line, studying the set-ups and the punch lines, then painstakingly crafting jokes of her own, syllable by syllable, sculpting them as carefully as any artist working in stone or clay.

The move to L.A. had been prompted as much by a desire to get out of the house and make a clean start as by the hope of making it in comedy. Tace's mother, a woman who laughed about as often as Nancy Reagan wore dominatrix leather, had gone ballistic at the idea of her daughter wanting to get up on a stage and tell jokes—especially dirty jokes. Her father might have stood up for her if he hadn't been dead for the past three years; on the other hand, he might not have, since his position in the family had always seemed to Tace a lot like Chamberlain's at Munich.

Davis came back with two bottles of beer. The band finished their set, leaving the air vibrating with unaccustomed silence. Davis said, "You handled that heckler pretty well tonight."

Tace took a long swallow of beer. "Y'know," she said, "a woman might think she's funnier than a man, and a man usually thinks he's funnier than other men. But a man *always* thinks he's funnier than a woman."

"Pithy," Davis said. "Nice sound-bite material."

"Instant aphorism, just add substance. Maybe I should run for office." She grinned at him.

Tace had met Davis Sands two months ago at the Joke Joint on Sunset. He was three years older than she and described himself as an "entrepreneur" when she asked him what he did for a living. His Los Feliz apartment was full of Ikea furniture, with nothing personal or idiosyncratic on the tables or walls. There were only a few books, most of them best-selling thrillers by people like Tom Clancy, Michael Crichton and Robin Cook. All in all, Tace was astounded that she had been, and continued to be, attracted to Davis. He was a card-carrying member of Generation X, and, while Tace shared his deep and abiding dislike of Baby Boomers—as far as she was concerned, the only good things to come out of the sixties were The Doors and Dr. Bronner's Peppermint Castile Soap—she did not feel that everybody over forty owed them a living, as Davis seemed to.

What made Davis worthwhile was his sense of humor—he had a quick and ready wit and was able to match her one-liners with comebacks—and the fact that he seemed truly to care for her. He never broke dates without good reasons, he brought her little presents—usually with a charmingly mordant twist, like tonight's dead rose—and he was, if not unfailingly considerate, at least much more often than not.

Two weeks after meeting they had had, to use his description, "wild, cautious sex," and he had proved himself considerate and caring in that department, too. He used what she called "bionic condoms": ribbed and ridged in all manner of imaginative ways. AIDS was, after all, nature's way of telling you you're fucked. Another legacy of the Love Generation, along with overpopulation and toxic waste, left for them to deal with.

She had even gone so far as to try out new material on him, which was, as far as she was concerned, a sign of true intimacy. "Is this funny?" she asked now, leaning across the table toward him. "Necrophilia is the ultimate passive-aggressive relationship." Davis sputtered laughter into his drink and Tace grinned, satisfied. She repeated the line into the microcorder just in time; a different local band calling themselves The Deadly Mantises had taken the stage. The stage screen began showing clips of truly bad old horror movies: juicy bits from Herschell Gordon Lewis extravaganzas like *The Blood Feast,* laughable special effects involving oversized locusts and Gila monsters, and so on. She recognized a few of the movies they came from: *Vampire Lover,* a Roger Corman cheapie from the late sixties starring that venerable old horror actor Franklin Conner, flashed by. When she'd been in middle school she'd had quite a crush on Conner.

She glanced at Davis, saw him tapping his fingers and nodding in time with the music. It occurred to her, abruptly and for no discernible reason, that anyone of the clientele here could be the Night Hunter she'd heard about on the news. He could have been in the audience at the comedy club, for that matter. He could have heard her, followed her here. . . .

Tace laughed, the sound swallowed up by the barrage of music, and downed the last of her beer. God, she loved L.A.

CHAPTER 11

Thursday, October 24

Jake Hull slumped low behind the wheel of the ancient city-owned Chevrolet with the bald rear tires and the paper-thin brake shoes, and yawned. It was early by his clock—three-thirty in the afternoon. He was parked across the street from La Brea Elementary School. The bell had just rung, and parents shepherded some children toward cars while other kids, backpacks slung over their shoulders, chased each other or began walking home.

Jake watched the gate, noticing for the hundredth time the spraypainted loops and spirals of gang graffiti on the stucco embankment from which the wire fence rose. A boy of ten, wearing jeans and a Power Rangers T-shirt, his left ear sporting a silver stud, left the gate and began hiking up the street. Jake watched him talking and slapping high-fives with some other boys, then trudging away until he reached the corner and turned left on Hawthorn.

From where he was parked he could watch the boy on his journey for a considerable distance, until the latter crossed an intersection and headed up a side street toward his house. He had no fear of losing the boy; he knew the route by heart. He knew that the boy would leap up and try to slap the box containing the WALK/DON'T WALK sign as he crossed the street. He knew that when he reached his house he would very probably throw his backpack onto the front porch, and his mother would have to make him go back out to get it so he could do his homework. He even knew what kind of cookies the boy liked to have for his snack.

He waited until the boy crossed the street before starting the car. He cruised past a taco stand, giving the teenagers who were congregated around a boombox there a quick profile to see if any of them had that particular stance and attitude that said they were packing. None did, this time. They eyefucked him, glaring with adolescent arrogance as he parked just past the intersection. From this position he could, by adjusting his rearview mirror slightly, watch the boy walk up the gently curving street. The boy stopped once to investigate something of interest in the tall grass next to the cracked sidewalk, stopped again to tie his shoe, and then continued without further distraction to the front door of his house.

When his son was inside the house, Jake started the car again, made a U-turn and headed east.

It wasn't like he'd always wanted to be a police officer. It had just seemed like the right thing to do at the time. He'd been twenty-eight, with two years of college in liberal arts, and was working as an assistant manager in a swimming pool supply store. One morning he had woken up and realized that the rest of his life was going to be nothing exciting, nothing heroic, nothing special.

He couldn't live with that. That afternoon he went down to the City Court Building and signed up for the Civil Service

Exam. He took a lie detector test, a physical exam and a battery of psychological tests, and qualified.

He spent six months in the police academy studying penal law, self-defense and the use of deadly force. It was boot camp, pure and simple. He wore khakis and a shaved head and was put through a grueling regimen every day. "The more you sweat now, the less you'll bleed later," they told him. Eventually he stood in a group of graduates, swore an oath with his right hand raised, and received a badge, a gun and the congratulations of the Chief of Police.

Then the real education began.

Jake drove east on Hollywood Boulevard. It was shaping up to be a warm day, the sort of dry desert weather that sometimes lasts in L.A. well into November. He wished the air-conditioning worked in the company heap he was driving. The Santa Anas hadn't been blowing in the Valley, but they were starting up here: gusts of cool, parched air that gave momentary relief from the heat of the sun. He'd been born and raised in Redlands, a town about eighty-five miles southeast of Los Angeles, notable chiefly for its orange groves and large number of churches, and so he'd never experienced truly cold weather. The only time he'd ever seen snow was on occasional family fishing trips up to Big Bear or Arrowhead. Jake glanced up the street, squinting against the glare, trying for a moment to picture Hollywood Boulevard with snow covering the inlaid sidewalk stars and capping the palm trees. He shook his head. Impossible to imagine.

Stratton had questioned the motel manager night before last about Jimmy Ray and learned next to nothing. Tate had rented the room for the first time, no doubt to rendezvous with a john; hardly an unusual occurrence at the swank Flamingo. The manager had seen no one else enter or leave the building. Neither had any of the street people they had questioned. No one had come to see the corpse at the morgue, either. The trail had been cold from the start.

As cold as his marriage had been, those last few years. . . .

Jake parked, walked down the block and entered a bar. The door had the name OSCAR'S painted on heavily tinted glass. He wondered if it were a reference to the Academy Awards or to Oscar Wilde. He wondered if any of the K-Y cowboys who habituated the bar had ever heard of Oscar Wilde.

It was dark inside; Jake lingered by the door for a minute to let his eyes adjust. Oscar's was a hole in the wall occupied mostly by a bar that ran the length of the room and a few tables. The chairs and the bar stools were covered with cracked and beer-stained leather. A few men sat at the bar. The bartender, a man with a lined face and silver temples, glanced his way. Jake approached the bar and flipped open the leather case that held his shield, letting the sunlight streaming in the doorway reflect from the badge into the bartender's eyes. The latter raised an eyebrow but otherwise did not seem unduly impressed. Jake pulled a snapshot of Jimmy Ray's face, taken after the morgue had cleaned him up somewhat, and showed it to the bartender. "Know him?"

The bartender glanced at the photo, shook his head. Jake turned to the nearest barfly, a man in his twenties with short-cropped hair, wearing tight jeans and a tasseled leather vest over a tanktop. "How about you?"

Leather Vest took the photo, studied it. "I seen him on the street a few times."

"Know anything about him? Where he lived, who he hung out with?"

Leather Vest shook his head. Jake showed the picture to the others in the bar, all of whom had similar reactions. It was frustrating, but not surprising. Someone with Tate's lifestyle didn't make a lot of close friends. If the decedent had been someone with roots in the neighborhood, it would be just a matter of time and footwork before Jake found somebody who could give him some history. As it was, he was trying to back-track an invisible man.

He started for the entrance. Leather Vest scooped a hand-ful of peanuts from a bowl on the bar, stuffed them in his mouth and mumbled around them, "Heard he was into some weird shit."

Jake stopped, turned. Leather Vest looked uncomfortable. "You know, like—black magic?"

Jake jotted down "black magic" on a field report card. "Anything else?" The barfly shook his head and gave his drink his undivided attention.

Jake stepped back out into the bright sunlight and gusting winds of October. He walked slowly back to his car, thinking.

Assuming Leather Vest was telling the truth—which was a big leap of faith right there, since everybody on the street considers it their solemn duty and sacred trust to lie to the police—it sounded like Jimmy Ray might have been flirting with Satanism, devil worship or something along those lines. It wasn't inconceivable. While not the spiritual plague sweeping the nation that Fundamentalists claimed, devil worship, satanic and voodoo rituals certainly weren't unknown among teenagers. He remembered vividly the bedroom of a sixteen-year-old boy suicide he had seen: a crucifix mounted upside down above the bed and heavy metal rock posters covering the walls, along with crude drawings of naked, erect men with goats' heads buggering screaming women. His parents had told Jake their son's obsession with the devil was a "complete surprise" to them.

He squinted into the afternoon sun, pulled a pair of sunglasses from his pocket and put them on. The car's engine started with its usual reluctance and he pulled away from the curb. It was time to call in reinforcements.

CHAPTER 12

Thursday, October 24

Jake parked his car on a trash-strewn street just above Fountain and east of Highland and walked into a small court of bungalows. They had been built back in the thirties and forties, he had heard, for the express purpose of housing young starlets and providing a quiet and convenient place for studio execs to slip away for a tryst. Now the run-down units housed ancient pensioners, hookers and one of Jake's stoolies.

Croaker answered after the third knock, peering warily out from behind the iron grid of the screen door. He relaxed almost imperceptibly when he recognized Jake. He did not invite the detective in, which was just fine with Jake; the cat litter that hadn't been changed in weeks was more than enough to keep him outside.

Jake filled him in on the details of Jimmy Ray's death. "Ask around. Get me some names; you know the drill." He folded the picture and slipped it through one of the openings in the grid's mesh. Croaker took it, hands trembling slightly. He glanced up at Jake and rubbed two tobacco-stained fingers together, grinning yellow teeth. Jake took out his wallet and passed a twenty through the hole. It disappeared into the pocket of Croaker's tattered sweater. With his other hand the stoolie raised a small gray cylinder, pressed one end of it to his larynx.

"Heard about it on the news." The electronic voice had no inflection, but the wheezy laugh that followed indicated Croaker's amusement. "Vampire killer. I love it." A scrawny cat appeared out of the bungalow's darkness, rubbed against the baggy trousers.

Jake tried not to gag at the ripe odor of cat shit that wafted from within the apartment's dark confines. "See what you can turn up," he said. "There's thirty more for you if you get me something I can run with." He headed back down the path through the overgrown bougainvillea and bird-of-paradise. Talking to Croaker always gave him the creeps, even though he'd dealt with far worse cases of poverty and disease. It probably had something to do with the fact that Croaker, despite appearances, was the same age as Jake.

Back in his car, he pondered his next move. There were a few more snitches he could put the word out to, though it would eat up what little discretionary funds he had pretty fast. He paid his informants out of his own pocket money, and trying to get the department to reimburse him was about as productive as preaching Jesus on a street corner.

Jake drove up to Sunset, turned and headed east. The palm trees whipped back and forth as the wind picked up. Dust and pieces of paper spun in momentary dust devils. It was five-thirty, the sun was touching the horizon, and the evening was turning cold fast. The air had that peculiar quality of luminous clarity that is rarely seen in Los Angeles outside of tourist postcards.

At the corner of Sunset and Ivar a lone hooker stood, wearing a short pink skirt and halter top. Jake could see gooseflesh marbling her dusky skin. He pulled over, rolled down the window.

She leaned down, giving him a look at her varicosed breasts. She was in her late twenties, early thirties, he judged; the wear and tear was starting to show. "Hey sugar, you lookin' for a party?" she asked, unable to keep the boredom out of her voice.

"What're we talking here?" Jake asked.

"Twenty-five to clean your pipes, fifty for the whole thing." She waited a moment; when he said nothing, she said, "C'mon, sugar, time is money, you know what I'm sayin'?"

Jake raised the leather wallet, let the lower half drop so that she could see the shield. Her expression hardly changed, though her eyes became a little more dead.

"Aw, man," she said. "C'mon, don't fuck up my day. I already been inside three times this month, I got to make some money."

Jake looked straight into her eyes. She fidgeted, looked away, then met his gaze, held it for several seconds. She straightened, walked around the car, opened the door and got in the passenger side, letting in a gust of cold dry air as she did so.

Jake pulled around the corner into an alley and parked. He turned the squawk box down, triggered the seat back release and lowered it until he was half-reclining. The hooker leaned over the emergency brake and unzipped his fly. Jake felt cold October air on swollen flesh.

She lowered her head, swallowing him, her black curly hair moving rhythmically up and down, her lips massaging the rigid shaft. She was good; he did not feel her teeth at all. He stared at the purpling sky beyond the windshield, the pennants on the lampposts rippling in the wind. He tried to think of nothing at all.

When he came he put his hand on her head, held her down on him until he finished spasming. He released her then. She straightened, looked at him; for an instant he thought she was going to spit a mouthful of his own come in his face. Then she opened the door and was gone, slamming it behind her.

Jake zipped himself up, then sat in the alley until the long twilight was nearly over.

CHAPTER 13

Friday, October 25

Franklin Conner slipped the pin into the weight stack and lay down on the incline press bench. He took a few deep breaths to steady himself and rev up his blood, then he pushed, feeling the muscles of his arms and chest protest the weight, feeling the plates move up the greased poles of the machine. He stopped before locking his elbows and then lowered the hundred and forty pounds slowly.

After eight repetitions he sat up, toweling away the sweat that had moistened his forehead and gray hair. He debated getting a drink of water, decided it could wait until he finished two more sets.

The YMCA was crowded today; in addition to the regular patrons, most of whom had been coming here for years like himself, there were a fair amount of new members, mostly young men and women. One woman—in her middle twenties, Conner judged, skin-tight Spandex outlining a figure that he thought verged on anorexic—glanced at him as she peddled a nearby Lifecycle. He knew the look well; the vaguely puzzled, "Don't I know you?" reaction that was both the pride and lament of lesser known actors like himself. His standard reply for several years now to such queries when they came was simply, "I have that kind of face." He'd given up telling them that they'd probably seen him in dozens of movies on late-night TV or cable. After a certain age tooting one's own horn that way becomes vaguely embarrassing, Conner felt. Especially since answering the inevitable question, "What have you done lately?" was becoming harder and harder.

He slipped back under the chrome bar and did another set of six reps, his glasses fogging slightly with the exertion. The weight moved a bit harder this time, but it was still nothing he couldn't handle. There had been a time when he'd been able to handle quite a bit more, but that was then and this was now. Now he was happy that, at sixty-three, he was able to delay the inevitable as long as possible.

Conner finished his third set on the chest machine and moved over to the free weight rack. He selected two thirty-five pound dumbbells and placed them carefully on either side of a padded bench, then spread his towel on the bench before lying down on it. He was not overly fastidious, but this was the season of sniffles, after all. He'd gotten a free influenza vaccination at a local Hollywood clinic, but it would do little to protect him against colds or some of the other strange viruses that seemed to be floating around these days. It was more than a matter of not wanting to feel bad; having been asthmatic all his life, and having spent most of that adult life breathing the polluted air of Los Angeles, he did not want to take the chance of catching something that might lead to bronchitis or pneumonia.

He lifted the weights slowly, arms bent, over his chest, bringing them together with a slight clink and then lowering them again. His right shoulder protested; legacy of having done his own stunts for several years. Conner wished, not for the first time, that he had taken better care of himself when he was younger—both physically and financially. If he had made a few different choices, maybe hadn't done quite so much work in those schlock horror films that Castle and Corman and the others had ground out in the fifties and sixties. . . .

Conner shook his head slightly, both to clear his eyes of sweat and to clear his head of such thoughts. There was plenty of room for regrets, in both his career and his life, to be sure. But things were as they were, as much a result of luck as talent. Nicholson and Coppola had worked for Corman at the same time he had, after all. It was hard not to be bitter.

He finished his third set, stood and regarded himself in the mirror. His posture was not what it had been when he was younger, but then, neither was anything else. His stomach was still reasonably flat, though he had never been able, even with strenuous dieting and exercise, to make the after-forty bulge disappear completely. Still, he could still touch his toes without bending his knees; more than many men his age—and many men a good deal younger—could do.

Conner regarded his reflection with the actor's constantly critical eye. Certainly still good-looking enough for character parts; the thick glasses gave a scholarly touch. The receding hairline was offset, he felt, by letting it grow more full around the ears and neck. The chest and shoulders were pumped and defined quite nicely for the moment. Conner nodded, satisfied, and moved on to the next exercise.

Conner did not shower at the Y, since he lived only six blocks away. He strolled down Hudson toward Sunset, wearing sweat pants, a T-shirt and running shoes. A black crew jacket bearing the logo THE TWILIGHT ZONE in Ralph Steadman-like lettering (he had guested in one of the syndicated episodes shot in Toronto back in '86) protected him from the chill morning wind. The smogless days when the wind blew always lifted his spirits; the dry weather kept the arthritis in his right hip at bay—thank God that fog last night had not lasted—and he felt in general quite pleased with himself and the world.

Oh, there was certainly room for regrets in his life. A pity, for example, that he and Helen had never had children—one of them might have struck it rich and been able to afford to support the old man in high style now. Sometimes he almost envied Helen; what remained of her resided in a pewter urn on the mantle in his apartment. Conner smiled sadly at the memory of her final days in the hospital. No, it was better to be alive, even though at times he had to wonder where his next meal was coming from. His last steady job had been almost a year ago.

He turned right, walked down a block and crossed the street to the Chansen and Delancy Mortuary. He picked up the newspaper, unlocked the side door and started up the stairs. He lived in a small apartment on the second floor above the mortuary. The rent was cheap in exchange for Conner's acting as a sort of unofficial night watchman for the place.

The irony of it all was not lost on him; a has-been character actor who had specialized in horror films living over a mortuary. Still, it had its advantages. He certainly couldn't complain about noisy neighbors, and it was close to the YMCA and the convenience stores over on Highland and Sunset. This last was especially good, since Conner did not drive. His astigmatism had grown steadily worse over the years, and the last car he owned had been over fifteen years ago.

The building dated from the forties, back when they knew how to build. The ceilings in his apartment were high, the doorways wide and linteled, as were the windows. The light switches were the old push-button kind. Practically every inch of wall space was covered with mementos of his career. The one-sheets, lobby cards and production stills ranged from his first appearance as a teen-aged juvenile delinquent on *Alcoa Presents* through the late fifties and early sixties, when

he had been a semi-regular on *Song of the City*. Then there
had been his salad days in the movies: the Edgar Allan Poe
and H.P. Lovecraft pastiches, the low-budget horror flicks and
the three films for AIP in which he had played Jonathan Skull,
the Vampire Slayer: *Vampire Lover, Bride of the Night* and
Cult of the Undead. After that had come increasingly infrequent parts in slasher films like the *Walpurgis Night* series.

There were also other keepsakes: the mask and hands of
the Embryon from *Shadownight*; a statuette of a vampire in
white tie and opera cloak given to him by the Vampire Ap-
preciation Society for his portrayal of Jonathan Skull; a thick
leather-bound book with iron hasps, the "Grimorum Dae-
monum," from *Hellspawn*. Conner had been asked by the
owner of the mortuary, when he was moving in, if he was sure
he wouldn't be nervous living in a building full of dead bodies. He had replied that, could the dead see his collection, they
would be the nervous ones.

Conner dropped his gym bag and headed for the kitchen.
He was always ravenous after a workout, and he lost no time
heating up a wok and preparing a meal of stir-fry with chicken
and vegetables. He had grown increasingly health-conscious
since Helen died. His own mortality was becoming more and
more real to him, and his health insurance was of a sporadic
nature, depending on the amount of work he did for signatory
companies. Things would have been much better had not
Helen's doctor bills and the chemotherapy eaten up what sav-
ings they had had.

In a few minutes Conner was sitting at the kitchen nook,
the wok's steaming contents spread over brown rice. From
this position he could see most of the living room and his
bizarre collection. Sometimes he wondered why he had been
so obsessive in collecting and preserving these souvenirs of
his work. The obvious answer was that they were the symbols of what he had done with his life. One likes to look back
and feel that one has done good work. He had always been
fond of horror and the supernatural, and had enjoyed the work

he had done, though one could certainly argue that it had been less than high art. Still, when all was said and done, Conner felt that he would not have done anything differently.

And his career was by no means over. He still did the occasional hour episodic guest appearance, and his agent was getting him work in commercial voiceovers. Plus he kept busy in other ways; two or three nights a week he did volunteer work over at Phoenix House, serving food and just talking to the constant parade of street kids who hung out there. A few of them even knew who he was, thanks to his stint in the *Walpurgis Night* movies as the psychiatrist tracking a demon who possessed teenagers and drove them to slaughter their peers in imaginatively grotesque ways. It was at times a draining experience, watching young lives being wasted, but he had the satisfaction of knowing that he was doing something, however small, to help stem that particular tide.

He opened the paper as he ate. The main story concerned the bombing of a van with someone inside over on Selma, but it was a sub-headline on the front page that caught his eye: POLICE BAFFLED BY "NIGHT HUNTER" SLAYING.

Conner read the article rapidly. He had not had a chance to catch the local TV news last night, and so this was the first he had heard of the strange killing only a few blocks from where he lived. After a couple of bites he forgot about his food as he read the piece, which told of a young transient found with a stake driven through his heart. There were no leads and no apparent motive for the slaying.

Conner went into his living room and stopped before a glass-fronted bookcase. Within were two rows of loose-leaf binders containing TV and feature scripts—everything he had been in, no matter how small the role, since 1956. He pulled out a volume entitled *Mask of the Vampire*. The script's final draft date was January 13, 1972. Conner opened it, leafed through it. His part had been highlighted in now-faded yellow marker. It had been a three-week, low-budget shoot, he remembered; a quickie designed to cash in on the drive-in crowd. Due to distribution difficulties, however, it had hardly been shown. The story was about a small-town sheriff who investigates a dead body found with a stake in its heart. He ultimately discovers, with the help of a Van Helsing-like local doctor, that his town is being preyed on by a vampire. Conner had played the doctor. The part had led directly to his starring in the three Jonathan Skull films.

Mask of the Vampire had been a mediocre effort, quickly condemned to late-night television and later video release. Still, Conner wondered, could there be a connection somehow between the film and what was now going on in L.A.?

He tried to recall if he still knew anyone who had worked on the film. Eddie Gray, who had played the sheriff, had died two years earlier of emphysema. Curt Caldwell had been the vampire; he was a regular now on a soap opera out of New York. The director had been Joe Fortes; he was also still working as far as Conner knew, directing hour episodics. The A.D. had been a guy named Ed Thayer, who had gone on to put together his own production company in the mid-eighties. Conner remembered reading in the trades that Thayer had died a couple of years ago in a fire up in San Francisco.

He glanced at the script's title page, unable to recall the writer's name. Phil Fitzgerald. Conner had no idea what he was doing now, if anything.

He leafed through the script a bit more, gratified to find that some of the lines, though they had been memorized twenty years before, still sounded familiar to him. One of the side benefits of acting was a well-developed memory; he could vividly recall the shoot, which had taken place in Altadena as a stand-in for a small Northern California town. His death in the film had been a somewhat imaginative one, improvised by himself and the director when budget constrictions had made the scripted finale impossible. He had been hurled by the vampire onto an electrified fence, and the fiery cruciform outline of his burning body had driven the undead fiend back into range of the sheriff's crossbow. Conner glanced around the wall, located the framed production still of his wax effigy ablaze against the night sky. He shut the script and put it back on its shelf.

It could be a coincidence, of course; it wouldn't be the first time life had imitated art in a particularly horrific manner. Still, it was worth looking into. He sat down in the easy chair next to his phone and dialed his agent's number. Marty had been known to drum up notoriety for his clients out of news-related incidents. He could possibly get some work out of it. It was a long shot, but, given the ephemeral quality of his bank account right now, worth pursuing. At his age any publicity was better than no publicity.

CHAPTER 14

Friday, October 25

It was four-thirty in the afternoon when Dan Stratton came into the station, looking smug. He dragged a chair over to Jake's desk, straddled it and grinned at the detective.

Jake studied Dan's expression warily. "What?"

"Something interesting on Jimmy Ray," Dan said. "Got Latham to give me a copy of the lab work-up." He pulled a folded piece of paper from his hip pocket, smoothed it out. "According to this, the garlic bulb in Jimmy's mouth bears evidence of digestive enzymes at work. It was soaked with saliva." He glanced at Jake, who looked blank. "You punch out, all systems shut down, right? Garlic is potent stuff, Jake. Put some in your mouth, your mouth waters, the digestive process kicks into high gear right away. Which is what happened here."

Jake took the lab report, looked at it. There was a jaw-breaking list of various enzymes found on the garlic clove:

ptyalin, acid phosphatase, lipase, lysozymes . . . he glanced
back at Dan. "You're saying Tate had the garlic in his mouth
before he was whacked." Dan nodded.

Jake tossed the report back to him. "So?"

"So," Dan said, "if you're going to kill a vampire and you
want him to stay dead, doesn't it make more sense to put garlic in his mouth *after* you stake him?"

Jake looked thoughtfully at Dan for several moments, then
nodded. "Okay," he said. "I'm asking McNamara to put you
in plainclothes on this assignment. You'll be working with me
on this."

Dan grinned tightly and pumped a fist. Jake, who was
reaching for the phone, stopped and looked at him. "This is
not, repeat, *not,* a promotion. It's an assignment. *If* I can swing
it."

"Understood," Dan said. "But if this works out, maybe I
can skip P-III and make Detective Trainee." He stood.
"Thanks, Jake. You and me, we're gonna bust this fruitcake."

Jake shook his head. "Ah, youth," he murmured. He started
to punch in the extension, stopped when his line rang. "Homicide, Detective Hull."

The wheezing, atonal voice was immediately recogniz-
able. "Check out a small-time dealer they call Ziplock,"
Croaker said with some effort. "Skinny kid, blond buzzcut.
Marijuana leaf tattoo on his right arm. Word is he knew Tate."

"Good work, Croak," Jake said. "I'll kick in an extra ten
for getting back to me so fast." He hung up and leaned back
in his chair, the springs protesting indignantly.

Dan looked at him. "You gonna tell me, or do I have to hire
a detective?"

Jake said, "We have a lead."

Every cop in the Hollywood Area knows that a prime place
to score dope and/or tail is Mister Mack's, a burger joint on
Gower near Willoughby. In the shade of its fiberglass awning
teenaged girls and boys, their bodies tanned as Pop-Tarts and

rife with STDs, play the old *Space Invaders* arcade games or lounge on the orange picnic benches, sucking down Cokes and fries for breakfast, lunch and dinner and eyeing the passing world with a strange mixture of naiveté and jaded weariness. Any of them can be penniless one day and twenty-four hours later have five or six hundred bucks wedged into the pockets of their tight-fitting jeans. Most are in the grip of crack cocaine or methamphetamines like a mouse in the talons of a hawk, and as quick as the money comes, out it goes to buy a few precious hours of mindlessness.

Jake parked the car a block or so down the street on the east side, near where the imposing walls, topped with razor wire, of Paramount Studios rose like some modern-day castle stronghold barricaded against the Third World neighborhood. He and Dan strolled up to Mister Mack's, feeling the weight of various appraising stares as they approached. It was just after seven, the sky above them the color of a bruise. The wind buffeted the area, causing the corrugated awning to rattle and hum.

There was no point, Jake knew, in pretending they weren't cops. These kids could smell a badge ten blocks away and against the wind. It was also worse than useless to come on like a social worker, all warm and friendly. Most runaways were one step up from feral; the only thing they understood and respected was a no-nonsense don't-fuck-with-me attitude.

At first look none of the burger stand's clientele matched the description they were looking for. Jake and Dan stopped by one of the arcade games, where a boy of perhaps seventeen was maneuvering a joystick intently. Despite the gusts of cold wind, he wore a net tank top over well-developed arms and chest. A scraggly beard covered his cheeks like crabgrass on a lawn. Jake leaned against the garishly painted cabinet of the game and said, "Looking for Ziplock. Seen him?"

The boy's cheek twitched. "He don't come around no more," he said in a hoarse voice.

Jake put a hand over the game's firing button, causing the starship on the screen to be blown into hyperspace. The boy slapped the console in frustration. "Shit, look what you made me do!" He glared at Jake. His eyes, the detective noted, were yellow; not just slightly bilious, but the color of ripe lemons. Hepatitis. The pupils were blown as well; that in combination with the raspy voice said ice smoker to Jake.

The boy took a step toward Jake. Jake was aware of the rest of the crowd watching him and Dan. He stared back, giving the kid cop's eyes. Back at the academy they had called it "command presence." After a tense moment the boy shifted his gaze groundward.

"Ain't seen him for days, I told you," he mumbled.

Without changing expression Jake spun him around and hiked his right arm up between his shoulder blades, then slammed him across a picnic table, scattering greasy fries and onion rings. "You were saying?" he said.

The boy hissed with pain. Jake kept his eyes on as many of the others as he could. He caught a glimpse of Dan off to one side, looking surprised but ready to start crowd control should it come to that. Which it could, Jake knew. While bracing a crowd of runaways was not as dangerous as wading into a party full of Crips or Bloods, there was still no guarantee that one of them, his better judgment shattered by a recent hit of crack or dust, might not decide to grab up the nearest potted palm and try to brain Jake or Dan with it.

"He's over at Phoenix, most nights," Jake's dancing partner said through gritted teeth. Jake released him and stepped back, making sure none of the scattered junk food was under his feet should he have to move quickly. "Let's go," he said to Dan.

They walked back to the car. Behind them the party quickly resumed; there was little that could surprise the local street Arabs for long. Jake glanced at his watch. Phoenix House was less than five minutes away. The thought that a break in this case could come that quickly almost brought a smile to his face.

Dan Stratton didn't say much on the short drive across Fountain to Phoenix House. He couldn't help glancing occasionally at Jake out of the corner of his eye, however. What had happened back there at Mister Mack's made him uneasy. While it was true that no cop—including himself—could truthfully say that they had never laid a hand on someone with less-than-justifiable cause, still it was yet another piece of evidence that Jake was on a pretty short fuse these days. Stratton was beginning to wonder if the word "liability" was more suited to working with him than "asset."

Phoenix House had once been a laundromat and dry cleaning shop that had gone belly-up; it was essentially one long, high-ceilinged room with various plywood and drywall partitions set up within it. Stratton had been there once before on a call-related matter. It was a rundown place where runaways and the homeless could come by and get a few hours' respite from the streets, have a hot meal and a shower, maybe use the ancient washer and dryer left there from the building's previous incarnation. There were rules that had to be observed: no fighting, no stealing, no dealing drugs. Breaking these meant banishment for a week or a month or maybe forever.

Second-hand clothes, clean and mended, were available for the asking. Food was contributed by restaurants and local merchants. Phoenix House also supplied condoms and a once-a-week free clinic with volunteer health workers. Inside an old Westinghouse refrigerator, the kind that parents used to fear their children would suffocate in, there was locked a fair selection of meds—mostly antibiotics and painkillers.

All in all, it was a good service, in Stratton's opinion. It was always operating on a wing and a prayer, one jump ahead of the landlord and the city health inspector.

When they arrived, the last bit of twilight was fading. A crowd of teenagers, nearly all sporting tattoos and multiple piercings, were hanging around the entrance. Stratton noticed several top-flight running shoes, expensive leather jackets, Walkmans and other items that were no doubt stolen. One of the volunteer staff, a man in his early thirties named Simon Rhys, greeted them and led them into a small office furnished with mismatched chairs, desk and filing cabinet. On one wall were several dozen pictures of people—men and women of differing races, ranging in age from late teens to early thirties. "Our successes," Rhys said, gesturing to them. "The ones that managed to get off the streets and back into society. Reminds us of why we're here."

He gestured for them to sit on a worn couch while he leaned against the desk. Stratton was struck by the economy and focus of Rhys's movements as he crossed the floor. There was a power and grace to the man that made the cop certain Rhys was a martial arts practitioner.

"What style'd you study?" he asked.

Rhys looked startled for a moment and then grinned. "Chan Gen. I try to keep in practice. Yourself?"

"I dabbled a little in Shotokan and Tai-Kwan-Do while I was overseas. Had a sergeant who was pretty good; taught me a few moves. Just enough to hurt myself." Rhys nodded, his smile encouraging. "Chan Gen," Stratton mused. "Never heard of that one. Chinese?"

"It's still kind of new in the States," Rhys said. "I teach a little here; helps give the kids some self-esteem and ways to vent their anger." He changed the subject. "How can I help you, gentlemen?"

Jake told him who they were looking for and why. Rhys listened attentively, his expression somber. "Ziplock, yes, we know him here. Does a fair amount of dealing—crack, heroin, ice. Usually hangs around with another boy who calls himself Angel. His drug of choice is PCP."

"Are they here now?" Jake asked.

"Unfortunately, no. But I can tell you where you'll proba- bly find them. They and a lot of other boys have been hang- ing out with a rich chicken hawk who calls himself Anton Magus. Lives up in the Hollywood Hills somewhere." Rhys's voice had an edge of disgust in it. "He claims to be a warlock and a Satanist. It's a rap that the kids, particularly the boys, can't resist." He shook his head. "When you're as fucked-up as some of these kids, and all you've really got to look for- ward to is winding up lying in an alley somewhere drinking Mad Dog out of a paper bag—if you live that long—then the lure of some kind of forbidden power is very strong."

"Believe me," Jake said as he got to his feet, "if I thought it would do some good on my case load, I might try casting a few spells myself."

Rhys showed them to the door and shook both their hands. His grip was strong and powerful. Dan figured him for sev- eral degrees worth of black belt, at least. He was glad Rhys was on their side; the man would not be an easy takedown if it came to that.

"If I can be of any more help, let me know," Rhys said. "A lot of the kids who come in here are scared, believe me. The newspaper stories about this 'Night Hunter' have really got- ten to them."

"Maybe a little fear is good," Dan said. "Might give them the motivation they need to get free of this life."

Rhys shook his head sadly. "One of the little sayings we have around here is 'The street ain't under your feet, it's under your hat.' A lot of them have opportunities for jobs and stable lives, but they prefer the excitement of living on the edge. And when you live on the edge, sooner or later you get cut."

Outside, another fog was coming in. The moon was almost full, and its silvery light on the wisps of mist seemed some- how repulsive, like glistening strands of webbing spun by some monstrous spider.

"Talk to this guy, talk to that guy. . . ." Stratton said as they walked toward the car. "I'm getting a sore throat. How about we take a break, maybe get something to eat?"

"Later," Jake said as he coaxed the engine into firing. "I want to run that name through the computer, find an address. This guy Magus sounds like a real solid lead."

Stratton sighed. He had heard that Jake Hull could be as tenacious as a wolverine when working a case, but it was one thing to hear about it and another to be in the middle of it. The later it got, the more energy the detective seemed to have. It was, Stratton told himself, going to be a long night.

CHAPTER 15

Anton Magus was a self-described latter-day Aleister Crowley who, as Rhys had said, lived in a mansion high in the Hollywood Hills at the foot of Mount Lee, on one of the roads that ended in a cul-de-sac. Jake and Dan drove up a series of narrow, twisting streets buckled by tree roots and weather until they came to the residence, which was not far from the Hollywood sign.

The house was built of redwood and stone, its sharp angles somehow merging well with the rocky hillside behind it. A '64 Porsche was parked in the driveway; the license plate read SATAN.

"Don't worry," Dan said to Jake as they parked and walked to the front door. "I brought a cross and some holy water, just in case." Jake shot him a look, then rang the doorbell. Sonorous chimes sounded somewhere deep within the huge house.

The door opened, and a man—a butler, evidently, by his

clothes—looked down at them. Neither Jake nor Dan was short, but both were dwarfed by the butler, who was six-two or -three easily. Jake showed him his shield. "Detective Hull and Officer Stratton to see Anton Magus."

The butler nodded and turned back into the house. Dan glanced at Jake, barely suppressing a grin.

They entered a wide front hall, decorated with framed paintings. Small golden plaques on the bottoms of the ornate frames identified them. Dan managed to read one of them as they walked: Bosch's *Garden of Earthly Delights*. The paintings all seemed to be medieval in period, their subject matter disturbing.

The butler led them up a few steps, past a small indoor garden in which Dan noticed a human skull, or a replica of one, serving as a flower pot. The hall opened into a huge two-story main room, the walls of which were covered with more paintings and bookshelves. Dan had never seen so many books. All of them appeared to be hardcovers, and many seemed quite old.

The furniture was of dark wood, intricately carved, with huge backs and snarling lions' and gargoyles' heads decorating the burls and crests. Though not at all of the same style as the house itself, they seemed somehow to fit. Hanging over the far door was a large iron pentagram with a stylized goat's head in it. One of the five points of the star pointed directly downward—Dan remembered reading somewhere that such a positioning was an invocation of evil. He sniffed; he could smell some subtle incense flavoring the air. Tinkling music—generic New Age, it sounded like—played faintly from hidden speakers.

Anton Magus was sitting in one of the high-backed chairs; he stood as they came in. He was wearing a black silk shirt with a red tie under a smoking jacket. He was as small as his butler was large; no more than five-six or -seven, tops, Dan estimated. Stand him next to the butler and he would look like a child. His hair was black, obviously touched up at the temples, combed straight back and tied in the short ponytail that most cops referred to as a "dork knob." His beard was carefully trimmed, and silver-rimmed glasses magnified his brown eyes.

"Detective Hull and Officer Stratton," the butler said. His voice was surprisingly soft.

Magus shook their hands. His hand was cool and dry, his grip firm. Dan could smell some kind of cologne or hair oil wafting from him, vaguely astringent, like patchouli oil. "Please be seated," he said. "May I offer you refreshments?"

"No, thanks," Jake said, while Dan shook his head. Neither of them sat down.

Magus did not seem offended. He gestured to the butler, who quietly left. Magus crossed the room to stand beside a glass-fronted case, the shelves of which contained bottles of powdered substances, a mortar and pestle and what Dan assumed were other alchemical appurtenances. Magus leaned one arm on the case and waited, eyebrow arched quizzically.

Jake took the photo from his jacket pocket and held it out to Magus. "This boy was killed at approximately two-thirty on the morning of the twenty-second. We understand you might have been acquainted with him."

Magus glanced at the photo without taking it from the detective. "James Raymond Tate. Yes, he attended a few of our meetings. He did not find traveling the left-handed path to his liking. I haven't seen him for several months." He could have been discussing starving children in Africa for all the concern displayed.

"The cause of death was a wooden stake through the heart," Jake said.

Magus nodded, apparently not at all surprised. "His dealings with drug dealers of Hollywood were bound to result in violence sooner or later."

"You don't seem terribly upset," Dan remarked. Magus turned his gaze toward the cop. Dan tried to read that gaze and couldn't. There was something behind it, to be sure, but what it was—anger, amusement or some emotion he had no name for—was impossible to tell.

"You men are here," Magus said, his tone conversational, even friendly, "because Tate was killed and you suspect his involvement with me is somehow connected. The penny-dreadful manner of his death only strengthens your conviction. You assume we routinely cause such gruesome deaths, directly or indirectly. Oh, I'm very familiar with all the rumors, gentlemen: that people like myself and my flock brainwash women into becoming breeders for us, willingly giving up their children for sacrifice; that we force people to participate in sabbatic orgies and unholy ceremonies; that we poison or otherwise dispatch by Machiavellian means those who decry us. Harassment, in short.

"James Tate was not someone I knew well, so I feel no great sadness at his passing, particularly since it was not unexpected, given the company he kept on the street. Also, we view death not as a cause for mourning, as do the fish worshipers. I have never been able to understand how a religion which teaches that its adherents will ascend to paradise after death nevertheless allows, even encourages, such a bleak attitude toward the deceased." He made a dismissive gesture. "But never mind. It's apparent that I must somehow convince you that neither I nor my flock had anything to do with his death. How can I do this?"

Dan and Jake glanced at each other. "You can start by telling us where you were when he was killed and if anyone can attest to your statement," Jake told him.

"Ah, an alibi." Magus seemed genuinely amused now. "Fortunately this is easy to establish." He crossed to one of the bookshelves, pulled out a large volume, obviously very old, with what seemed to be iron hinges anchoring the cover to the spine. Dan could make out the black Gothic lettering of the title: *Liber Arcanorum*. Magus opened it, riffled through pages covered with faded spidery scribbling and illustrations of magical symbols. "I was conducting a study group with several of my students on the various categories of demons according to Michael Psellus. I can give you their names if you'd like." He closed the book and put it back on the shelf.

Dan was uncertain whether Magus meant the names of the students or of the demon categories, but Jake just said, "I'd appreciate it. And their phone numbers and addresses." He scribbled the information on a field interview card.

"Will there be anything else, gentlemen?" Magus seemed definitely amused now.

Dan glanced at Jake. The latter was gazing around the room, taking in the bookshelves full of ancient lore and the bizarre statuary and artwork. He stepped over to a table, looked at a large bronze sculpture depicting a winged and horned demon performing analingus on an extremely willing woman. Even from across the room Dan could see that the demon was hung like a fire hose and, judging by the woman's expression, was no slouch in the tongue department either.

Jake looked up at Magus. "You're really a sick shit, aren't you?"

Magus allowed himself a small indulgent smile. "How does the current argot have it, Detective? 'Different strokes for different folks'?"

"Sly and the Family Stone," Jake replied. *"Everyday People,* 1969. Not what I'd call current. Your lack of hipness is showing."

"People are often repulsed by that which they do not understand," Magus replied. He smiled, looking at Jake, his dark eyes glittering. "Or by that which, on a deeper level, attracts them."

Jake straightened and took a step closer to Magus. For a brief instant Dan thought the detective was going to slug the Satanist. But Jake merely smiled slightly, reached into his pocket and handed Magus a business card.

"If you have any further thoughts you'd like to share with us about Jimmy Ray, don't hesitate to get in touch," he said.

They started for the door. "Don't bother calling Lurch," Dan said, "we can find our own way out."

Magus seemed momentarily confused, then realized Dan was referring to the butler. Obviously not into popular culture, Dan told himself. Magus followed them to the front door.

"One last thing—was anyone in your coven friends with Tate, or an enemy of him?" Jake asked Magus as the latter opened the door.

"My advice to you," Magus replied, "would be to concentrate your efforts on the drug dealers and other human vermin that Tate associated with. You're far more likely to find the kind of person who would kill him there than among us.

"Oh, and by the way—'coven' refers to a gathering of witches. Satanism has nothing to do with witchcraft. Witches are pathetic souls who scrabble for crumbs of diabolic power to further their own petty ends. We, on the other hand, are an integral part of the eternal scheme of existence. Light, after all, cannot exist without the contrast of shadow. Lucifer's attempt to wrest power from God and his subsequent fall from grace gave us free will. His was a far greater sacrifice than Christ's."

"Thanks for the sermon," Jake said. "Don't leave town."

Magus smiled and gently closed the door.

As they walked back to the car, Jake said, "I like him."

Dan knew that Jake was not expressing a wave of personal regard for the Satanist. "I don't," he replied. "It's too neat. He's too perfect."

"One thing you learn, you been doing this for awhile, is that neat isn't necessarily bad. That's TV think, that's Colombo crap. 'He can't be the murderer, he's too obvious.' Well, sometimes they're obvious for a reason, and that reason is they did it."

They got in the car and started back down the winding streets framed with towering eucalyptus and *faux*-Mediterranean villas. Dan leaned back in the seat. "Maybe. But this guy doesn't come across as stupid. If I'm a major-league hitter and I'm gonna do somebody, I'm sure as shit not gonna beat him to death with a Louisville Slugger. Satanists, stakes—it's too fucking obvious."

"Maybe. Anyway, if these alibis check out, we're gonna have a hard time sticking him with it," Jake said.

They rode in silence until they were out of the hills. Then Dan said, "You believe any of that shit he was spouting about light needing shadow and all?"

Jake was quiet for so long that Dan thought he hadn't heard the question. Then he said, "We don't need more shadows. We need more light. A *lot* more light."

CHAPTER 16

Saturday, October 26

Brandon squealed with laughter as he looked at the reading on the scale. "Mommy, I only weigh ten pounds on the moon! Know why?"

"No, dear," Sarah said, with what she hoped was a patient smile. "Enlighten me."

"Because the moon has less gravity than Earth, *that's* why!" The boy leaped off the scale and ran toward another one. "Let's see how much I weigh on Jupiter!"

Sarah followed, trying to keep Brandon in sight amidst the crowd of people who milled about the various exhibits at the observatory. Even in here, deep within the massive stone structure, she could hear the winds howling outside. It was three P.M. on a Saturday and the Santa Anas had been blowing for nearly twelve hours straight all over the L.A. basin. They had started before dawn and now were gusting hard enough to warrant traffic advisories everywhere. She hadn't wanted to drive all the way over to Griffith Park—she was always nervous driving the Jeep in high winds—but she had promised Brandon for weeks to take him here. It was good to encourage the boy's interest in science, after all—get all the plugs for education while you can before he becomes a teenager and starts rebelling at everything in sight.

She treasured the times she had with her son more than anything else in her life. That the hours were so few made them all the more precious. According to Brandon, Matt rarely had time for field trips like these with his son, and so Sarah tried to take up the slack as much as she could. Someday, she promised herself as she watched Brandon—sidetracked from his quest to weigh himself on all nine planets by another, more fascinating exhibit—someday she would have him all the time. She only hoped she could make it happen before he was too old for them to enjoy times like this together.

She saw Brandon talking to another boy, perhaps a year younger. The two seemed to be making friends in that guileless, easy manner of which children are sometimes capable. Sarah automatically glanced around, seeking the adult or adults who would have their eyes trained on the boy even as hers constantly were on Brandon. She did not see anyone, and felt a small flutter of discomfort. Should she go up to the child, ask him where his parents were? Sarah knew at times she was overprotective, that you can't keep an eye on your child every minute of every day, but the knowledge of how quickly a kidnapper could remove her son and her sanity from her life forever was always lurking in the back of her mind. To be a parent is to give up the ability to relax completely for the rest of one's life.

She had already taken a step toward Brandon and his new friend when a familiar voice behind her said, "It's okay, he's with me."

Sarah turned and saw Jake Hull standing a few feet behind her. It took her a second to recognize him; he wasn't wearing the rumpled sports jacket and slacks that were his trademark uniform. Instead he was dressed in loose jeans and a T-shirt. The shirt was emblazoned with a quote by Tolstoy, to her surprise: "All great truths are simple."

"Fancy meeting you here," she said, regretting the clichéd phrase almost as soon as it left her mouth. "That's your son?"

"Max," Jake said. "I get him on weekends."

"Me too, with Brandon." Sarah felt a surprising sense of kinship with the detective; she had known he was a divorced parent, like her, but the thought of the two of them being in the same place on an outing with their kids had never occurred to her. "So much for nuclear families, huh?"

He smiled and was about to say something in return when the two boys suddenly turned and raced toward the huge swinging pendulum in the rotunda beneath the dome. The detective and the M.E. both turned in perfect unison and yelled, "Stay in sight!"

The boys slowed to a walk for a few moments before their enthusiasm got the better of them again. Jake and Sarah looked at each other and started to laugh as they both followed their offspring.

"It's like being a member of a club," Jake said as they walked. "Being a parent, I mean. It really gives you an 'us and them' way of looking at life. As bad as being a cop."

"I didn't think any club was as exclusive as being a cop."

Jake gave her a sidelong glance. "Oh, I can think of a few. Doctors, for example."

"Advantage—Hull." They stopped at the edge of the pit and looked down at the slowly swinging metal ball. Small pegs were arranged in a circle that marked the edges of the pendulum's swing; according to the informational plaque, the rotation of the earth insured that a peg would be knocked down every hour. The pendulate movement was mesmerizing; they watched it in silence for awhile, glancing up occasionally to make sure that the kids were still in sight.

Finally Jake said, "So, you come here often?"

She nodded. "I like the band. Food's not bad either."

He smiled slightly. The sight surprised her; she'd worked with Jake Hull on a number of cases, had seen him intense, angry, brooding and sarcastic. She had never seen him smile before.

"It's nice seeing you away from the job," she said. "You seem more—relaxed."

The slight smile that creased his face flickered but did not entirely vanish. "Appearances can be deceiving."

"Oh, come on—don't give me that 'cop's work is never done' shit. It's nice knowing you're the kind of guy who'll take some time off to be with his son. I like that."

He nodded as though considering the words very seriously. In the pit below them the tip of the pendulum knocked over another peg. Jake turned his head and looked at her, more directly than he had before. "Well, it's nice knowing the same thing about you."

Sarah felt her skin prickle slightly, as though the winds outside had somehow penetrated the walls to run invisible cold fingers over her. She smiled at him, feeling the twinge of cracked lips. "How about we get the kids out of this crowd?"

They sat on a cold stone bench and watched Brandon and Max crawl through graffiti-scarred plastic tunnels and swing on ropes over sand, which the childrens' imaginations had turned into swamps teeming with crocodiles. The small park was tucked away into a corner of the Hollywood Hills, just off Mulholland Drive, and the chill wind which howled and blasted down from the high desert did not touch them save for gentle eddies and backwaters of air.

"This is a nice little place," Sarah said. "I didn't even know it was here. Good to be able to let the kids run free without worrying."

"You never stop worrying." Jake's gaze seemed fixed, not on the children playing but on other, darker sights. Sarah saw him rub his stomach and wince in pain.

"Six weeks ago," he continued, "couple of *cholos* caught

an Asian woman jogging here. Took her up into the hills, back there—" he pointed "—and anally raped her. Had her face pushed into the dirt so she suffocated while they took turns getting off."

"I remember the case," Sarah said. She felt angry at Jake now; why had he spoiled the mood by bringing something like this up? There was no need to remind her that Los Angeles was rife with murder and danger. It wasn't like she was a civilian, skating through life with only the vaguest awareness of the horrors that lurked below the city's glossy surface.

Perhaps he felt they were getting too friendly. Perhaps this was his way of reminding her that they were two professionals, linked only by the need to bring to justice the sick and twisted dirtbags out there whose deeds kept them busy night and day. Well, fine, if that's how he wanted to play it. . . .

"I did some ER work over at County-USC a few years ago," she said. "We had a young girl brought in with a gunshot wound to the chest. Wrong place, wrong time, wrong end of the gun, you know? She's okay at first—even talking—then her blood pressure starts to drop. Fifteen minutes later her heart stops from shock and blood loss.

"We got it started again, but she needed surgery. Only the on-call surgeon wasn't there. He's banging some candystriper upstairs. Patient's heart stops again—we crack her chest, massage the heart, clamp the artery. She holds on for another half hour, then dies just as the surgeon walks through the door, zipping his fly."

Jake watched the kids, giving no indication at first that he'd heard her. Even shielded from the wind and with the sun high in the sky, the air was chilly. Sarah zipped her windbreaker a little tighter.

"Had a call last week," he said, still not looking at her. "Six-week-old baby found dead, his little asshole sewn shut with fishing line. Died of a blocked intestine. Found his mother—seventeen years old, a crackhead. Seems she just got tired of shitty diapers."

Sarah nodded. She'd never heard of a case like that, but she found it no stretch of the imagination at all to believe it. "One of my first times out as M.E.—a house over on Slauson. Some poor sonuvabitch dead as Elvis on the floor, multiple stab wounds. Not a hard call on cause of death. They're Mirandizing the wife when I walk in—she's still holding the knife and not exactly grasping the gravity of the situation. 'What, you mean he's *dead*?' 'Yes, ma'am,' one of the uniforms says. She kicks the body, says, 'You motherfucker! I stabbed you plenty times before and you never *died* on me!'"

Jake laughed. It was only a few sharp barks of humor, and it took Sarah a moment to recognize the sound coming from him. He looked at her then with an expression she could not quite fathom—mingled amusement, disgust and despair were all part of it.

"It grinds you down, you know? You're supposed to be one of the good guys. But you find yourself breaking the law all the time, in little ways and not so little ways, just so you can take down some asshole who richly deserves it. You find yourself being judge, jury and sometimes executioner. And at first you fight it, you say, 'Hey, this wasn't in the job description.' But it erodes you. After a while you just say, 'Fuck it. It's the whole wide world against me.'"

He was quiet again. The wind sang a distant, sad song. She wanted to tell him she understood; that if anyone other than another cop could understand, it was someone like her. Instead she said, "He would have killed you if you hadn't killed him. Just like he killed Nivens."

He was quiet for so long that Sarah thought he hadn't heard her. Then he sighed and said, "Yeah, I tell myself that, over and over. Doesn't help. I've looked at it six ways from hell, come up with angles even the investigation didn't. Doesn't matter."

"He was a gang member, Jake. He knew what he was doing. He didn't kill Tom by accident. And he would have killed you, too."

He looked at her, his eyes dry but haunted. "He was *eight years old,* for Christ's sake!"

He looked out across the playground. "He was the same age as my son. And I had to kill him. And because I didn't pop him right when he pulled the piece, Tom is dead. Nothing can make that all right."

There was nothing she could reply to that, Sarah knew. The silence between them lengthened as she looked away also, across the cold sand to where the two boys ran and ducked and hid among the playground equipment, pointing imaginary guns at each other and shouting, "Bang! Bang!"

CHAPTER 17

Saturday, October 26

The room was long and narrow, with a high ceiling that was lost in the dim light from the candles. There were six of them, arranged in a pattern that Ziplock said was a pentacle. Just beyond the foremost candle the man in the black robes stood behind the—altar Angel guessed you would call it; it looked like an upside-down cross resting on its point and one of its arms—and prepared to read out of some huge black book he had propped up there. Angel didn't like how dark it was. The candlelight seemed to make the darkness around the little island of light stronger somehow.

Angel knew he was supposed to have his head bowed, but he couldn't resist surreptitious glances around him. Not that there was a whole lot to see; just the weird cross, the guy behind it and some candles in big stands set around. And the nine youths, all in their late teens, who also wore black robes and knelt before the cross. Initiates, the man had called them.

Ziplock had been right about one thing, Angel thought; this was some spooky shit. Had to be, hands down, the strangest thing he'd seen yet in his time on the street. Zip, his friend and sometimes partner in crime, had invited him to come to the ceremony tonight, the—what had he called it?—the *invocation.* Angel hadn't known what an invocation was—he only knew that the fucking wind was carving chunks out of him right down to the bone. Any place inside was okay by him tonight.

The man made some kind of weird gestures with his hands and started reading in a tone that was straight out of some old black-and-white horror movie. "Emperor Lucifer, Master of all the revolted Spirits, we entreat thee to favor us in the adjuration which I address to thy mighty minister, Lucifuge Rofocale, being desirous to make a pact with him. . . ."

A weak movement of cold, dry air caused the candle flames to flicker. The swaying shadows flickered over the faces of the initiates as they listened to the man—his name was Magus, Angel remembered, Anton Magus—behind the inverted cross. Angel felt his skin prickle and the thin fine hair on his arms and neck stirring with more than just static. He hadn't had a toke all day, and he was missing it. Everything here was suddenly just a little too real for him.

Hey, now . . . was he imagining things, or was the light from those candles getting dimmer?

A quick nervous inhalation escaped from him. Ziplock, on his knees to his right, shot him a sharp look, as did one of the others. He knew he was supposed to keep quiet, but shit, he wasn't imagining it, those candles were definitely flickering down now, and when they went out it was going to be fucking *dark* in here. Angel had never liked the dark. Too many bad things happen in the dark.

"We beg thee also, O Prince Beelzebub, to protect us in our undertakings. Count Astaroth! Be propitious to us, and grant that our plea be heard—"

One of the candles guttered and died. A moment later another one went out as well. The darkness now felt like a living, breathing force that pressed in hungrily from all sides. Angel stared about him, no longer trying to be subtle about it. It seemed he could see vague shapes, patches of blacker darkness, roiling just beyond the feeble yellow light. . . .

Angel couldn't take it anymore.

The man in black stopped his chant abruptly as Angel jerked to his feet with a cry, his voice cracking with fear. The other initiates stared at him in shock, then looked back at their master as though expecting him to hurl a lightning bolt from his fingertips that would turn this heretic into a small pile of ashes.

Instead, Magus smiled and moved from the altar to one of the nearby walls, his black-robed form disappearing for a moment beyond the dim light. Then the darkness was banished by an overhead set of track lighting that brightened slowly, like an artificial dawn, as he turned up a dimmer switch.

"It appears the latest addition to our flock is a bit overwhelmed by all this," he said softly. His voice made Angel think of cats and velvet. "Forgive me," Magus continued. He crossed the long narrow room to Angel and put a hand on the latter's shoulder. "There is nothing to be afraid of. You are among friends here."

Angel said nothing in reply; he looked around in slight embarrassment. This was the first time he had seen the room clearly. When he had been led into it with the others the lights had already been down and the candles lit; it could have been the size of a football field as far as he could tell. Instead it was narrow, maybe twelve feet across, and nearly twenty feet long, with a high raftered ceiling. The illusion of limitless space had been heightened by the thick black curtains that draped the walls.

"Hope I didn't . . . you know, spoil anything," Angel mumbled. Magus gave his shoulder a reassuring pat.

"It is forgiven. Despite popular opinion, our Master can be

lenient with new blood. But such things are not lightly interrupted; it would be best if I closed the liturgy."

Magus turned the lights back down, then returned to the altar and raised his arms, making more cabalistic hand movements. "O Prince Lucifer," he announced solemnly. "We are complete in our petitions to thee. We now leave thee in peace, and adjure thy minister to retire to Pandemonium, and will be mindful always of our obligations and servitude to thee."

As the lights came up again, Angel whispered to Ziplock, "Now what?"

"Now we eat," Zip whispered back.

Angel had to admit that the food was the best he'd had since he'd hitched into L.A. Some kind of vegetable soup to start, then roasted chicken and potatoes with green beans. He hadn't known what to expect, but this seemed too—normal. That didn't stop him from chowing down with gusto, though.

He and Ziplock were sitting together at a long table along with the rest of the initiates, in a softly lit dining room. Angel felt somewhat nervous handling the silverware and heavy crystal glasses, but it certainly wasn't enough to blunt his appetite.

Magus sat at the head of the table. Plates were removed and replaced by a tall, saturnine man whom Ziplock said was the butler. Angel had heard of butlers, but he'd never really seen one before.

"This is fuckin' *great,* Zip," he whispered to his companion. He nodded his head at Magus. "What's he into?"

Ziplock grinned. "Nothing you ain't done for twenty bucks and a Big Mac. But here we got clean sheets, good food, a place to sleep . . . man, it's *heaven* next to the street."

It sounded too good to be true. Angel knew there were few things he wouldn't do or have done to him to get a berth in a house like this.

He jerked around at the pressure of a hand on his shoulder. Anton Magus stood beside his chair, looking down at him and smiling, his teeth white against the dark lines of his trimmed beard. "Well, my nervous young friend, I do hope our ceremonies and devotions have not prejudiced you against us."

"Uh, no, I guess not," Angel said. "I mean . . . I just kinda got spooked, I guess."

"Of course," Magus said. His tone and expression were kindly and reassuring. Angel felt himself relaxing, although normally he viewed anyone over the age of twenty with deep suspicion. "Of course, if you are to join our flock, you will have to accustom yourself to the tenets of our faith. But there will be time enough for that." Angel was aware of the others watching him, their heads like pink and brown bubbles floating above the high-collared black robes. "Gordon has vouched for you," Magus continued, and it took Angel a minute to realize that he was talking about Zip; he'd never known the real name of the boy who had been his friend for over a year. "What I ask from you, should you decide to join us, is unquestioning devotion and orthodoxy. What I offer you. . . ." Magus's eyes seemed to be burning within their sockets; their intensity kept Angel's gaze mesmerized. "What I offer you is a bliss beyond imagination—the utter joy of serving a master who was ancient before this world cooled and gave birth to life."

Angel winced; Magus's grip on his shoulder had tightened uncomfortably. With his other hand the man cupped the boy's chin and turned his head slightly, first one way and then the other. He smiled slightly. "What is your name, lad?"

"A-Angel." It was hard to move his mouth against the grip on his jaw.

Magus shook his head slightly. "No. Your real name, your"— he smiled as if at a private joke—"your 'Christian' name."

Those eyes seemed enormous to him now, and glowing as bright as the moon. Angel heard his voice as if issuing from another's throat, far away. "Randy. Randall. Randall Farrow."

It seemed that he could feel Magus's heart beating in time with his own.

"Randall. Tell me then, Randall—will you join us?" Magus's voice echoed within his skull.

Angel wasn't sure if he spoke out loud, or even nodded, but Magus seemed satisfied. He released the boy's chin and stepped back slightly, and Angel felt as if an electric current that had been running through him had suddenly been cut off. He blinked and felt momentarily dizzy.

"Very good," Magus said. His eyes were still glowing, but there was a different look to them now. It was a look that Angel knew well.

It was time to pay for dinner.

Like Zip had said, it was nothing he hadn't done before—at least at first. Magus's bedroom was huge, dominated by a modern four-poster covered with satin sheets. And Magus was fairly gentle compared to a lot of tricks he'd turned. Anyway, Angel had learned before leaving home how to tune out, how to shut down and pretend it was happening to someone else's body.

It didn't hurt so much anymore; certainly not like the first time, which had felt like something the size of a cannon crushing his guts from within. And the sense of shame, of helplessness, that had been even worse than the burning, tearing pain . . . he'd gotten over that, too. Because now it was his choice—he was in control, he got to decide who got the wild ride and who didn't. In a weird, fucked-up sort of way, it made him feel . . . powerful.

Sometimes it even felt almost good.

Angel could hear Magus breathing behind him, short, deep breaths that grew in intensity. Angel could tell from how the man gripped his shoulders, the way his thrusting was growing harder, more rhythmic, that things were coming to a head, so to speak.

Zip was right, he told himself; it was still better than the street.

Then, as Magus burst inside him, Angel felt sharp teeth bite savagely into his neck, felt his warm blood spurting into the man's mouth and heard him moaning in ecstasy as he drank.

CHAPTER 18

Saturday, October 26

Tace sipped her drink and watched the show. The crowd at the Joke Joint was a little more mainstream than she was comfortable with, but better middle of the road than dead in a ditch, after all. She spent a good part of her night life prowling places like the Improv, the Comedy Factory, the Joke Joint and others. Some of these places she had played; some she had yet to play. But all had acts that were worth studying. There was no substitute for listening to how an audience reacted to various styles of humor.

Right now Craig Alstadler was onstage. Tace had seen him before and thought he was pretty funny. Tonight, however, he seemed to be just going through the motions.

She glanced around the room to see how the audience was reacting. They seemed amused, for the most part, though none of them were in any danger of popping a hernia. Tace noticed one fellow who was watching Craig with an intent gaze. He had blond hair and handsome, regular features. He seemed compactly built, though it was difficult to tell since he was wearing a voluminous coat, like a range coat or duster. The room was warm from the combined body heat of the crowd and the lights, but the man did not seem uncomfortable. Something about his haircut and the intensity of his gaze made Tace think "gay." Well, that wasn't particularly surprising, given the neighborhood. Maybe he was planning on putting a move on Craig after the latter finished his set.

" 'Scuse me. . . ."

Tace turned to see a young man behind her . . . about her age, early twenties, she judged, though it was hard to tell; his sunken eyes, pallid skin and near-emaciated frame would have made Tom Waits look healthy. He wore a baggy over-sized pair of pants and a shirt that accentuated his cadaverous appearance. One ear had been perforated with rings from lobe to crest, and a microscopic diamond decorated a nostril.

He thrust a pad and pen in her general direction. "You're Tace Daggett, right?" he mumbled, just barely above the threshold of her hearing. "Sign this?"

Tace blinked in disbelief. An autograph—her first autograph! She resisted an overwhelming urge to leap up on the table and interrupt Craig's act with this momentous news. Instead she accepted the pen and paper, trying to act like this was an everyday occurrence—which she devoutly hoped it would soon be. "Sure, love to. What's your name?"

"K," he said. The monosyllable was rendered all but unintelligible by his low-pitched mumble; it took several repeats before Tace understood, or thought she did. "Kay? K–A–Y?"

"Just 'K,'" he said. "Like the letter, y'know?"

Okay . . . she scribbled quickly, "To 'K' (Joseph?)—Auschwitz, class of '42—Tace Daggett," and added the date. The autograph seeker accepted it with considerably less excitement than she would have preferred, mumbled something that was probably "thank you" and disappeared into the hazy, dim-lit rear of the club.

Tace settled back in her chair and took another sip of her drink, letting satisfaction warm her like the drink. She had heard it said that one's first autograph is like one's first sexual experience—for better or worse, you never forget it. And there was this to be said about signing an autograph—it wasn't nearly as messy, and she didn't have to pretend to like him afterward.

Craig finished his set and left the stage to a decent round of applause. He saw Tace sitting there and weaved over to her table, dropping into the chair like a sack of laundry. "Jesus," he groaned. "Give me some aspirin, some bourbon and a bed." He considered. "If those don't work, give me a gun."

"That's what I like about men—their stoicism." She regarded him. He did look pretty bad; pale, red-rimmed eyes, generally lethargic. He had his collar pulled up; now he tugged it closer around his neck and shivered, hugging himself in the warm air. Tace asked, "Are you taking anything for it?"

"You kidding? They didn't mix this many drugs at Woodstock." He sagged lower in the chair. "Nothing's working, though." He groaned.

"Eloquently put. Maybe you should stay off your feet for a few days."

"Thanks, doc. What do I owe you—my car, my house, what?" He squinted up at the dim lights. "Bright in here."

"Seriously," Tace said, "you better get home and hit the sack." She stood. "C'mon . . . I'll drive you." She knew that Craig's car was perennially in the shop. She pulled him to his feet and steered him toward the door. The acts were winding down anyway. She glanced over to where the man in the duster had been sitting as they left the room, and saw that the chair was empty. Probably figured Craig was straight when he saw me talking to him, she thought.

Outside, the cold October wind slammed against them like some malevolent force. Tace and Craig walked, both slightly unsteadily for different reasons, down the street to where

Tace had parked her '68 Mustang. "Hey," Craig said, "this really is nice of you, Daggett. I hitched over here, but it woulda been hell getting back."

"Yeah, I'm a fucking angel of mercy. Get your feet in the car."

"But don't think you're gonna get any sexual favors from me by taking me home," Craig said as he slumped in the sports car's seat. "Way I feel, I couldn't get it up with a fork-lift."

"Thank God," Tace replied as she put the car into gear. She drove carefully east on Melrose, aware that there was probably a little too much alcohol in her blood to pass if she was pulled over.

There was still a fair amount of traffic at four-thirty A.M. L.A. was a city that never really slept. Maybe, she thought, that was why it was so psychotic. Even cities need to dream.

The funky glamor of West Hollywood gave way to boarded up storefronts, auto repair shops and fast-food outlets with signs in Arabic. By the time she passed the Paramount gate the eastern horizon was beginning to lighten and Craig was asleep. A few minutes later she was deep in the hills of Silverlake, pulling up next to the small cluster of bungalows on Hyperion where he lived.

She stopped the car, got out and opened his door. "Your stop, pal." He was motionless, snoring slightly. Tace shook him, gently at first, then hard enough to rock the car. "Come on, Mac, I gotta schedule to make." Nothing—save for the faint glottal sounds of his snoring, she might have been shaking a corpse.

Well, this is just *great,* she thought. There was no way she could drag him out of the car and up the steep stairs to his place. And it seemed that nothing short of a thermonuclear device was going to wake him up.

After a few more moments of trying to come up with options, Tace faced the fact that she had none and got back in the Mustang. She could go home, but she knew she wouldn't have any more luck getting him into her place. And she couldn't just let him sleep in the car. If he had arrived at this condition by being drunk or stoned it might be tempting to do so, but being sick wasn't his fault.

She yawned—the combination of alcohol and no sleep was getting to her. She fished a Preludin out of her pocket and dry-swallowed it. It should keep her going for the rest of the day, though when she crashed it would be hard.

"Okay, asshole," she said to her sleeping companion. "Guess we'll go for a drive 'til you wake up." She let out the clutch and headed back toward the flatlands. She cranked up the volume on a Concrete Blonde tape, but even Johnette Napolitano belting out the lyrics to "Still In Hollywood" didn't put a dent in Craig's slumber. Tace drove in no particular direction, waiting for the dawn, feeling like the last surviving soul in a city full of vampires.

CHAPTER 19

Sunday, October 27

Jake sat in T. Martin McNamara's office, listening to the captain express a litany of worries about Jake's ability to do his job. This was not anything new. McNamara had been on Jake's ass ever since the shooting last spring. The department had taken serious flak about it, and somehow in all the hue and cry no one had really seemed to care that a good cop had gone down because some kid had a gun and knew how to use it.

Jake had been cleared of any and all charges by the investigating board, but McNamara had not been satisfied with that. From then on he had watched Jake like a hawk watches a henhouse. The irony of the situation was not lost on Jake: a heavy bit of additional stress caused by the burden of proving to McNamara he wasn't under any undue stress.

"This isn't personal," McNamara was saying. He was a big man, soft around the belly but still built like a cinderblock everywhere else. He'd been a uniform for nine years, a detective and lieutenant for nine more before getting his present position. "I want the same things you want—what's good for the department, and what's good for you. That's why I think you should put the badge away for awhile, get some serious R and R."

"I'm glad it's not personal," Jake said. "I'd be very depressed otherwise." He winced, tried to hide the pain roiling in his gut. It felt like a rat gnawing at him from the inside.

"Look," he said, interrupting another of McNamara's speeches about how we're all only human. "The bottom line is, unless you order me to stand down, I'm not gonna do it. This job may be shitty, but it's familiar shit, and I do it well."

McNamara looked at him with unreadable eyes. Jake looked back, not defiantly, just calmly, waiting, the same stare he had given a hundred different jerkoffs on the street who were always the first to blink.

McNamara did not blink. He held Jake's gaze steadily as he said, "Well, then I guess we're done talking. For now."

Jake and Stratton had lunch that evening at the Hollywood Bar & Grill. It was after seven, and the sky was purpling from dusk to full night. Stratton was wearing civilian clothes instead of his uniform.

"This night shift really has me turned inside out," he said. "My circadian rhythms are all fucked up."

"Your what?"

"Circadian rhythms. The way your body gets used to sleeping and waking up." The cop took another bite of his burger, wiped catsup from his mustache with a napkin.

Jake just nodded. Stratton was full of all kinds of weird information, some of which was making him useful on this case, some of which was just annoying.

"I got a call today," he said as he sliced another piece of steak. "Some has-been actor named Franklin Conner. Says this Night Hunter case is just like a movie he was in twenty years ago and wants to know if he can be of help." Jake chuckled as he chewed.

"Franklin Conner," Stratton said reflectively. "I remember him." His face brightened with memory. "Yeah, *Mask of the Vampire*. He's right—there are similarities."

"You think he's worth talking to?"

"Not really. The resemblance seems pretty coincidental to me." He grinned. "Though I wouldn't mind meeting him."

Jake chewed and swallowed. "I still think our best shot is Magus."

The waitress brought the bill to their booth, and Jake began scrounging his pockets for dollars and change to pay his half. Stratton watched him for a minute, then put a twenty on the tray. "I got it, Jake."

The detective looked at him for a moment, then said, "Thanks." They left the restaurant. The air was cold and crisp, the mountains and the Hollywood sign clearly visible.

"Darlene's been on me for the alimony," Jake told Stratton as they got into his car. "I'm only a week late, she's acting like it's a felony." He started the car, headed up toward Hollywood Boulevard.

They turned right on the boulevard and drove east, passing the boarded-up structure of the old Aztec Theater. The movie palace of the twenties and thirties had been closed for almost thirty years. The Meso-American carvings had been defaced by graffiti, the glass of the marquee long since shattered by rocks and bottles. Stratton stared at it as they passed. "My dad used to go there to see Saturday matinees all the time when he was a kid," he said. "The old Republic serials. Ever see any of them? Rocket Man, Captain Marvel, Dick Tracy?"

Jake said, "What do you think?"

"Things were simpler then," Stratton continued, ignoring Jake's tone. "Ralph Byrd as Dick Tracy, man. *He* didn't have to fuck with Mirandizing skels, getting sued for false arrest, any of that shit. He chased the bad guys, he shot the bad guys. End of story."

They rode for awhile in silence. Then Jake said, "I say we put a tail on Magus."

"What the hell," Stratton replied. "It's something to do."

CHAPTER 20

Sunday, October 27

Four hours later, Stratton said, "Somebody'd told me detective work was this boring, I wouldn't have been so hot to get into it."

They were parked across the street and down the block from Magus's house up in the Hollywood Hills. They had been there since dusk—it was now fully dark. There were no streetlights on this particular avenue, so, save for a few isolated porch and interior lights, the street was darker than sin. This worked both for and against them—they could watch the house without fear of being seen, but unless people were considerate enough to arrive by the front door there could be a Satanic Mass complete with ritualistic sacrifices going on inside without their being aware of it.

After a considerable time of silence, broken only by the crickets and other night noises, Stratton said, "So, I hear you and Dr. Allen have been seeing quite a bit of each other."

"Christ," Jake said and slumped lower in his seat. "We met at the observatory and had dinner together. That was it, that was all. How'd the hell you hear about it?"

"My network of spies is everywhere," Stratton said in a portentous voice. Then he added, "Actually, a couple of uniforms saw you and her and the kids coming out of the Hamburger Hamlet on Beverly." He was quiet for a few seconds, then said casually, "So you're saying this wouldn't really qualify as a date, huh?"

Jake grunted. "You want more information, read the society pages."

Stratton chuckled. Then he looked out the windshield and sat up, as did Jake. "Satanist at twelve o'clock, I think," the cop said.

Jake lifted a small pair of binoculars to his eyes and adjusted them. "That's him," he said. Magus was backing his Porsche out of the driveway. They slid lower in their seats as he drove past them, then Stratton cranked up the car, turned around in a driveway and followed.

Magus drove within the speed limit, his brake lights alternately brightening and dimming as he went around curves. Jake and Stratton kept a reasonable distance behind him. At the bottom of the hill a traffic light changed to amber. Magus put on a burst of speed and shot through the light just as it turned red.

Stratton came to a stop. "Think he made us?"

"Maybe. Maybe he's just late for a meeting with Lucifer."

Stratton let the car get about a block ahead, then eased through the red light and continued to follow. Out of habit, Jake profiled the crowd moving aimlessly along the streets, picking out the pipeheads, the hookers, the garden-variety dirtbags.

They followed Magus by a circuitous route down to Santa Monica Boulevard. The Porsche moved fairly quickly eastward, turned south on Gower and slowed down when it reached Mister Mack's.

They watched as Magus pulled over near the burger joint. A street kid in his late teens strolled over to the car. He was wearing tight black jeans and a T-shirt beneath a tattered studio crew jacket, his hair long and lank.

"Could it be that we've struck paydirt?" Stratton mused as the kid got into the Porsche.

"Sometimes God gives you one for free," Jake replied. They pulled back into traffic after Magus.

The Porsche moved up Gower, past cheap houses and apartment buildings, up to Franklin and then east. They kept behind him until the Satanist was back at his house.

"Let's see," Jake said as Magus and his young entertainment entered the house, "worst-case scenario: we bust him for soliciting. Best case—we got our Van Helson."

"Helsing."

"Either way, we got to go in. My only concern is that, if he's not the killer but he is somehow connected to the case, we maybe lose a good lead if we bust him."

"Yeah, but that's still better than a poke in the heart with a sharp stake," Stratton said, "which is what the kid might get if we don't go in."

Jake nodded. There was no way around it. "Let's do it."

They moved quickly across the lawn, avoiding the front walk, guns out and ready. A panel by the front door with a glowing green light said that an alarm was off. Thank God for small favors, Jake thought.

They were halfway up the walk when the door opened. Magus and the boy stood there, backlit by the light from the entryway. Jake and Stratton stood before them, guns raised.

Magus looked calmly at the boy and said, "Go wait in the car, Jordan. These officers won't do anything to stop you." The boy hesitantly moved past Jake and Stratton and headed for the Porsche.

"Detective Hull, Officer Stratton," Magus said politely. He seemed not to notice the guns in their hands. "So good to see you both again. Would you care to come inside?"

"No, we would not," Jake said. He and Stratton had both lowered their guns, but had not holstered them. "So what exactly were you doing with Jordan, Mr. Magus?"

"I don't really think that's any of your business," Magus replied imperturbably.

"Oh, I think it's very much our business," Jake replied. "I think we are talking, at the very least, soliciting, at the most felony child endangerment. I think you're going to take a ride with us, Mr. Magus."

Magus was smiling slightly, as though Jake were an amusing but not particularly bright child. Dan caught a whiff of that hair oil or cologne or whatever it was Magus was wearing and wrinkled his nose.

"You have no evidence that anything untoward was taking place between Jordan and me," Magus said. "If you must know, the lad is one of my flock—I brought him back here on 'church' business. Ask him; he'll corroborate this. He came of his own free will. And he is over eighteen. I'm sorry, Detective, but you have no case here."

Jake stared at Magus for a moment, then surged abruptly forward, putting his arm across Magus's chest and propelling the latter back to hit hard against the door. Magus grunted with the impact, but did not otherwise react.

"*I* decide whether or not I've got a case, you oily piece of shit," Jake hissed. He stared into Magus's eyes, which were like glittering black stones.

Stratton said, "Ah, Jake, this might not be the best procedure under the circumstances. . . ."

Jake held Magus for a moment longer, then relaxed his arm's pressure. Magus calmly smoothed the silk shirt he wore. His gaze was still locked with Jake's.

"You hate me, don't you?" he asked softly. "You consider me the antithesis of everything you stand for. But what you don't realize, Detective, is that you see in me a reflection of yourself. There is a darkness within you—it is quite evident. It is not the things I do that repulse you—it is the attraction you feel for them that repulses you. You are a kindred spirit. Why don't you admit it?"

Jake lunged for him again, his fist cocked, ready to smash the smirk on Magus's face into a bloody mess of splintered teeth and pulped lips. Stratton lunged as well, barely managing to grab Jake's arm in time. Magus retreated a step, his composure cracking momentarily.

"Not good, not good," Stratton said in a low voice. "Lawsuits, suspension, famine, pestilence. Get a grip, Jake."

Jake turned and headed down the walk, back to the car. Stratton gave Magus a chilly smile. "I'm sure we'll be talking again—real soon," he said. Then he turned and followed his partner.

CHAPTER 21

Monday, October 28

Craig Alstadler couldn't sleep. The goddamned head cold had kept his sinuses on the verge of meltdown for yet another day. He tossed restlessly on his water bed, exhausted but wired at the same time from the antihistamines. They were supposed to make you sleepy, but the doctor had said that if you keep taking them something called "rebound syndrome" caused them to have the opposite effect. Just another one of God's little jokes.

He looked at his luminous watch in the dark and groaned. In a little over four hours he was supposed to do another gig at the Comedy Factory and he had never felt less funny in his life. This was the third cold he had had in two months. He never used to get sick this often. He had taken enough vitamin C to kill a dozen lab rats, but it was no use; his immune system had obviously crashed and burned.

There was no way out of the gig—he needed the money,

and he needed the exposure. He was starting to build up a following; the other night at the Improv he had gotten a smattering of applause when he'd been introduced.

It hadn't been easy, and this spate of ill health sure hadn't made it any easier. The only thing that kept him from wondering if he hadn't contracted AIDS was the fact that a monk had a better sex life than he did.

But he couldn't quit now. It was starting to happen; Craig could feel it, *taste* it. Not stardom, maybe, not yet, but at least a little money in the bank. Anyway, he'd been feeling somewhat better when the sun went down and the heat abated slightly—

He sat up, not quite sure what the noise was that had startled him. The water bed roiled gently beneath him, sloshing slightly; other than that, the only sounds were the omnipresent traffic and the *mariachi* music from next door. His bungalow was one of nine in a part of Silverlake that even the SWAT team was reluctant to visit. Craig had never experienced any violence toward himself so far, but he had seen plenty of it in this neighborhood. A few weeks ago he'd been awakened by screams and looked through the door peephole to see a couple of Puerto Ricans stomping the living shit out of the old Nicaraguan man who lived two doors down. Prudently, he hadn't rushed to the old man's defense, though he did call 911. The cops had arrived after an hour or so; by that time the old man's tormentors had gone and he had dragged himself back into his house.

Craig heard it again: definitely the creaking of a floorboard. He swung his legs to the floor and picked up a letter opener from the bed's headboard, next to the pile of bills and junk mail. He'd been intending for some time to buy a baseball bat or some other form of protection—now he wished he had. He took deep, quiet breaths, trying to calm the surge of adrenaline through his veins.

Though it was just after sundown, it was very dark in the room; he had kept the western windows covered with aluminum foil during the summer to bring the oven-like temperature down a few degrees, since he couldn't afford an air conditioner. Though it had turned cold in the last few weeks, he hadn't gotten around to taking the foil off yet.

How could anyone get in? The doors and windows were all locked—

Forget about that now. Just find out what's going on.

He moved quietly to the bedroom door, feeling ridiculously fragile in his underwear, and reached for the knob. He usually slept with the door shut because the intermittent rattling of the refrigerator kept him awake otherwise. Maybe the noise was just the building settling—this place had been built in the forties, after all, a wonder it was still standing—

The door slammed open, hurling Craig backward; he staggered against the water bed's frame and fell onto the shifting mattress. Before he could even think about getting up another body landed on top of him, ramming a knee into his gut and driving the air from his lungs in a painful explosion.

Holy shit, this is it, this is really it! Craig stabbed frantically up at his unseen assailant. He missed; the letter opener arced down, plunging through the sheet and tearing a hole in the polyvinyl mattress. Water welled up around him; he could smell the sharp scent of chlorine. Then he felt a gloved hand seize his throat, squeezing painfully. Bright explosions of fireworks seemed to go off in his eyes; he was pushed backward by the hand, pinned down by the knee in his midsection. He tried to strike at the dark form crouching over him, but his arms abruptly had no strength. Another hand rammed something into his mouth, and even in the terror of the moment he was surprised by the strong taste of raw garlic. Then the hand left his throat, and at the same time he felt something hard and sharp strike his chest, breaking the skin and grazing against a rib. The stunning pain of it paralyzed Craig; he could not have screamed even had his bruised throat been capable of it.

Then there was the sound of wood hitting wood, and a

burst of fiery agony inside him, worse than any pain he had ever before felt—

Then nothing.

Tace parked her Mustang at the foot of the concrete steps that rose between two beds of ivy to the nest of bungalows on the side of the hill. The evening shadows were darkening, and the Santa Anas had slackened, but the dry air now seemed charged with a subtle tension. Either negative ions or positive ones, Tace could never remember which were bad and which were good. But whichever ones were filling the air tonight seemed to invest every sound, even innocuous ones like far-off barking dogs and the tinkle of running water, with a sense of menace.

Tace shook her head and ran her fingers through her hair, hearing it crackle with static. Too little sleep and too many drugs, she told herself as she started up the stairs.

She had come back to check on Craig, since he hadn't answered his phone. After he had finally woken up in her car just after dawn, he had barely been able to get up the steps and into his house. Probably it was just the flu, Tace told herself—in which case she was crazy for putting herself in danger of catching it—but she wanted to make sure he was okay. Starving comics had to look out for each other, because it was for stone certain that no one else gave a shit.

The sound of trickling water grew louder; a small stream was running down the walkway and just starting to drip over the first few steps. Tace blinked in surprise as she saw that the water was leaking from beneath the door to Craig's bungalow.

The door was ajar; she pushed it open slowly. It was quite dark inside; there were no lights on and the windows had been covered with tinfoil for some reason. Tace felt the hair on the back of her neck struggling to rise, and she knew it wasn't just the static charge of the dry air. The thought of setting foot inside that dark house suddenly seemed about as bright a move as turning out all the lights on the spaceship and splitting up to go look for the Alien.

She could hear water dripping from inside, in an oddly rhythmic pattern. Jesus, what if Craig had somehow torn a hole in his water bed and drowned in the resulting flood? Or. . . .

Or, her mind whispered, what if there was someone in there sporting a chainsaw and a hockey mask who had just reduced Craig to chitlins and was ready for another victim. . . .

Tace felt her heart hammering. She pushed the door open slightly; the dim evening light illuminated no more than a few inches of worn hardwood floor, the dull brown bisected by the darker stain of the flowing water. She felt an overpowering urge to turn, to run back to the car and drive like the wind, away from Silverlake, maybe away from L.A. and all the way back to Baltimore. . . .

But Craig was her friend, and he might need help.

"Craig?" she called, her voice sounding unfamiliar, the voice of a timid stranger. "Craig, are you all—?"

She did not, could not finish the question. She was looking down at the water where it dripped from the floor to the first step, pooling slightly around her feet before continuing on down.

Even in the fading light she could see that the drops were tinged with red.

Suddenly the door was pulled open, hard enough to slam against the wall. A hurtling form struck Tace, knocking her back and to one side. She had a brief, surreal impression of a dark figure coming toward her before her head struck the fleshy bole of the banana tree growing beside the porch hard enough to cause an explosion of colors inside her head.

It got dark real fast after that.

CHAPTER 22

Monday, October 28

Remind me never to doubt you when it comes to murder,"
Sarah Allen said to Jake Hull. "You said he'd do it again."

Jake didn't answer; she really hadn't expected him to. He
stood quietly near one wall of the small bedroom, watching
as the E.T. members dusted for prints and carefully gathered
items to place in paper bags. Flashbulbs strobed at intervals,
etching the grisly spectacle in stark black and white as the
crime scene photographer documented the body.

Sarah moved over to the water bed where the corpse
floated, half-submerged in sodden tangled sheets and blan-
kets, the legs dangling over the wooden frame. Water tinted
red with blood dripped slowly onto the grimy wood floor. One
of the techs dipped a Q-tip in the blood and deposited it in a
stoppered vial. Sarah opened her bag, a small leather valise
worn and supple from several years of use, and pulled out a
pair of latex gloves.

Craig Alstadler had died in bed, like Jimmy Ray, but there didn't seem to be much resemblance between the two other than that. Tate had been a teenager with a washboard belly and ropy muscles on his chest and arms; Alstadler was twenty-four, according to his driver's license, and possessed of a soft and pasty body which had probably not been able to put up more than a token resistance to his killer.

She glanced at Dan Stratton, standing in one corner taking the statement of Tace Daggett, the woman who had found the body. From the bits of conversation she had overheard the woman had dropped by to check on Alstadler, whom she knew to be sick. There had been no answer to her knock, and the door had been unlocked. She had been about to enter when someone had run out of the house, knocking her down and stunning her for a few moments. When she came to, she had managed to reach the living room phone and dial 911.

Sarah checked the hands for transfer of materials: cloth fibers, skin scrapings or hair caught under the fingernails. There was not much else to look for; the water would most likely have washed away any other evidence that might have been left.

Sarah glanced around the small room. It was barely big enough for the queen-sized water bed and a cheap pressed-wood dresser by the door. Taped to one wall was a poster of Lenny Bruce in silhouette before an audience. It was fairly easy to figure out what profession Craig had aspired to before someone had decided to plant a tree in his chest.

She sighed and motioned to Jake, who came over and sat down on the damp rim of the frame beside her. "They'll have to move him now," she said. "I can't take his temperature in this mess." She glanced over at the white-faced woman in the black jeans and leather jacket who stood staring at the body. "Better get her out of here before we do it."

Jake nodded, crossed to Stratton and spoke to him in a low voice. Stratton nodded and took Tace Daggett gently by the upper arm, leading her out of the room. Jake then made a gesture to two cops, who came over and carefully lifted Alstadler's body out of the slashed vinyl mattress. They laid him down on a tarp another officer had spread out, trying to maintain the original position of the body as closely as possible. Sarah stifled a yawn while this was going on.

She squatted down beside the body, tilting the hips to one side. Alstadler had been sleeping in a T-shirt and boxer shorts. There wasn't much left of the shirt, but the shorts, soaked in water and blood, were still around his waist. Sarah pulled a pair of scissors from her bag and cut the shorts diagonally, exposing the corpse's damp and pallid buttocks. She took out a chemical thermometer and inserted it, ignoring the inevitable coarse cracks this action always inspired in the cops present.

Jake knelt down beside her. "How long, you think?"

"I'll know better when this comes out. As a guess, I'd say two or three hours. Rigor's started already." She glanced at the techs who were dusting white powder on various surfaces. "Better make sure they print the deceased before his fingers curl up."

"They're professionals," Jake said dryly. He glanced at his watch. She looked at hers as well; it was just after two A.M. "Any idea how he got in?" she asked.

"Snapped the bolt on the front door." He was glancing around the room as he spoke, gaze flicking from one spot to another, searching for something—anything—that might have been overlooked.

Sarah pulled the long thermometer out and checked it. The reading was ten degrees below normal; that might have placed time of death at five hours or more in the past, but the fact that the body had been soaking in tepid water had to be taken into account. She said as much to Jake, then stood, feeling her left knee pop. "That's all I can do." The officers who had moved the body before came forward again, lifted the mortal remains of Craig Alstadler and placed them on a stretcher. A sheet was carefully pinned in place over him, and then the body was carried out.

"Wait," Sarah said abruptly. The officers stopped at the door, looking back at her quizzically. She moved over to the corpse and carefully pulled the sheet away from the face. This was something her sleepiness had caused her to forget to do the last time, and it had been left to Todd Latham to find the garlic bulb in Tate's mouth.

She pushed the jaw down gently, using a pencil flashlight to peer into the mouth. Sure enough, there it was—a tiny clove resting against the victim's cheek. She fished it out and deposited it in an evidence bag.

Jake was watching her. "You forgot to check for bites on his neck."

She looked at him as she stripped the gloves off. "No," she replied. "I didn't. There weren't any."

Jake looked soberly at her for a moment, and Sarah had to stifle a sudden bubble of laughter that rose in her throat: *He's going to tell me I'd better start wearing a cross.*

"Come on," was all he said. "We need to talk."

She followed him through the small living room with its mismatched furniture and down the outside stairs. Several TV vans were parked behind the patrol cars. A reporter thrust a microphone in Jake's face.

"Detective Hull? Is this another murder by the Night Hunter?"

"No comment," Jake said, pushing past the man and moving toward his car, Sarah right behind him.

Once in the car Jake steered a cautious course down the narrow street, through the crowd of curious neighbors and on-lookers. Sarah watched their faces blur past the car window, expressions of confusion, exhaustion, and most of all, fear. The sight of the police investigating the murder did not seem to reassure them at all.

She looked at Jake, his profile strobed by streetlights and neon as they drove west on Sunset. There had been no change of expression that she could see when he had walked in and seen the body in the water bed, even though it had confirmed his fear that "Van Helsing" was a pattern killer.

He pulled into a parking lot a few blocks away from the crime scene, shut off the engine and turned to her.

"When this hits the news, this case will be top priority," he said. "The whole department's going to have to drop everything else and stick to this like gum on shoe leather. I'll need help. I've got Stratton on it with me; I need you, too. Everything you can correlate between this killing and Tate's; every possible extrapolation on who this nutcase is and why he's doing this. I don't want this to be a celebrity case. I want this fucker caught before he becomes a household word, if he hasn't already."

She nodded, a little intimidated by his intensity. She knew it was hard not to get involved on some level with cases, especially the strange ones, but there seemed to be something somehow personal in it for Jake now. She wondered what it was.

"Whatever I can do, you know I will," she told him.

"There's one more thing," he said, and took her by the shoulders, firmly but not roughly, pulled her to him and kissed her. Sarah was caught by surprise as he pulled her forward. She put a hand out to maintain her balance; her palm came to rest in his lap, and she felt his erection beneath the cloth.

She was surprised, and also a little bit shocked at this sudden horniness on Jake's part right after finding Alstadler's body. She pulled back; he released her, did not meet her eyes. "Sorry," he said.

"Not a problem; I just didn't expect it."

"I don't know what came over me," he said softly. "I didn't mean anything by it."

"Felt pretty sincere to me," Sarah said. His gaze flickered at her for a moment. She kept her expression neutral; she wasn't sure if she wanted this to go any further or not.

After another moment he started the car and pulled back

onto the street. Neither said anything further as they drove back to the crime scene where she was parked.

This could get complicated, Sarah told herself. Fishing off the company dock was never a good idea. If she was going to continue her post as an M.E., she would in all likelihood have to work with Jake Hull quite a lot. Were either of them adult enough to handle the added intensity of a relationship?

There was only one way to find out. The problem was, of course, that by then it would be too late.

CHAPTER 23

Monday, October 28

It had always astounded him, this fascination people had with the undead. The immortals, in all their various guises, had been a large part of myths, and the ongoing infatuation they caused humanity was perplexing. Perhaps there had been a time when he had felt the same way; if so, he could not remember it, which wasn't surprising.

In his attempt to know the enemy he had read quite a few of the novels and stories devoted to this theme, and seen several movies as well. A common thread he had noticed among the imaginary undying ones was a hubris that almost inevitably led to their downfall. Fictional vampires in particular seemed prey to this mindset. True, they were crafty and cautious, hiding their coffins from casual discovery and using human servants for their eyes and ears in the daytime. But inevitably it was the contempt they felt for mankind, the sense of superiority over these cattle fit only to serve the nutritional needs of the lords of darkness, that led to their destruction. Time and again the vampires would underestimate their opponents; in their smug complacency they would make some fatal flaw, and in short order find themselves exposed to the dreaded sunlight or pierced through the heart with a wooden stake.

It was not that easy.

To add to his problems, now the police were on his trail. First this detective, this Jake Hull, had not simply dismissed the killing of Jimmy Ray Tate as another of the many unsolvable murders that overwhelm the Los Angeles police force. It was the stake, of course; the unusual manner of killing. But that could not be helped—it was the only way to accomplish what had to be done. The irony of this was not lost upon him.

He had underestimated the glee with which the media had pounced upon the slaying. As always, the people must have their bread and circuses, he thought wryly. And now, with another body found, the hysteria over the "vampire killer" was mounting. Once again he had been interrupted before he could properly dispose of the corpse.

But in the long run—and he was certainly used to taking that view—it would not matter.

He realized he was walking too fast, and slowed his pace. It would, of course, take quite a bit more than a rapid pace to draw attention to himself on the Sunset Strip, but he could not afford to take any chances. He let the crowd flow by him: the would-be gang members with their baggy clothes and strutting attitudes, the drug addicts with their vacuous stares, the yuppies with their moussed hair and electronic pagers on their belts.

How many of them, he wondered, had something in their lives to give it meaning? A passion, a quest, a crusade—even a hobby . . . how many lived lives utterly devoid of purpose, more animal than human? A great many, judging by the dead flat quality of their eyes. . . .

One thing the books and movies never dealt with was how the undead gave meaning to their immortal lives. Immortality was considered its own reward. For the most part, it would seem, people would gladly trade deathlike sleep during the day and the grim necessity of killing and living on blood every night to survive for centuries. As if that were incentive enough.

But mere survival was not enough. There must be purpose, even to a vampire's life. That was the great secret—that was what he knew that no one else did. And that was why he would ultimately triumph.

He passed a nightclub from which raucous music thundered. Young men and women, dressed in leather and chains, loitered by the entrance. They watched him pass, their pupils pinpoints in the dim neon light.

In the lining of his coat was a stake of sharpened ash wood, carefully prepared according to the ancient ceremonies. In his pocket were cloves of fresh garlic. The time to use them again would be soon. And then his time in this city would be done, and he would move on before the police could find him.

He continued walking, just an anonymous face in the crowd. According to the books and the films, the undead were easy to spot if you knew what to look for.

It wasn't that easy.

"Same shit," she said wearily. "Always the same shit."

Jake watched as Darlene paced the threadbare carpet—the carpet he'd been intending to have replaced for three years, only there was never any money, and now why should he even think about the fucking carpet since he didn't live there anymore, hadn't for eight months. First separation, now divorce, final six weeks ago and still he thought, sometimes, late at night when driving his car, watching life pulse along the sidewalks like a cut vein, that maybe there was still a chance, maybe they could make it work again. They weren't like the pathetic souls he saw night after night, the ones chained together in marriages of mutual pain and torture, the men who get drunk and carve up their wives like London broil, the women who won't press charges even after losing an eye or worse. . . .

They weren't like that. They were two reasonable adults, with differences, yes, but none that couldn't be resolved if they both would just *try.* In his years on the force, Jake Hull had seen the worst that love could offer. They weren't like that. There was hope. They could make it work. He knew they could make it work like it had in the beginning.

He thought about the carpet. He thought about the right rear tire on Darlene's Honda Civic that was losing its tread. He thought about his son's growing need for orthodontia. He thought about all these things instead of the sadness in her eyes and the weary anger in her voice, because to acknowledge these things was to acknowledge what he only knew in her presence—that the two of them didn't have a chance in hell of making it work again.

"He's a *child,* Jake! Only eight years old! He came home *crying* after you took him to the goddamn observatory!"

"He needs to *know,* Darlene! Like it or not, the bad guys are out there, and he has to know how to protect—"

"You think I don't teach him that? You think he doesn't get enough lectures on safety and not trusting strangers from me? He doesn't have to hear in detail about the horrors lurking behind every car and bush in the state!"

He felt cold. He always felt cold in this house. It had nothing to do with the temperature. "That's the world."

"No—that's *your* world. He doesn't have to live in it, and neither do I."

"Oh, you're in it," Jake said. "You're in it up to your eyebrows, Darlene, whether you want to be or not, and so is Max. I'm just trying to do what I can to keep him safe. You don't even walk him to school and back—"

"It's *three blocks*! He doesn't want me to walk him; he'd rather go with his friends. He's just at that age—"

"A lot can happen in three blocks. Less than a mile from here a little girl was taken from her front yard. They found her a week later in a Dumpster. She'd been—"

"I don't want to hear it!"

He was starting to feel angry now, finally. It was a relief to feel something, even if it was anger.

"Nobody wants to hear it! But that doesn't make it go away. God damn it, Darlene, he's my son, too, and I *will* do what I think is best for him! You can hide your head in the dirt all you want, but—"

Her gaze abruptly shifted from his face to over his shoulder. Jake turned, saw Max standing in the doorway to the hall, watching them. One hand held an X-Men action figure, dangling by the cape.

To Jake, the scene seemed to go on for an excruciatingly long time—in reality it was no more than a second or two before Max turned and ran back down the hall to his room. Darlene brushed past Jake with a muttered "Asshole . . ." as she ran after their son. Jake heard the door to Max's bedroom slam.

He stood alone in the small living room, looking at the picture of some English manor over the couch, the fake Tiffany lamps on the end tables, the silk flowers on the mantle and feeling the hot red pain like a laser in his middle. A cop would know by the decor exactly what sort of people lived here: people without lives, people without hope.

He thought of the last vacation they had taken, nearly six years ago: Catalina in November, the off-season. They had taken the water taxi over from San Pedro, spent a long weekend in one of those little hostels by the water. The streets of Avalon had been almost deserted that time of year, the narrow lanes and crowded houses making him think of pictures he had seen of British villages, even though the architecture was completely different, too quaint and picturesque to be real. They had rented one of those electric golf cart cars which were the only vehicles allowed in the city limits and gone tooling up and down the hills, the whole place like some bizarre miniature San Francisco. Eaten clam chowder and toured the bay in the glass-bottomed boat, Max still young enough to be in the chest-carrier. He could, right now, detect some faint ghost scent of the sea air, an olfactory hallucination brought back by yearning.

Jake blinked, brought his vision back to focus on the dust motes dancing in a slice of sunlight through the door's beveled window. Very faintly he could hear the muffled sound of Max's voice and his mother's soothing replies: no words, just voices in abstraction, subdued human tones . . . emotion without language.

Abruptly he crossed the shabby carpet and pulled the door open, the glass doorknob all hard angles against his palm. Tempted to slam it, he closed it gently instead, stood on the front porch breathing deeply of the dry, crisp air.

From where he stood he could see one of the windows of Max's bedroom; the shade was drawn. A ghost made of cotton balls glued together, looking more like a Christmas snowman than a Halloween revenant, hung from the sash against the glass.

His son's life was going on without him. He was granted occasional glimpses into it, grudging connections on weekends and holidays, but that was all. His boy was growing up, while Jake spent his days in uneasy sleep and his nights living on Maalox and Mylanta and trying to stem the endless red tide on the streets. His shoulders sagged as he moved down the walk toward his car.

On the fence across the street was a smear of graffiti that he recognized as belonging to one of the local gangs. Jake felt resentment flare within him at Darlene's attitude. It wasn't *his* fault that the world was a cesspool. You had to give up your innocence when you became a cop, or when you married a cop. It's a terrible thing to see the world as it really is, that he knew, but the truth could keep you safe, while fiction could kill you.

"You can't hide us from life," she had said to him once. But that wasn't what he was trying to do. There was a difference between hiding someone and protecting someone.

Jake slid into the warm interior of the car, feeling suddenly and completely overwhelmed. So many children who disappeared and were never found again. There was nothing to keep Max from being one of the thousands who stared solemnly out from fliers and milk cartons, the images growing silently by computer aging as the years passed, a hideous two-dimensional mockery of maturation, while the children themselves most likely moldered in shallow graves, their last moments cacophonies of pain and betrayal and terror.

Jake gripped the steering wheel, feeling his heart hammer within him. It suddenly seemed impossible to get a full breath of air. The air seemed even brighter and clearer than the Santa Ana weather could account for, the distant mountains almost preternaturally sharp and detailed, like the peaks of the moon.

Lately he'd taken to carrying two guns with him at all times: his Colt Special in its belt holster and a 9mm semiautomatic in an ankle holster. He drew the latter now, pulled the slide and checked the clip. He hadn't told anybody back at the division that he was packing a second gun, even though it wasn't an unusual thing for a cop to do. He gripped the piece, holding it below window level. He knew it was foolish, a prime example of tombstone courage, but he felt more secure with the gun in his hand even sitting in his car on a quiet residential street.

The bad guys were out there. Maybe it was an exaggeration to say they were behind every bush and fence within sight . . . but maybe not. Just because you're paranoid doesn't mean they aren't out to get you. Being a civilian as opposed to being a cop, Tom used to say, was like living in TV instead of living in the real world.

His ex-wife and child didn't know it, but they were naked

in this world. No matter what Darlene said, he would do everything he could to make sure they were safe.

Jake started the car and drove away down the street, leaving the house behind, one of countless small forts surrounded by faceless enemies.

CHAPTER 24

Tuesday, October 29

"M.E.'s report on Alstadler is pretty much the same as the one on Jimmy Ray," Stratton said, glancing over the papers in his hand as he sat on the edge of Jake's desk. "Died as a result of winding up on the wrong end of a wooden stake. No sign of sexual molestation or other incidental trauma. However, we did find a couple keys of grass in his closet."

"Big surprise. What about the garlic?"

"Same thing—one small clove found in the victim's mouth. Analysis indicates it was placed there before death." Stratton shuffled papers. "And speaking of the dark side, have you by any chance seen this?" he asked, holding out a rolled-up newspaper. Jake took it. It was a copy of the latest *Midnight Star*, a weekly tabloid. Their offices were in San Francisco, but they found L.A. fertile ground for stories, and it appeared that this was no exception. LOS ANGELES OVERRUN BY VAMPIRES! screamed a banner headline. Beneath it, in slightly

smaller type, Jake read, LONE VIGILANTE STANDS BETWEEN
PUBLIC AND THE UNDEAD.

He quickly scanned the story, which informed him that the
LAPD were faced with a deluge of corpses, their blood
drained and sporting the obligatory two small puncture
wounds on the neck. L.A. residents were stocking up on garlic and wolfbane to keep the undead—who, according to the
Star, were prowling the city streets in droves—away. The
city's sole hope for survival seemed to lie with the mysterious "Van Helsing," who had already staked several vampires
and was searching for the elusive leader of the bloodsuckers.

He sighed. "Are we famous yet?" he asked as he tossed the
paper back to Stratton.

"Why I do this job," Stratton said, chucking the paper in
the wastebasket. "The fame and respect. And the money, of
course."

Jake was quiet for a few moments, staring at the swirl of
cream in his coffee. The chipped mug was a gift from Darlene; black letters on its side read IT'S NOT MY FAULT. Through
the half-opened blinds, the fading light was crimson and ma-
genta. Somewhere deep within him he felt an uneasy sense
of relief that the day was ending.

He glanced up at Stratton. "You're not married, right?"

"Not yet. Probably not ever, with this job." Stratton studied the papers in his hand. A silence grew, threatening to become awkward.

"Yeah," Jake said. "It's tough. Nobody understands a cop's
life except another cop." He stared across the big room at a
stack of cardboard file boxes piled high against one wall.

Stratton said, "You guys tried therapy?"

"She wanted to. We saw a marriage counselor once or
twice." He gave a snort of disgust.

Stratton said nothing. Jake continued, "She says I bring my
work home with me too much. What the fuck am I supposed
to do, leave it somewhere to be cleaned? It doesn't stop happening when I take off the shield. . . ."

Another silence, broken only by the ringing of phones and the buzz of conversation at other desks. Stratton started away from Jake's desk, then turned back. "Look, Jake—there's been a whole lot of shit come down on you these past couple of weeks. I mean—everyone expected you to take some time off after what happened to Nivens."

Jake was silent for a moment. Then he said, "Maybe I should have. It can't happen now, though—not with Lon Chaney on the streets and the press stroking it like the second coming."

Stratton nodded. "Just try to do something for yourself. Go to the gym, ride a bike, I don't know . . . shave your head and hang around the airport if it'll help. Something."

He started out of the room, then turned and added, "Lon Chaney was the Wolfman." He left.

Jake stared at the wanted posters on the far wall. "It figures," he said softly to himself.

Sarah was having trouble keeping her mind on her work. A long and tense phone conversation with Matt last night had left her furious enough to beat the living hell out of a pillow with the side-handle baton she kept by the bed. He was making well over a hundred thousand dollars a year compared to her forty-plus, and he still had the gall to ask her to pay half of Brandon's private school tuition. He had pointed out that his expenses matched his income, just as hers did, to which she had answered that no one had put a gun to his head and forced him to buy a beach house in Malibu.

The talk had ended with nothing resolved, and with considerable bad feelings on both sides. And now, today, she was having trouble concentrating on the Night Hunter case.

Todd had done the postmortem and found, as before, no indications of molestation or fetishism. Jake told her he felt certain the killings were somehow hooked up with Anton Magus. They still did not have a linking motive for the Satanist, however.

She yawned and poured another cup of coffee. She wasn't

used to working nights, would never get used to it, had drunk so much coffee today that she felt simultaneously wired and exhausted—her brain seemed to be vibrating in the casing of her skull. When she reached this stage of fatigue she was unable to bring anything new to a problem and unable to let go of it. The *Res Gestae*—the facts of the case—chased themselves around and around in her head, with no new insights offering themselves.

In an attempt to break the pattern, she thought of the weekend afternoon she had spent with Jake and their two boys. Thinking about Jake was perilously close to thinking about the case, and Sarah knew her thoughts could easily slip back into the same tired maze, but she wanted to think about him. She had known Jake Hull as an acquaintance since she had begun her practice as an M.E., and he had always been polite but distant, the kind of cop who had no life outside of his work. This was not a mark in his favor. She certainly had no desire to get involved with another Type A—being married to a doctor-in-training had been bad enough. Although, she admitted to herself reluctantly, she was not exactly guiltless of workaholism herself.

She found herself thinking about his eyes, about the way his hair fell in untidy strands over his forehead. Dwelling on such things was a bad sign, she knew, but she felt no desire to stop. He was interested in her—that had been quite apparent the last time they had seen each other—and she wondered what it would be like. He seemed very reserved and restrained in many ways . . . would those walls break down in bed? Would there be a flood of passion?

The sudden kiss in the car certainly indicated that that would be the case. She pictured them in her apartment, necking on the couch, saw him with his shirt off, felt his hands cupping her face. The skin of her neck and upper arms tingled as she sank deeper into the pleasant reverie; she felt warm despite the chill air of the room.

We're not talking a prize catch here, Sarah warned herself.

He's divorced, a career cop . . . but telling herself those things was no good, and she knew it. For better or worse, Jake Hull was on her mind.

She was thinking about his eyes when there was a knock on the door, and a moment later he walked in.

Sarah blinked in surprise, feeling oddly flustered, as if he somehow knew she had been thinking about him. He did not seem to notice her embarrassment, however. "Latham said you were down here." He picked up a carbide scribe from the machinist's toolbox that served as her evidence kit, examining it as though he'd never seen one before.

"How certain are you about the time of death?" he asked her.

"Fairly certain. It's not possible to pinpoint it exactly, as I'm sure you know. Lividity was fixed, and rigor fairly extensive. He was cool to the touch. It's in the report."

"I read it." He wasn't looking at her. Sarah became aware of a dripping faucet somewhere nearby. "No indications this was a sex crime?"

"Swabs for semen in the mouth and anus were negative. No come on the skin or clothes either."

He nodded, still apparently fascinated by the contents of her evidence kit. "Drugs?"

"Tox screen was negative, except for traces of OTC antihistamine. Like I said, Jake, it's all in the report."

Jake put down the anti-putrefaction mask he was inspecting and looked at her for the first time since he'd entered the room. "Okay. Thanks." He hesitated, then added, "You looked a little—I don't know, maybe upset to see me when I came in. Anything wrong?"

"No." Then she said, hearing the words as though they were issuing from someone else's throat, "I was just wondering what you'd be like in bed."

If this had been a movie, Sarah thought later, they probably would have done it right there in the morgue, tearing each other's clothes off and humping like mad rabbits on one of the gurneys, oblivious to the naked sheeted traffic accident parked against one wall. But neither of them were sufficiently overcome with passion to consider that. Instead they had driven back to her apartment, Jake following her through the neon California night.

Once there, he had seemed somewhat shy, which only increased his attractiveness in Sarah's eyes. As in her fantasy, they sat on the couch, kissing, exploring each other's faces with their fingers, tracing skin in erotic Braille.

He seemed in no hurry, and for that she was profoundly grateful. They left their clothes in a trail leading to the bedroom; Sarah gave only a fleeting thought to the piles of unfolded laundry and the unmade bed.

The only awkward moment was when she insisted on a condom. He groaned, but acquiesced, and seemed somewhat mollified when she offered to put it on him. Sarah was afraid for a moment that the mood had been spoiled. But there was no way around it—she had seen too many skeletal street victims of the plague.

He was slow and deliberate, his thrusting measured, almost thoughtful. She dug her fingernails into his shoulders and watched his face, half-shadowed in the moonlit darkness. When he came, it was punctuated by the wail of a far off unit racing Code Three through the streets, and they both pretended not to notice. She peaked a few moments later, and afterward they lay side by side, his arm beneath her neck, her fingers entwined in his pubic hair.

"We have a lot in common," he said quietly.

She nodded against his arm. She never felt much like talking after sex; it was supposed to be a female thing, but she felt fairly certain that men were apt to do it more than women.

He pulled his arm from beneath her neck, raised himself on one elbow and looked about the room. "Nice place," he commented. She felt a subtle tension from him, a straining to make conversation.

"You don't have to stay," she told him gently.

He looked at her with surprise and a little bit of suspicion. She smiled. "Look, I'm not picking out china or anything because of this. I want to take it step by step just like you do. I was the one who asked you here, remember?"

She could feel him relax. He lay back down beside her, put a hand on her stomach, moved it in slow, easy circles. "I guess I panicked for a minute there."

"I know the feeling." Sarah studied him for a moment, then said, "You want to talk about the case?"

He grinned at her, more relaxed now than she had ever seen him. "Yeah," he said. "Let's talk about the case."

CHAPTER 25

Tuesday, October 29

Franklin Conner stood before the microphone and script stand, wishing he had brought a jacket with him; though the weather outside was warm and sunny, the temperature in the recording studio was just this side of chilly. It was too late to worry about that now, though.

He glanced at the script on the stand before him; his part was highlighted in yellow ink. His agent had called him yesterday to tell him about the part, that of a recurring villain in a toy-inspired action-adventure cartoon series. The producers were dissatisfied with the actor originally cast and had called Conner in to audition.

He had been glad to do it. Money had been getting quite tight, and scale plus ten percent would pay his rent and living expenses nicely. If he got the part, it would be his first role in animation, and, with any luck, might lead to a second career for him in voice-over work. Conner hoped so; there was a lot to be said about doing voices for cartoon characters. The pay was more than decent, and sitting in a recording booth for a few hours a week reading off a script was certainly more pleasant than going through makeup, wardrobe and everything else that was part and parcel of a live-action shoot. This was something he could do, theoretically, even after he was too old to walk. He had heard a story once about Bill Brecht, who had been the voice of Scamper for many years on the popular sixties cartoon *Boondoggle.* When the show had been revived in the eighties as a TV movie to satisfy baby boomers' nostalgic cravings, Brecht had been brought back to do Scamper's voice, even though adult-onset diabetes had left him almost totally blind. They had fed him the lines one by one and he had recited them back flawlessly. Obviously, Conner thought, the only thing an aging voice-over actor had to worry about was losing his voice.

The director, an intense thirtysomething with a ridiculously long ponytail, was explaining the character to him. "You're not just a guy out to conquer the world. It's like, you really *believe* that humanity is fundamentally flawed, and that machines are the way to go. See, you're half man, half computer, so there's this war always going on inside you. Let me hear that struggle when you talk about turning the President into a toaster."

Conner nodded, trying not to smile. Okay, maybe it wasn't Shakespeare in the park, but it was honest work, certainly no worse than hunting vampires for American International and a hell of a lot easier.

He read the audition piece in a quiet, contained voice, on the theory that someone equal parts man and machine would show little emotion. At the same time he tried for an undertone of menace and aloof confidence. It was drawing heavily from the calm self-assurance of Jonathan Skull, whom Conner had always played as a borderline fanatic, eerily detached even when facing hordes of the living dead.

Evidently it was the right way to go. The producer, who

looked barely old enough to shave, asked him to tweak a few lines, but overall seemed more than satisfied with his performance. The writer, a thin man with an earring and a salt-and-pepper beard, shook Conner's hand enthusiastically afterward, telling him what a huge fan he had been since junior high. Conner thanked him for the compliment and tried not to feel too old.

The studio was on a side street in Echo Park, just south of Glendale Boulevard. Conner strolled toward the bus stop, hearing Latin music serenading from open apartment windows and smelling the spicy aromas of *chorizo*. He tried not to be nervous. When he had first moved to Los Angeles in the fifties he had dated a woman who had lived in Echo Park, and he remembered it then as a charming and quaint neighborhood, its hills covered with Spanish and Mediterranean-style bungalows and apartments. Now graffiti marred the buildings and street signs, rusting cars sat on blocks with their engines disemboweled, and men lounged on porches in torn undershirts, passing bottles and joints. Something crunched like a dead autumn leaf under Conner's shoe; when he looked down he saw he had stepped on a syringe.

He decided that if he got the part he would indulge in taxis to and from the studio rather than taking the bus. The daylight hours were growing steadily shorter, and he had no desire to walk through this neighborhood after dark.

There were times—more and more, lately—when Conner fantasized about leaving Los Angeles entirely. He had thought several times of moving to some small Northern California college town and teaching acting and drama. Certainly he had the credentials, and it seemed a more dignified way to live out the rest of his life than scrabbling for work in a city that was rapidly turning into a war zone.

He really wasn't quite sure why he stayed. Perhaps it really was the old joke about the man working in the circus shoveling elephant shit: "What, and give up show business?"

Somehow he still felt umbilically connected to it. Even though he knew the neighborhood he lived in was growing increasingly dangerous, the thought of leaving saddened him beyond words.

Conner sat down on the bus stop bench beside an old woman with shopping bags piled about her feet. The problem, he told himself, was that people could no longer tell the difference between reality and fantasy. They acted out murderous daydreams now with no thought to the consequences. It was fashionable these days to blame this lack of impulse control on movies and television, a trend Conner found highly questionable. When he was younger and working steadily no one had been all that concerned about violent subject matter in film and TV. True, the sponsors were always nervous, but their concerns had primarily been about granting subliminal free advertising to competitors, which was why Chevrolet would insist that lines like "fording a river" be deleted from a script. Foolish, but in the end relatively inconsequential.

But in these days of the rampantly politically correct it seemed as if all subjects were taboo, particularly the genre he had happily worked in for so long. Now lawsuits flew thick and fast whenever someone was foolish enough to mimic a dangerous action on TV or in a film. The networks were all terrified of what they called "imitative behavior." Darwin had a term for the results of such actions, Conner thought sourly; he called it "natural selection." As a child he had spent long afternoons at the local bijou in Teaneck, watching cartoons, newsreels, double features and comedy shorts. He had sat in the dark, enthralled, as John Wayne and Humphrey Bogart fired hundreds of bullets in westerns and gangster movies, had thrilled as Karloff and Lugosi and Chaney stalked their victims across the mist-shrouded moors, had howled with laughter as Moe poked Larry and Curly in the eyes and Elmer Fudd blew Daffy's beak off with a shotgun. And, though he had sat through all those films unsupervised during his formative years, Conner could not once recall ever having had the urge to shoot a man, bite a woman's neck or stick a pair of pliers up someone's nose in an attempt to twist his head off.

He sighed. It made him extremely resentful that his livelihood could be circumscribed and curtailed because people were no longer willing to take responsibility for their actions. He had hoped that, as he grew older, the world would gradually make more sense. Instead it seemed to grow more and more incomprehensible.

The bus pulled to a stop amidst clouds of diesel exhaust. Conner paid his fare and sat down. Across the aisle an old man dressed in cast-off clothes stared out the window, his toothless jaws mumbling to himself. Conner could see tinfoil lining peeking out from beneath the shapeless hat he wore. A few seats down a pair of teenagers in baggy clothes, baseball caps perched backwards on their heads, huddled over a Game Boy. A young pregnant woman a few seats over was reading a tabloid; the headline said something about vampires infiltrating L.A.

He leaned back and closed his eyes, wondering if the case that the press referred to as the Night Hunter really did have anything to do with *Mask of the Vampire*. Though he didn't believe in censorship as a way to avoid parental and personal responsibility, he was not blind to the fact that a few disturbed people could be prompted to crime by something they watched or read. He had called the police and offered to discuss the matter with them, and had received a polite "No, thank you" for his trouble. Still, Conner couldn't let go of the idea—the similarities between fact and fiction, in this particular case, were too many to be denied.

Of course, he did not for an instant believe that an actual vampire was haunting the streets of Los Angeles. He had no trouble discerning fantasy from reality, after all. But it seemed quite believable that someone might be patterning murders after the methods of a vampire hunter. . . .

Conner felt a sudden chill wash over him. *He* had played

a vampire hunter in more than one film . . . what if this psychotic somehow became fixated on him? Stranger things had certainly happened; he personally knew two actors who had been stalked by obsessed fans. It had never happened to him, though he once had to change his phone number to an unlisted one after the last Skull feature came out on video and a fellow from Cleveland kept calling him to talk about the films.

He shook his head. "Ridiculous!" he said, then felt foolish for having spoken out loud. No one seemed to care, however . . . one would have to perform much more bizarre actions than talking to oneself to be noticed on the RTD.

Though Conner knew he had no proof and that it was purely paranoia, the uneasiness he felt at the thought of the killer becoming obsessed with him would not go away. It persisted for the remainder of the bus ride up Hollywood Boulevard and the short walk back to his apartment through the gathering dark. He was quite relieved to be able to close and lock the door and glad to be back once more in his macabre sanctuary.

CHAPTER 26

Tuesday, October 29

Once back in his living quarters, surrounded by the photos, one-sheets and other memorabilia of his career, Conner thought the disquietude would go away, but it did not—if anything, it increased. Normally he felt no concern whatsoever about living over a mortuary, but this evening, as the sun slipped behind the horizon and long shadows crept through the streets, he was acutely aware that somewhere beneath his feet a host of cadavers rested. He could not shake the image of them as a sort of vile hive, quiescent now but capable at any moment of lurching to some horrific semblance of life.

He sat in his favorite chair, trying to read a nonfiction book about the England of Charles Dickens, but finding his eyes unable to resist looking at the door in the far wall of the living room. It had not been opened in the six years he had lived here, for the very good reason that he did not have a key to it. It was the connecting door to the stairs leading down to the mortuary. On it he had hung a framed poster for the last Skull movie, *Cult of the Undead.* It was a lurid painting showing a vague likeness of himself in Edwardian garb, beset by a spiraling horde of pale zombie-like cadavers boiling out of a distant graveyard. Though he knew it was foolish, Conner could not shake the image of the bodies below him—some bedecked in suits and dresses, rouged and coiffed for their final appearances in expensive lace-lined caskets, others lying naked and eviscerated in the building's basement—but all of them stirring, rising stiffly to their feet, formaldehyde pulsing sluggishly through their veins instead of blood, driven by a hideous hunger, stumbling toward the stairs that led up to his apartment. . . .

Conner sighed, closed the book, got up and went to the stack of stereo equipment. He picked out an old vinyl recording of New Orleans jazz—he hated compact discs, thought they sounded exactly like what they were, soulless electronic reproductions of music—and put it on. In a moment the slapping bass and tinkling ivories of the Johnny Dodds Trio's *Blue Piano Stomp* filled the air.

He stood in the center of the room and let the music wash over him, trying to shake his nervousness. It was absurd that, after a lifetime's career of scaring people, he himself should now be starting at shadows. Still, there it was; he could not deny it.

Conner was not a big fan of alcohol, but he occasionally enjoyed a glass of white wine after dinner, and there was a bottle of Chardonnay in the kitchen. He filled a wine glass and sat back down with his book, sipping the wine and listening to the music. He could feel himself beginning, almost imperceptibly, to relax. These fears were ridiculous, after all. The dead below him came and went, true enough, but not under their own power. Vampires did not stalk the streets of Hollywood thirsting for blood.

Louis Armstrong's *Alligator Crawl* came to a stop and silence marked the end of side one. That was one advantage

CDs had over records, Conner thought as he got up to turn the vinyl disc over. The music and the wine together were beginning to work—he felt a mellow, pleasant glow suffusing him. He flipped the album and started to set the needle in the beginning groove of side two.

It was then that he heard the scratching at the locked door.

Conner froze, feeling every drop of blood in his veins alchemically transformed into ice water. He stared over his shoulder, twisting his neck uncomfortably, not daring to move. The sound came again: a faint, almost imperceptible scratching.

Like that of long nails being drawn slowly over wood. . . .

It was definitely coming from the other side of the door.

From the mortuary. . . .

He heard a faint hissing sound escaping from his throat. In an instant, it seemed, everything he knew about reality had been shattered—this was a new world now, some sinister alternate dimension into which he had somehow been hurled, in which the dead *did* walk and hunger and hunt. . . .

Conner managed to straighten up, and it was then, at this late date in his life, that he learned something about himself for the first time—he learned that he really was a brave man. Though every nerve in his body screamed at him to flee the apartment, he approached the connecting door to the mortuary—slowly and with stiff legs, it was true, but nevertheless he approached.

The room was no more than twelve feet across, but it seemed to stretch impossibly as he walked, the walls elongating and the door warping in his vision like some fish-eye lens effect. Even so, he found himself standing before the door all too soon.

Whatever was on the other side of the door was quiet now. *It knows you're here,* his mind screamed at him; *it can smell your blood.* . . . The air about him seemed to hum with tension. Conner licked his dry lips. He imagined a fist suddenly hammering through the wood, bludgeoning a hole in the heavy door with impossible strength, rotting flesh scraped from ivory knuckles by the force of the blow, skeletal fingers groping for his throat. . . .

He heard the scratching again. Now that he stood next to the door he could tell exactly where it was coming from—down near the bottom. He looked down, and even as he saw the flicker of the cat's paw in the space between the door and the floor he heard the faint meowing.

The relief that flooded him was so intense that Conner literally became dizzy; he staggered to one side, bumping into the bookshelf by the door and nearly knocking over a framed picture of him and Roddy McDowall. A short bark of annoyed laughter escaped his throat, and he delivered a petulant kick at the door. He was rewarded by the faint sound of the cat on the other side scampering back down the stairs and a sharp pain in his big toe.

A *cat,* for the love of God—either a stray that had gotten into the building somehow or a new pet. Conner couldn't believe it. He had played this very scene a dozen times, reacting in terror to an unseen menace that turned out to be something embarrassingly prosaic.

Of course, his mind whispered as he headed back to his chair, *the way it works is to set up tension and release, and then sucker-punch the audience.* Which meant that the vampire should come crashing through the window right about *now. . . .*

Conner realized he had stopped again, posed warily, listening. He heard nothing. Somewhat annoyed with himself, he sat down, taking a gulp of wine.

There were no such things as vampires, he told himself. And even if there were, they would know better than to mess with Franklin Conner, the man who had slain legions of them. He glanced toward the door to the bedroom, where a wooden mallet and stake—props from *Vampire Lover*—rested in a Plexiglas case. Let them try to bare their fangs anywhere near him. He had garlic in the kitchen and he knew how to use it.

He smiled slightly and picked up the book again, trying to lose himself in nineteenth-century England. But somehow the rules of whist and fox hunting did not intrigue him as they had a few minutes before. Nor did he feel an urge to listen to the album's second side.

Instead he decided to go over to Phoenix House for a few hours of social work. This was not one of his usual nights to go, but they certainly would not turn down more help, as they were always chronically understaffed. The thought of going out into the night after the scare he had just had was not upsetting in the least; in fact he rather looked forward to it, feeling that it would prove on some obscure level that he was back in touch with his own familiar reality.

Of course, he was not going to walk over there in the dark. There might not be anything to fear from ghosts and goblins and things that went bump in the night, but the streets of Hollywood were no less dangerous because of that. No, Conner would do what he usually did; call a cab to ferry him the few blocks over there and back. The tragedies that were constantly being played out among these non-supernatural children of the night were heartbreakingly sad, but they did accomplish one thing for him; they made him forget his own troubles.

CHAPTER 27

Tuesday, October 29

Conner arrived at the halfway house just before nine P.M., the time when the group activities—which usually consisted of watching videotapes or playing board games in the big front room—were winding down. Several of the kids there recognized him and greeted him; his status as a film actor from years past had risen considerably when Phoenix House had run several of his old movies on the VCR.

Rhys put him to work updating the job referral listings. He did not seem surprised that Conner had come in for an additional night; Conner had the impression that nothing could surprise Simon Rhys.

As an actor he was fascinated by Rhys; he found the man's every movement to be a paean of graceful choreography. Conner had, at times, watched with complete fascination the other doing some menial task like folding clothes or alphabetizing the house's lending library; Rhys performed every job with an economy and surety of motion and a concentration that seemed worthy of a Zen master. It was not that the man seemed arrogant or dangerous; rather, he was—Conner could find no other word for it—*peaceful.* The actor had asked Rhys once how he had developed this fascinating trait, and Rhys had smiled and said, "Years of practice."

One of the kids Conner recognized there that night was Angel, a teenaged boy who, when he wasn't blasted out of his skull on PCP, liked to work out with the free weights kept in the rear room. For someone who lived on junk food and drugs he was surprisingly muscular. Usually Angel was a nice enough sort when he was straight, and he had taken quite a shine to Conner after watching the Skull movies. The boy talked longingly of being a movie actor. Conner thought that, given his physique and that sort of charming naiveté that he had when he wasn't dusted, he might have a chance if he could only stay clean.

Tonight, however, Angel seemed nervous and upset. Conner noticed the boy was wearing a grimy gauze pad held in place by adhesive tape strips on his neck, and he overheard him asking one of the known dealers where he could find some angel dust.

This couldn't be condoned. Conner moved over to the two and said, "You know the rules, Angel. What you do on the street is your own concern, but there's no dealing in here."

Angel gave him a resentful look, but turned and headed for the door, followed by the dealer whose name Conner didn't know. Conner shook his head sadly and returned to his categorizing. It was hard to maintain a firm attitude with some of these kids, especially the ones who knew how to play on your sympathies for special favors. But it was necessary; if you got too emotionally attached, the sadness and horror of it all could burn you to an emotional husk.

Once again Jake Hull and Dan Stratton sat in an unmarked car parked across and slightly down the street from Anton

Magus's house. Dan muffled a yawn as he listened to crickets chirping in the cool hillside night. They had been on stakeout here for nearly four hours, and they hadn't spoken for the last hour and a half. Before that, the conversation had consisted mostly of various clever observations and one-liners on Dan's part—at least, that was his opinion—and terse answers or grunts from Jake.

He tried again, just for something to do. "I checked out that fighting style the guy at Phoenix House mentioned," he said. "Chan Gen—thought it was some kind of Chinese kung fu." Jake gave no indication that he'd heard anything; Dan continued doggedly. "It's not. Had one of the research guys track it down. *Changen;* it's Middle English. You know, like Shakespeare? Five, six hundred years old. Means 'change.' "

Jake didn't even grunt in response. No wonder he got divorced, Dan thought in disgust; his wife probably couldn't keep up with that sparkling wit.

He gave it one more try. "What kind of gun you carry?" Odd that he'd known Jake for over a year and never thought to ask him that; it was the first thing cops usually talk about.

For a minute he thought Jake was going to stonewall that subject as well, but then the detective reached under the left side of his jacket and pulled a snub-nosed Colt .38 Detective Special from its belt holster. He handed it to Dan, who shook his head wryly.

"Jesus, an antique. Same gun Jack Webb used in *Dragnet.*" He handed it back, pulled his Glock. "This one's mine."

Jake glanced at it, then turned his eyes back to Magus's house. "Yeah, you guys are all hot for those Tupperware guns." He put the Colt back in its holster. "This piece is good enough for Joe Friday; it's good enough for me."

Dan thought about saying, "Friday's dead, Jake," but couldn't really see any point in it.

Jake asked, "How often you hit the range?"

"Twice a month."

Jake shook his head. "Not good enough. You should go

shoot at least once a week; more if you can make time. And
don't just plink at the target; really get into it. Concentrate.
Shoot with your left hand, practice re-loading with your eyes
closed. They say you've got to do something at least 3,500
times before it becomes muscle memory. When was the last
time you tested your Mace?"

Dan was beginning to think he liked Jake better in surly
mode. Fortunately the detective did not press him for an answer to his question. Silence reigned in the car again.

Dan's worry that Jake was losing perspective on this case
continued to grow. The detective's obsession with Magus was
by far the greatest example. Dan had no problem whatsoever
with the concept of the Satanist as a sleazy motherfucker who
deserved several decades in a jail cell, preferably in the inti-
mate company of a large black man named Bubba. But they
had nothing to go to the D.A.'s office with yet, nothing with
which to build a case. Nevertheless, it looked like Jake had
completely convinced himself that Magus was their boy. It
was one thing to play a hunch, but this wasn't the way one
went about solving a murder—even though Dan was still a
uniform, he knew that much about detective work. You had
to work horizontally, not vertically—spread yourself over the
immediate area of the murder, letting people lead you to other
people, working the neighborhood. That way, ideally, you
came up with a number of suspects whom you then win-
nowed down to the one or two most likely.

Jake hadn't done that, not even close. He had fixated on
Magus and didn't want to hear about any other possibilities.
Not that there were any at this point, but that was the problem, Dan thought. You solved a case by assembling the clues
and finding whoever fit them best, not by picking someone
and trying to jack the case around to fit him.

Jake suddenly sat up and reached for the key. "He's on the
move," the detective said softly.

Dan saw Magus's Porsche backing out of the driveway. The

car's finely tuned German engine purred softly in the night air as it headed down the street, a sleek metallic predator. Jake let the sports car get about a half block down the winding street before putting their vehicle in gear and following.

Dan tried again. "What if he isn't the guy, Jake? I mean, you got no one else at this point. This case is a real live wire— we gotta be able to show more than one suspect—"

"This is the guy," Jake said, in a tone that brooked no discussion. Dan opened his mouth to protest, then closed it, his teeth making an audible snap.

Jake was quiet as they followed Magus's car for a block or two; then, as the Porsche turned west on Franklin, he said, "Jesus Christ, Dan, you need a haunted house to fall on you? Magus is *perfect*. He's the guy."

"Hey, I don't care how fucking perfect he is." Dan was unable to keep the annoyance out of his voice. "The bottom line is, we got no evidence. Without that we got no case. All I'm saying is, let's go back to the scene before things get any colder, *talk* to some people, for God's sake. Basic investigative procedure. . . ."

"When you've been doing this as long as I have," Jake said, "you learn to trust your instincts. I'm telling you, I got a feeling about Magus. He's our guy."

Dan opened his mouth, then closed it again and settled back against his seat. Hopeless. For the past two days Jake had been talking more and more like a TV show. Not good, Dan thought. Not good at all.

They did not speak again as they followed the Porsche over to Phoenix House. Magus parked in front of the building and shouldered his way through the crowd that immediately gathered around the car. Jake and Dan parked across the street and about half a block up. As he passed under a street lamp Dan noticed that Magus was wearing a small gauze bandage patch on the left side of his neck.

"No place you can go that I can't follow," Jake said softly, his eyes fixed on the halfway house's entrance. Dan rolled his eyes. Fucking Mickey Spillane, he thought. The next thing you know we'll be having goddamn car chases—if this city-issue piece of shit could do above sixty for more than a block without throwing a rod. . . .

CHAPTER 28

Tuesday, October 29

Conner watched with mild surprise as the man in the black leather trench coat entered the main room. A pimp? he wondered. But there was a different, more sophisticated air about him than pimps usually projected.

The man looked about, spied Conner and stepped over to him. "I'm looking for a boy they call Angel," he said.

"He's not here." Both Conner and the man in the trench coat turned at the quiet but authoritarian sound of Rhys's voice. "And you have no business here, Mr. Magus."

The man Rhys called Magus frowned. "The boy is one of my flock, Rhys. He has asked me to show him the virtues of the left-hand path, and I—"

"Bullshit," Rhys said, his voice softer still. Several of the kids who had been watching the exchange with interest now backed away and out of the room. "Angel told me what you did to him—what you've been doing to Zip and the others as well. He doesn't want anything more to do with your sick games." Rhys moved fluidly to stand in front of Magus. "Now get out of here while your legs still work."

Conner felt his skin prickling with awe. He had no doubt that Rhys was perfectly capable of breaking Magus in half and that he would be totally justified in doing it. Conner had heard the boys speak of Anton Magus, although this was the first time he had seen the man. He felt like adding his voice to Rhys's, but he knew the other needed no help.

Magus stared at Rhys for a moment, then dropped his gaze, clearly the loser in the confrontation. "This will not be forgotten," he said in a low voice. "Offend me and you offend Lucifer."

"Out," Rhys said, pointing toward the door. Magus's eyes narrowed; then the Satanist swept past Rhys and out of the building.

Rhys watched him go, then stood, apparently lost in thought, for a moment. Conner cleared his throat, and Rhys turned toward him with a smile that seemed almost rueful, as if he were embarrassed by the melodramatic overtones of the past few minutes.

"Never a dull moment, is there?" he asked.

"I hope he stays away from here," Conner said, the vehemence in his own tone slightly surprising him. "These kids have enough problems without having to deal with the likes of him."

Rhys nodded, introspective again. "Don't worry," he said. "He won't come back." The certainty in his voice intrigued Conner; the actor was about to ask how Rhys could be so sure, but before he could speak the other man left the room as well.

Conner shrugged and turned back to the tasks at hand. It had certainly been anything but a boring evening.

Jake cranked up the car as Magus stormed out of Phoenix House. The Satanist spoke with several of the kids congregated about his Porsche, then got in the sleek black German machine and drove away with a screech of tires. Jake followed, the Chevy's engine protesting the rapid increase in speed.

"Looks like something twisted his tail in there," Jake mused as Magus sped east to Vine. He turned south there, following it down past Melrose, where the street name changed to North Rossmore, a tree-lined avenue that passed stately old apartment complexes and mansions built decades ago next to the Wilshire Country Club.

Magus followed Beverly east, cruising past the fast-food stands, clothing outlets and porn theaters toward downtown. Within twenty minutes they were heading down Figueroa. Dan could see the mirrored towers of the Bonaventure Hotel silhouetted against the moon. They turned east on Temple, driving past the heart of the city's business and financial district.

Dan had always found the downtown area depressing. He had seen pictures of Los Angeles back in the forties, had come to know it well from all those old Republic serials he had loved as a kid. All in all, the years just prior to World War II were his favorite time for the city, though he had missed living through them by almost thirty years. Back then City Hall had been the tallest building around at a measly twenty-seven stories. There had been an identity to the city in those years; now towering corporate monoliths like the First Interstate and United California Bank buildings dwarfed the more interesting structures and made the downtown area look like any other major city. In trying to establish a character for itself, L.A. had achieved only anonymity.

Magus's glossy black car turned south on Broadway, leading them down a thoroughfare that was an uneasy amalgamation of barrio and business district. They passed the Bradbury Building, the Million Dollar Theater and the Orpheum—rococo remnants of a bygone age. The area really didn't appear all that different from the way it looked in *Blade Runner,* Dan thought. All that was needed was rain and flying squad cars. . . . It was not yet nine o'clock, and both car and foot traffic were still relatively heavy, which made it easy to keep close to the Porsche without being noticed.

Magus turned east, paralleling the Santa Monica freeway. Within twenty minutes they were in a run-down area of dilapidated warehouses, manufacturing plants and other commercial buildings, most of them long-abandoned or half-destroyed, their empty husks rising starkly against the glowing towers to the west. This was a part of Los Angeles the tourists never saw, a desolate locale that was more like East St. Louis or the South Bronx. A place where the living envied the dead, Dan thought grimly. Derelicts warmed themselves over trash can fires or shuffled aimlessly down the dirty streets. "Strawberries"—addicts who traded sex for crack— stood on corners. Infrequent streetlights cast a bilious glow that reflected from painted-over windows. There was little graffiti scrawled on the walls; this territory wasn't worth claiming even by gangs.

Dan had only been in this area three or four times in all the years he had lived in L.A. It was a strange urban dystopia of sheet metal, razor wire and cinder blocks, bounded by the concrete banks of the Los Angeles River, San Pedro Street, Little Tokyo and the elevated lanes of the Santa Monica Freeway. There was an entire subculture surviving down here, he knew, staying alive in a multitude of illicit ways such as scrounging bulk produce and cut-rate electronics to sell for crack and cheap booze. Transients lived like troglodytes in empty warehouses, finding meager sustenance in Dumpsters. A few artists still clung to their cheap spacious lofts, trying to pretend that this underbelly of the city could yet give birth to an artistic renaissance. Illegal underground clubs sprouted like mushrooms in the deserted warehouses, lasting at most a couple of nights, drawing adolescents in search of raves full of illegal drugs and cutting-edge music. But for the most part this area belonged to the disenfranchised and the damned. Prostitutes, addicts, thieves and drifters . . . together with the bleak buildings that jutted like rotten teeth, they made the region look like some post-apocalyptic vision of hell.

Dan wondered what Magus could possibly be after in this blighted landscape. Chicken, possibly; hard though it was to believe, this was an area that rich men habitually trolled for young male prostitutes. But why, Dan wondered, would Magus come all the way down here when he could have easily gotten some willing young hardbody back in Hollywood?

Magus's car wended its way through a confusing welter of industrial side streets. The two cops followed slowly, their lights off, since there were no other cars around. At last the Porsche came to a stop before an old deserted building that had apparently once housed some kind of chemical factory. Magus, looking absurdly out of place in his black leather trench coat and snakeskin boots, got out of the car, locked it— Dan heard the alarm cheep—and went to the door. It was apparently unlocked, for he entered without difficulty, vanishing into the building's black interior.

Dan and Jake had parked a block back, Jake cutting the engine and rolling the last fifty feet or so before coming to a stop. They got out of the car and moved quickly and quietly toward the building.

Dan was wondering if maybe Jake's hunch was right after all—this looked pretty suspicious. There weren't many things that someone like Anton Magus could be after in this neighborhood at this time of night, and all the ones Dan could think of were illegal. Maybe they couldn't bust the guy for the murders of Jimmy Ray Tate and Craig Alstadler, but it was looking more and more probable that they would be able to bust him for something—most likely possession. Dan could live with that.

The door was open. They slipped quickly inside. The interior was a huge barn-like space dimly lit by moonlight filtering through grimy skylights far overhead. A maze of wrought-iron stairways and catwalks zig-zagged over huge dry vats.

Dan swallowed, feeling his stomach clench with uneasiness. He started hearing a little voice in his head whispering seriously about backup. This kind of place was a cop's worst nightmare, rife with potential ambushes and deathtraps. But beyond that, it was *spooky*. The description came easily to mind, even though it was a word he had not had occasion to use seriously since he hit puberty. Spooky described it perfectly, though—the silence, save for skittering sounds that were almost certainly rats, the deep liquid shadows that cloaked the walls and ceilings, the half-seen railings and catwalks above him where bad guys—

Or worse, his mind whispered . . .

—might lurk.

Jake, however, did not seem concerned. He moved quickly ahead through the darkness, and Dan had no choice but to follow.

CHAPTER 29

Tuesday, October 29

At first Jake thought crack house, but the place was too big, too quiet and much too easy to get into. He wasn't sure what was going on here, but he knew that Magus was involved in it somehow right up to his tinted hairline.

He also knew he should call for cover units. This was a stupid Hollywood thing to do, going into a potential situation without backup, but Stratton's harping on the way he was handling the case had gotten to Jake somewhat. He wanted eyeball evidence that Magus was involved in something before he called in the Marines.

He moved through the soft darkness, his .38 in his hand, trying not to let his nervousness escalate into outright fear. He had been in tight situations a few times before, and he had gotten the job done, despite the fear. He'd never known a cop who hadn't admitted to being scared shitless on occasion. And fear was a perfectly appropriate emotion to be feeling right now, given the circumstances.

Nevertheless, Jake had to admit that what he was feeling now was more than just the worry of someone throwing a cap into him. Though he was loath to admit it, he was afraid of the dark itself. Maybe the sensational aspects of this Night Hunter case had gotten to him; whatever the reason, he felt spooked in a way he could not recall feeling since he had been a small boy hiding in bed.

It was a vague, amorphous fear, but none the less intense for that. The worst thing about it was that there was no real way to get a handle on it. He didn't believe in ghosts, vampires, any of that crap, so he knew nothing like that lurked, red-eyed and waiting, in the vast dark spaces of the building. He knew it, and yet the fear lay heavy on him, and there was nothing he could do to dispel it.

They moved through that first big room and into a narrow corridor that was a tunnel of utter darkness leading out of the gloom. Jake could hear Stratton behind him, his breathing sharp and quick. Jake had thought it couldn't get much worse than being in that large, echoing chamber, but this corridor was far worse—he felt claustrophobic, pressed in by the walls and ceiling as though they were moving slowly together to crush him.

He stopped for a moment; his heart was pounding as if he had just run a mile uphill. His gut was trying to chew itself in half again as well, but there was something almost comforting about that pain—bad as it was, it was familiar, a connection to a life lived outside this building.

He was about to continue when he heard voices ahead.

Jake frowned, listening. He could clearly make out Magus's tone, but the words were not distinguishable. There was another voice as well, and something about its tone caused Jake to swallow dryly. If asked, he could not have said exactly what it was about the voice that disturbed him, only that there was something *wrong* about its cadence and timbre.

The corridor ended at an office door. Behind the pebbled glass was a dim cold radiance, more like foxfire than a real light.

Jake drew in a long, shuddering breath through his nose. *Fuck it,* he thought. And lunged forward.

He kicked the door open and stepped in, immediately putting his back to the wall beside the door. *"Police!"* he shouted.

Something grabbed him.

As Jake went through the door, Dan had a brief, confusing glimpse of a small cramped office, moonlight filtering through a flyspecked and dirty skylight, a metal desk and filing cabinets against the far wall, everything covered with dust as thick as that of an Egyptian tomb. Then someone grabbed Jake and hurled him—a man who had to weigh one-eighty, at least—across the room as though the detective were made of cardboard.

Before Dan could draw down on the shadowy figure that loomed before him, a hand lashed out, knocking his gun from his fingers with a force that numbed them and sent the cop spinning back against the wall.

Jake landed with a crash and a cry on the desk, sliding over it and hitting the floor on the other side. A smaller figure, standing near the door, tried to lunge through it, and Dan, reacting out of instinct, body-slammed the guy against the door-jamb. He got a good whiff of that distinctive odor that identified Magus.

Magus went down and Dan grabbed his cuffs, pulling the Satanist's arms behind his back, letting his hands do their work automatically while his eyes desperately scanned the room, looking for the guy who had just shot-putted Jake a good twelve feet.

He saw Jake pull himself to his knees. Incredibly, the detective still had his gun in his hand. Dan saw the larger figure, a hulking shadow, moving toward Jake. Before Dan could scream *"Shoot the motherfucker!"* Jake shot him. Once, twice, three times, a half dozen times, flames blossoming dazzlingly bright from the Colt's muzzle, the flat thunder of the gun deafening in the enclosed room. Dan could see the attacker jerk with the impacts.

And keep coming.

Jake knew he hit the guy, hit him at least five times in the torso, saw the slugs impact, saw the bursts of blood that trailed from the wounds, at least two of which were square in the chest, if not in the heart then right next to it. And yet the guy kept coming, and Jake was seized with the terrifying conviction that the only bullets that would drop this asshole were silver ones.

Jake was still dry-firing his gun when his opponent grabbed him and lifted him over his head once more with superhuman strength. Jake could clearly see his assailant's face below him, lit by the filtered gray moonlight. He could see the teeth that looked like sharp fangs bared in a snarl, saw the bite marks in the neck. He tried to reach the other gun on his leg, but couldn't.

Before Jake could be thrown across the room again, Dan leaped in from behind, swinging a straight-backed office chair like a club. Jake heard the heavy thud as the wood slammed into his assailant's back, knocking him off balance. With a startled cry, he released Jake. The detective managed to land mostly on his feet, and both he and Dan grabbed the guy's arms and pulled him down to a prone position. Jake heard a hysterical voice within him telling him to run, that there was no way to keep this dirtbag down because he *wasn't human,* that the only way to survive was to find someplace to hide until the sun came up and this horror they were wrestling was forced back into its coffin or wherever the hell it came from. . . .

The guy, still writhing beneath them with such strength that they were barely able to hold him, suddenly screamed, a high, quavering note. Blood burst in a black torrent from his mouth and nose. Then he gave a final convulsive shudder and went limp.

For a moment neither of the cops released their grip, un--able to believe that their attacker might actually be dead, sure that this was some kind of ploy to lower their guard. While maintaining his grip as much as possible, Jake managed to press two fingers against their opponent's neck. There was no pulse.

Jake suddenly realized that Magus was shouting at them. The Satanist lay on the floor where Stratton had cuffed him, and even in the dim light it was apparent that he was livid with rage. "Fools! *Idiots!* I had everything under control until you showed up! Now he's dead, and you Cossacks *killed* him!"

Jake rolled away from the body and sat up, his coat and shirt sodden with blood and sweat, his eyes wide, his voice breaking on the edge of hysteria. "How do you know he's dead? He's a fucking vampire!"

Magus managed to struggle up to his knees, staring at them in furious disbelief. "A *what*?"

"A vampire! He took five slugs, threw me around like a toy . . . what the hell else could he have been?"

Magus was silent for a moment, slack-jawed with amazement. Then he shook his head and began to laugh, harsh, bitter laughter that sounded almost like sobs.

CHAPTER 30

Tuesday, October 29

Tace stepped down from the stage, the applause long and warm, bathing her in the audience's approval. Maybe she hadn't killed tonight, but she had left them mortally wounded, without a doubt. Her timing had been perfect, her delivery impeccable, her material clever and trenchant, and her reward had been the roar of laughter, the sounds of palms slapped against tabletops and the sustained cheers at the end. It had been one of those nights when Tace knew without a doubt why it was her life's mission to make people laugh until they ruptured themselves.

She had needed this in a big way. Having someone you know be a victim of Los Angeles's latest serial killer was bad enough, but to be the one to find the body. . . . Tace felt gooseflesh crawl over her as she approached her table. That was a little too far out even for her. She had to admit that she'd been worried the last twenty-four hours, afraid that the mysterious and sinister Night Hunter might be sizing her up as the next candidate for a stake implant. She had seen him, after all, although the encounter had been over too quickly for her to be able to give the police any real information. Still, she had not been able to keep from wondering as she stood on the stage if he was in the audience, watching, waiting. . . .

She sat down at the table near the wall where Davis waited with a grin. He held up a napkin on which he had scrawled in ball-point "9.9." Tace grinned in response. Even her uneasiness about the Night Hunter couldn't completely undermine the rush that vibrated through her.

"Did you see it?" she demanded. "I had them, man—they were *mine*. I could've sent them out to kill the President and they would've done it! Jesus, that felt so fucking *good*! Let's have sex right here on the table."

Davis just grinned at her, so obviously proud of her, so obviously sharing in her joy, that she felt a rush of affection for him intense enough to almost frighten her. It's just the adrenaline, she told herself; everything's amped to the max at the moment. Now was definitely not the time to be thinking about falling in love.

Still, his support for her needed to be acknowledged. Tace put her hand on Davis's and leaned forward. Before she could say anything, however, her attention was distracted by someone approaching the table.

A guy in his thirties, sporting the Gap look, smiled down at her. "You're a funny lady," he said.

Tace looked up, felt a brief adrenal jolt of fear, masked it with a joke. "Oh, shit, it's my parole officer." The line caused Davis to nearly pass most of his beer through his nose.

Mr. Gap's grin grew wider. He dropped a card on the table—one of those thin translucent plastic ones. It lay beside her drink upside down, and Tace could see through it, see the guy's name in reverse, looking like it was printed in Russian. She could also see the stylized logo of Universal Pictures on it.

She scooped the card up, turned it over. The name on the card was Jerry Todd. The title beneath it was "Executive in Charge of Development."

She looked back up at him. He grinned, obviously enjoying the moment, and said, "Have you ever thought of pursuing a career in show business?"

Tace glanced at Davis. "Change in plans," she said. "I'll have sex with *him* on the table."

"Call me," the Gap ad said. "I'd very much like to talk to you. We're putting together something you might be good for." He raised a hand in a farewell gesture and walked away.

Tace watched him go, unable to believe what had just happened. She looked at Davis, wanting him to share in her moment of triumph, but Davis seemed oddly preoccupied with the last few sips of his beer.

"Did you hear that?" she demanded, when he didn't say anything. "The guy just offered me a part in a movie! Well, maybe not quite, but—"

"Don't get your hopes up," Davis said, his tone like a splash of cold water in her face. She stared at him; he refused to meet her eyes. "Davis," she said, "what's wrong?"

He picked up a swizzle stick on the table, tapped it uncomfortably against the table's edge. "I just don't. . . . Look, you know these guys are constantly blowing smoke. Okay, maybe every once in a while something happens, but. . . ." He was silent for a moment, then looked up at her. Tace was surprised at the guarded look on his face. "I just don't want you to get all worked up, you know? 'Cause it might be for nothing."

"Don't you think I know that? Do you see me running out to put a down payment on a Maserati? I don't need reality now, Davis. I want you to be happy for me, congratulate me, take me up to a viewpoint on Mulholland and say 'Someday all this will be yours!' "

Davis looked back down at the dregs of his beer and didn't

answer. Tace felt her bewilderment at his actions giving way to anger. She really needed something like this now. Davis had always been so supportive of her career—but now, all of a sudden, he was pulling back. Why? How dare he, at this most important point? A number of scathing putdowns leaped to mind; Tace had to clamp her teeth together firmly to prevent them from escaping. Instead she got up and headed for the ladies' room.

The room was tiny, only one stall and a sink, with a latch on the door. She stared at herself in the mirror, seeing in her face an echo of the bleak, haunted look she remembered wearing nearly all the time back in her mother's house. Odd, Tace thought, how she never thought of the place as "home." In her mind it was always her mother's house.

She scrutinized her face, looking for hints of crow's feet around the eyes, even though she knew she had several years left before that, looking for any signs that her face was turning into her mother's face. She realized what she was doing and pulled back from the mirror with a grimace of disgust. She pulled a paper towel from the dispenser and blew her nose. Then she left the room.

When she got back to the table, Davis smiled at her as if nothing had happened. "How about hitting Club Zero for an hour or two?" he asked.

Tace hesitated, tempted not to let him get away with it, considering telling him just how pissed she was at him for spoiling the evening's high. Instead she said, "I don't think so; I'm not feeling so good."

"What's wrong?" The tone solicitous, an amazing imitation of the Davis Sands she had come in the door with a few hours before.

"Oh, the usual end-of-the-month problems: headache, cramps, bloating, internal bleeding . . . all that stuff that makes women so special." She leaned over, grabbing her purse at the same time that she gave him a quick and passionless peck on the lips.

"I'll call you," he said, as she wended her way through the tables toward the door.

He probably will, too, she thought as she pushed open the door and went out into the cold night air on Melrose. And I'll probably be glad to hear from him. Jesus Christ, she thought; aren't I too young to be this fucked up?

CHAPTER 31

Wednesday, October 30

Yyou're reassigned," McNamara said.

Jake stared at his superior's desk, the edges of his vision gray with fatigue. He said nothing.

The captain leaned back in his chair and stared at him. "You're off the street for awhile anyway; that's mandatory. I think it's for the best, Jake. I really do."

Jake focused on the battered woodgrain that marked the edge of the desk. "What should I have done," he asked softly, "let the guy kill me and Stratton? He would've had us for breakfast if I hadn't shot him."

McNamara looked uncomfortable. "Any cop there would've done the same thing," he said. "But Anton Magus has said you were calling this Randall Farrow a 'vampire.' He's raising a pretty big stink about it."

Jake felt slow, sluggish stirrings of anger deep inside him. "Old Randy was dusted out of his mind. Guy took a slug through the heart and kept on ticking. He nearly killed me. And you blame me for . . ." he stopped. He was going to say, ". . . for thinking the guy was a vampire," but he knew how absurd that sounded. Every cop knew that angel dust could sometimes turn a normal human being into a raging unstoppable machine. He had leaped to a ridiculous conclusion.

But in the dark, given the circumstances, it had not seemed ridiculous at all. Jake remembered being held high over Farrow's head, looking down at him, seeing what looked like long fangs glittering in the asshole's mouth. Even the medics who got there later admitted that the guy's incisors were a bit long and pointed, though not unnaturally so. His imagination had done the rest.

The anger he was feeling didn't go away, though. If anything, it increased. "So, what—I shoot some shitbag who should have been drowned at birth and you're taking me off the case? It isn't right. I don't deserve this."

McNamara stared at him, his face a mask.

"What about Magus? What was he doing in some warehouse in the middle of the night with a duster? Has anybody thought to wonder about that?"

"He says he was trying to help one of his 'flock,' whom he had been told was scoring drugs down there." McNamara shrugged. "The guy's got guts, even if he's not particularly high on brains. Anyway, we're not talking about him. We're talking about you."

Jake stood, feeling a little giddy, knowing he was crossing the line and enjoying the feeling. "Fuck this," he said. "*Fuck* this."

"What're you gonna do?" the captain asked. "Is this where you throw down your badge? You know I don't have any choice here, Jake. This thing is high visibility, and Magus is flogging it for all it's worth. I can't have the media accusing us of carrying silver bullets on patrol."

Jake stared at him for a moment, then raised his hands in

a gesture of disgust and dismissal. "Do what you gotta do," he said, and turned toward the door.

In the hall, he leaned against a bank of filing cabinets and squeezed his eyes shut in pain as his ulcer kicked in with a vengeance. Fuck this, he thought again. Fuck the entire thing.

He tried to make his feet carry him back to his desk, where he would spend the rest of the morning writing reports and discharged-weapons forms on the incident, but instead he somehow found himself down in the evidence locker, staring through the cyclone fence that surrounded the metal shelves. Stacked on them were the various murder weapons, stolen items and other bits of urban flotsam and jetsam that, with luck and hard work, might help write *finis* to the many cases listed on those three-by-five cards upstairs. Jake went in and moved slowly down the rows of shelves, looking for one particular item. There were hundreds of guns, knives, iron pipes and other killing tools listed and categorized there, but only two wooden stakes.

He found the one that had recently been pulled from Craig Alstadler's body and opened the heavy-duty sealed polyurethane bag that protected it. He reached in for it, and when his fingers came in contact with the sanded, bloodstained wood, he staggered and cried out in surprise and pain. He dropped the stake to the concrete floor; it lay there, rocking slightly, the polished surface of the wood reflecting the light in rhythmic pulses from the fluorescent tubes overhead.

Jake leaned against one of the metal racks, breathing in sharp gasps. Touching the stake had felt like touching a live wire; the shock that had coursed through his body had left his hand and part of his arm numb. His heart was thudding in his chest like he had just taken a hit off a crack pipe. After a moment he knelt down beside the stake, feeling muscle tremors in his legs. Cautiously he poked at it with one finger. There was no further shock, not even a tingling. He set his teeth and picked it up.

The only sensation he felt was that of holding a piece of

wood. Had he imagined it? he wondered. No way; his arm was still jerking in spastic tics from the jolt. Jake licked his dry lips, then stuffed the stake back into the evidence bag and put it back on the shelf. Quickly, before anyone else might come in and see him, he left the locker.

What the hell was *that* all about? None of the work-ups on either of the two victims had mentioned any kind of electric shock from touching the stake. If Latham or Sarah or anyone else had felt that, they sure as shit would have mentioned it. Thinking about it, Jake realized that the shock hadn't felt like electricity; in fact, there had been a definite sense of exhilaration to it. His initial mental comparison of it to some kind of drug rush seemed more and more appropriate the more he thought about it.

This was too fucking weird. . . .

He stepped out in the parking lot, blinking up at the bright morning sun. He saw it so seldom these days that it seemed a strange, otherworldly thing to him. The thought crossed his mind that this was probably how a vampire thought of it: a sight as fearsome and deadly as the face of God.

"Jake." He saw Stratton coming out of the building toward him. Jake turned away, heading for his car, moving through the warm dry air slowly, as though it were water, still flexing the hand that had touched the stake.

Stratton caught up with him. "Boy, this is some fine shit, huh?" He paced alongside Jake. "Look, I just wanted you to know that I appreciate what you did last night. Saved both of our lives. No one can say you didn't."

Jake stopped and swung around to stare at Stratton. "I blew it," he said. "We shouldn't have been there in the first place."

Stratton regarded him for a moment, his eyes unreadable behind aviator's sunglasses. Then he said, "Well, since you bring it up, I was getting a little worried about you. I mean, high motivation is one thing, but you were starting to act like *Lethal Weapon* on crack, man. I'm glad you got straight on it." He was quiet for a moment, looking uncomfortable, then shook his head and asked, "So what're you going to do?"

"Do? I'll tell you what I'm going to do. I'm going to put that cocksucker Magus behind bars."

Stratton pulled his glasses off and stared at Jake in disbelief. "You're *serious.* Ah, Jesus, Jake, you can't do this! Even TV cops don't act this stupid! C'mon—it's somebody else's headache now. Let it go. Tell you what—we'll go someplace, get drunk, do a little male bonding. How about it?" He took Jake's arm, tried to move him along.

Jake pulled his arm free. "I thought you wanted to make detective," he said.

"Yeah, I do. Call me old-fashioned, but I don't think it would be a real good career move to lose my badge in the attempt. This is fucking nuts, Jake. We can't work the case on our own."

Jake turned away, knowing he was being an asshole and feeling a sense of perverse satisfaction from it. "You don't want to help, fine. I'll do it."

"You'll do *what*?" Stratton shouted, exasperated. "You buck McNamara on this, he's gonna cut off your head, scoop out your guts and use you for a fucking golf bag!" He lowered his voice persuasively. "Jake, Jake, it's just a case—not a crusade. Let's go have a beer or nine and forget about it, okay?"

"I tell you what," Jake said, "why don't you have mine for me. I've got work to do." He got in his car, keyed the ignition and burned rubber leaving the lot.

He knew that everything Stratton had said was true. Maybe cops in movies could go vigilante and come out of it with their jobs and pensions intact, but there was no way that was going to happen to him. Best to just let it go, write his reports, take the desk work and be glad of it. Maybe even take a week or so off—he had enough sick leave accumulated. Try to release a little of the pressure.

The dry bright air caught in his throat, making him cough. It wasn't like he had a real stake in this case, for God's sake.

He hadn't reacted this strongly when Tom was shot. He couldn't understand his motivations. When it came right down to it, he didn't give two shits if some street hustler like Jimmy Ray was staked, drawn and quartered or burned alive. Ditto the other guy, Alstadler, and anyone else they might not have found yet. Any caring or sympathy he'd felt for the hundreds of vics he'd seen over the years had been ground out of him by their endless parade. It wasn't even that he really believed something supernatural was going on, that he was a lone crusader holding back the forces of darkness—although last night he'd sure as shit believed it for a few heart-stopping minutes.

He didn't know why. All he knew was that he couldn't let go of this case.

Unfinished business.

Jake drove, the windows down, feeling gusts of wind hammer at him, dried palm fronds crunching under the wheels of his car. After ten minutes he realized he had no real destination in mind; like so many of the cars on the freeways and streets, he just seemed to be driving, with no purpose or goal, hypnotized by the rhythmic pulses of sunlight off windshields and signs, the Doppler sounds of other cars passing, the endless similarity of the buildings and the streets.

CHAPTER 32

Wednesday, October 30

Sarah had just made the Y incision on the corpse's torso when Jake walked into the autopsy suite. She could tell immediately that he was pissed off. He had that tight-lipped intensity that Matt used to get during his internship, when some tenured surgeon would start leading him around by his nose for the simple reason that he could do it.

She put the scalpel back on the tray and came around the stainless steel table to him. "I heard about what happened. I tried to call you—"

"I'm desk-bound until the hearing. Meanwhile, this psycho's still out there pounding his stakes."

She tried to look him in the eyes, but he refused to meet her gaze. "There's nothing surprising about this, Jake. You know that. It's standard procedure." She peeled the double gloves from one hand, tried to touch his cheek with her fingers, but he turned his head away.

"This dirtbag is out there *laughing* at me—I know it." He started pacing across the tiled floor. He looked bizarrely out of place here, his shabby coat and wrinkled slacks dark against the sterile lights, the gleaming white refrigerators and sinks.

She glanced back at the body on the table. "Look, I've got to get these organ temperatures before this guy cools off. . . ."

He waved one hand in a dismissive gesture. "Hey, don't mind me. Carve away. I'm just here to bitch."

Sarah put a new set of gloves on and peeled the skin away from the abdomen. Jake watched impassively as she inserted the chemical thermometer into the liver. "Anybody we know?"

She shook her head. "Just some homie wearing the wrong colors." She pulled the thermometer and read the temperature into the mike hanging over the table.

Jake kept watching as she continued to examine the organs, cutting away at the connective tissue around the heart. He wrinkled his nose at the rich odor rising from the intestines, which the heavy reek of disinfectant that saturated the morgue could never completely disguise. "Funny how we all look the same on the inside," he commented.

Sarah lifted out the stomach, sliced it open to check the contents, then spoke into the mike. "Last meal looks to have been Chinese food."

She looked back at Jake, who was examining the Stryker saw as if he had never seen one before. "So what are you going to do now?" she asked.

"They can stop me from being the detective of record," he said, "but they can't stop me from investigating the case."

"Are you sure that's a good—" she began, then stopped when he dropped the saw with a loud clang and wheeled about to glare at her.

"Christ, first Stratton and now you. Look, I *know* it's crazy, okay? But I also know that slick shit Magus is in this up to his eyebrows, and I *will* nail his ass."

She raised gloved hands slimed with blood and offal in a

pacifying gesture. "Okay, Jake, okay. You do whatever you have to do. You know I'll be on your side." She hesitated. "I'd just—like to see you take a few days to think it over. There's been an awful lot of pressure on you lately, and—"

"What, you think I should go talk to a shrink?" Contempt riddled his voice.

Sarah felt annoyance rising within her. She walked over to a sink and rinsed her hands, then looked at him and said in a calm, measured voice, "You're trying to pick a fight. I don't know why, but it's real obvious. So back off, Jake, because I won't take this."

He glared back at her for a second; then his shoulders slumped and he looked away. "I just want some understanding, that's all," he said, his tone surprisingly close to a whine.

"I understand your frustration. I sympathize with it. But I also know there's not a thing you can do about it, and so do you. You can't get your ego in an uproar, Jake. You have to let it go."

"He's laughing at me," Jake said again, quietly this time. "I know it. He's . . . *daring* me. Out there somewhere, scoping out the next vic, thinking there's not a goddamn thing I can do about it."

"Assuming that's true," Sarah replied, "and there's no reason to think it is—so what? So *what,* Jake? Why do you care what some sick asshole thinks about you? Whether you take him down or somebody else takes him down, the important thing is he gets taken down. And that'll happen—we both know that. This isn't some random drive-by or motiveless killing. This guy's got an MO, and once you or whoever figures it out, end of story. He's done. Even if you don't put the cuffs on him, you're a part of it. So my advice to you, Jake—and, as someone who recently slept with you, I think I'm qualified to give advice—is forget this Dirty Harry shit. Get back on your other cases, be available for consultation when they need you, and when this psycho is in jail you can wave your dick at him all you want."

Jake watched her while she was speaking, his face a mask. After she finished, he turned and headed for the door.

"It's been comforting," he said over his shoulder as he stalked out. The door *whooshed* shut, and Sarah could hear his footsteps diminishing down the long corridor beyond.

"Well," she said out loud. *"That* was fruitful." She suppressed an urge to abandon her work and go after him—if he wanted to be an asshole, he could do so without any more help from her.

She walked back over to the other man in her life at the present and picked up the saw to begin cutting through the skull. As Sarah rounded the table she caught a glimpse of the corpse's penis, shrunken almost to invisibility in the thick black curls of the groin, and she snorted in recognition of a momentary urge to start cutting from that end instead.

CHAPTER 33

Wednesday, October 30

He had read all the news coverage and was highly amused at being described as "Van Helsing." He knew who the character was, of course—he had read Stoker's book years ago. There were certain similarities between those vampire hunters and his own methods, but the ends that they were means to were quite different.

It was simultaneously exhilarating and frightening to have so much media exposure. It was the first time this had happened to him. All the other times he had stalked and dispatched his nocturnal victims, in cities all over the world, he had managed to do so without bringing attention to himself. Now it was different. It lent, he admitted, a new spice to a task that had grown somewhat pedestrian over the years. But he was not blind to the peril that it brought, not by any means.

Still, he had to say that he was enjoying the game. He knew he was in no real danger—after all, he had only one more time to strike, and then it would be over again. Then he could leave this city of neon night, resettle somewhere else, sink back into obscurity once more. He always had to maintain a certain level of vigilance, of course—those he hunted could easily turn the tables and hunt him—but at least he would not have the police on his trail as well.

There was no doubt that the detective was a worthy adversary. A shame that they had to be pitted against each other—after all, in an obscure way, they were fighting the same battle, each trying to turn back the night. He felt a certain kinship for this Jake Hull. . . .

Dan paced the halls of the division for awhile, fuming. His worry for Jake was all but overshadowed by his anger—the man was being a Grade-A, USDA-approved prick. Dan knew it, and he knew Jake knew it, too. He admired the detective's independence, but felt it needed considerable leavening by common sense.

Well, fine—Dan had done his part, had tried to talk him into behaving rationally. That was all he could do for Jake. Now he had to give some thought about what to do for himself.

He had looked upon this case as a way to bootstrap himself to detective quickly, and he was still hoping that might be possible. He knew it was pointless offering his help to the ones who had been re-assigned to the case; they would want to work it themselves and keep whatever glory came from it. They had inherited the meager evidence accrued so far; all he could offer was guesswork and some knowledge of old horror movies, neither of which, Dan was sure, would make them fall all over themselves to invite him back on the case.

No, the way Dan saw it, he had only two options: forget about it and go back to uniform work, with the possibility of making detective in another five years or so, or work with Jake unofficially on the case.

Well, there *was* a third option: continue a *sub rosa* investigation on his own.

He sat down on one of the waiting benches and thought about it. Working with Jake right now was not going to particularly endear him with the powers that be, since Jake seemed to be on a mission from God to piss off everybody in sight. On the other hand, if he came up with something significant to contribute to this case on his own, he couldn't help but look good. That was the kind of initiative that paid off big time, career-wise. After all, Jake was barred from investigation on the Night Hunter matter, but Dan wasn't.

Dan frowned, wondering if by doing this he was being somehow disloyal to Jake. But if Jake wanted to shoot himself in the foot, Dan could see no reason why he should take a bullet in his own extremity out of friendship.

He would have to be careful, of course. Although he was not technically forbidden from working the case, he felt fairly sure that the detectives involved would be less than thrilled if he tried to horn in on their territory. But there were ways to avoid that.

One thing he felt reasonably sure of: Magus was a dead end. He decided the smartest thing to do would be to go back to the comedy club where Alstadler had worked and see if he could find some leads there.

Dan nodded to himself and stood. Having made the decision, he felt energized, even though it was late in the day. Even if nothing came of this, the stand-ups at the Joke Joint might provide him with a few laughs, and God knew he could use that.

Franklin Conner sat at a table near the back of the Joke Joint, watching someone on the small stage setting fire to a rubber chicken with an acetylene torch and trying not to let his imagination drift back to the subject of vampires. He had gone over the few books he had containing information on the undead, had reread all three Jonathan Skull scripts, had even checked out some more material from the library. Finally, in an effort to fill his mind with something different, he had come here.

So far it hadn't helped much, but that, he felt, was largely due to the fact that no one had been particularly funny yet. Conner had attended the club more than once in the last few years, and some of the new comedians he had found quite amusing. The fellow up there now, however, was definitely not one of them.

He looked about the room restlessly, noticing others at the tables. He recognized a woman sitting not far from him: Tace Daggett, one of the better acts he had seen recently. A sharp, insightful wit, and looks to boot—his private prediction was that she would go far.

He had had just enough alcohol to contemplate going over to her table and offering to buy her a drink. True, he could easily be her father, but thank God for double standards—an older man dating a young woman was not frowned upon all that much. Conner ordered another drink, thinking idly that it might give him the wherewithal to approach her.

Before the notion could become reality—if, indeed, it had any intention of so doing—Conner saw another man, much closer to her age, step up to her. Her reaction of pleased surprise left no doubt that the two were already acquainted. Conner pressed his lips together in slight annoyance, then shrugged. Ah, well. No doubt she would be happier with someone from her own generation.

He kept watching the two during the course of the next act, however—they were more interesting than what was going on on the stage. There was something about the man—his mustache, his general bearing—that said he was a cop. The thought made Conner's skin prickle slightly. The second victim of the Night Hunter had been a comedian, he now recalled, who used to play here. Conner took another sip of wine. Had his subconscious, knowing that, led him here under the pretense of trying to get away from the subject?

He shrugged the thought away—one can only be so paranoid, after all. Then he noticed the young man looking at him. The man glanced away, glanced back, then said something to Tace. She turned her gaze toward him, too, and Conner saw a brief smile flicker over her face. It was a smile of recognition; he knew it well, though not, he sometimes thought, as well as he might have liked.

The man said something to Tace, then got up and walked toward Conner's table. Conner felt a slight flicker of nervousness—he was still fairly certain the man was a cop.

"Excuse me," the man said. "Aren't you Franklin Conner?"

Conner felt his face slipping easily into the smile reserved for fans. "I am," he said, putting out his hand. He saw Tace Daggett approaching as well. Good—of the two, he would much prefer talking to her.

"I'm a big fan," the man confessed, with just enough of a gosh-wow element in his voice to make Conner feel amused. *"Cult Of the Undead, Vampire Lover. . . ."*

"It's always a pleasure to meet an admirer of my work," Conner said courteously. "I'm sorry, I didn't get your name . . . ?"

"Dan Stratton." Stratton was silent as Tace introduced herself.

"I've seen your act, Ms. Daggett," Conner said. "You're a very funny lady."

"And you're a very scary guy, Mr. Conner."

He smiled again. "I try."

"Mr. Conner," Stratton said, "I'm with the LAPD. . . ."

"I knew you were a policeman," Conner said. "You have that look."

"Yeah, I've learned to live with it. . . . Didn't you call the Hollywood Division a couple of days ago offering some help with the Night Hunter case?"

Conner felt the stab of wariness all people feel when being questioned by the police. "Yes, I did. I thought it might be worthwhile to point out what I felt were some similarities between a movie I was once in and what I read about this case."

Stratton nodded. *"Mask of the Vampire."*

Tace said, "I was the one who found Craig Alstadler, the man who was killed night before last."

Conner felt a small charge of excitement course through him. He had called the police on the vague hope that he might somehow cadge some publicity out of all this. Perhaps that hope was now about to rise, vampire-like, from its grave once more.

"Fascinating," he said. "Do tell me more."

CHAPTER 34

Jake cruised Hollywood Boulevard, starting at Laurel Canyon and heading east all the way down to where the street merged with Sunset in Silverlake. Halloween decorations were up everywhere: articulated paper skeletons dangled in shop windows, plastic jack-o'-lanterns leered, cutouts of black cats arched their backs and snarled. Halloween on the Boulevard was a real freak show—in a way he was almost glad he was desk-bound and wouldn't have to deal with it this year.

He drove past the endless Fellini parade on the sidewalks, automatically profiling them, sorting them into various categories: hookers, druggies, gangbangers, vagrants . . . all going nowhere on this boulevard of broken dreams. The neon signs merged into a psychedelic blur as he drove. Snatches of gangsta rap, heavy metal and other jarring music for which he had no names pounded at him from passing cars and from boomboxes riding the shoulders of strutting young boys. Boys barely old enough to shave, many of whom had probably already killed more than once.

He had given up the 9mm he kept in the ankle holster, but not his revolver. No way was he going out after dark without being packed.

Jake thought of the likelihood of his son growing up to be one of those downy-cheeked sociopaths. The concept made him tighten his grip on the wheel, his knuckles whitening in the passing headlights. He knew it was a possibility without the presence of a strong father figure to keep the boy on the right path.

In a way he wished he had never had a child. He could remember when Max had been a baby, how he had lain awake nights listening, waiting for him to cry, poised to leap out of bed at the first sounds of distress, trying to hear the boy's breathing all the way down the hall. He had lost count of how many times he had awakened, heart hammering, from dreams of abduction. He remembered vividly the first time Max had gotten the stomach flu, when the boy had been a few months shy of his second birthday—how quickly he had lost weight while unable to keep anything in his stomach, how his delicate ribs and collarbone had begun to show, how unnervingly still he had been, so different from the usual hyperkinetic bundle of energy. Jake remembered sitting on the couch, trying to get his son to take a bottle of Pedialyte, staring into those solemn brown eyes. . . . Riding in the car now, Jake was surprised to feel his own eyes brimming uncomfortably, and a fullness in his throat. The pain of his separation hit him like a sudden hammerblow. It wasn't Darlene that he missed so much—he could admit, at times, that they'd had their run, given it their best shot, and found that it simply couldn't be made to work, a square peg in a round hole. It was a sadness he could deal with.

But God, how he missed his son. . . .

He drove aimlessly for several hours, noticing a half dozen potential troublemakers on the street whom, under normal circumstances, he would have shaken down. Around three A.M., he pulled into an all-night topless bar down on Pico. He sat drinking a watery beer and watching young listless women gyrating in G-strings to the deafening strains of Creedence's *Born on the Bayou.*

He had several more beers; around four-thirty he left the bar, staggering. Driving north on Vermont he saw a black hooker trolling restlessly on the corner of Beverly Boulevard. At first Jake thought it was the same one who had blown him a few nights before, but as he pulled up alongside her he realized he was wrong. Not that it made any difference.

She bent down to look in the car, smiling around her gum, giving him a look at her tits the way the other one had. The smile died when Jake fumbled his badge out and flashed it at her. "Get in," he said.

He could see in her eyes the thought of running away, but knew she wouldn't—a lifetime of abuse had trained her to stay there and take whatever the man of the moment was prepared to dish out. She crossed around in front of the Nissan, opened the door and slid into the front seat, looking at Jake as he turned the corner and drove up a dark side street.

"Are you a vampire?" he asked her. The thought seemed abruptly, absurdly funny, and he startled to giggle, the giggles giving away to hiccups. The whore said nothing, just watched him warily as he parked the car.

"Here," he said, "I got somethin' for you to suck, vampire." He groped at his fly, trying to unbutton and unzip his pants, but the periodic spasms of his diaphragm, combined with his drunkenness, prevented him from accomplishing this.

"I'll do it, sugar," she said, reaching over. Her fingers adroitly opened his fly and slid inside. Her long nails touched his dick, which shriveled as though trying to escape as she pulled it free. He felt a sudden burst of rage at her. "Leave it *alone!*" he shouted, cuffing her on the side of her head with his open hand. She fell sideways against the dashboard. A whimper escaped her lips, but she made no move to get out of the car. Jake pulled his .38 and pointed it at her. Her lips parted slightly, but otherwise her expression did not change. He extended the gun, touched the barrel to her nose. She closed her eyes. Jake realized that his dick was stirring, growing hard.

Shame filled him then, as suddenly and completely as the rage had before, slamming into him with such force that he felt nauseated. He swallowed hard against the surging bile and holstered the gun. "I'm sorry," he mumbled. She opened her eyes at his words, but did not move.

"Look," Jake said. "I wouldn't. . . . I'm sorry, I was just. . . . It's my wife, I guess. Aw, fuck." He dug his wallet from his inner coat pocket, managed to get it open, pulled out two twenties and a handful of singles, all he had in it. He thrust the handful of bills at her the way he had thrust the gun a moment before, then dropped them when another set of violent hiccups hit. She gathered the money up, watching him warily.

"Go on," he said. "Go." She found the door handle with her free hand and opened it, backed awkwardly out of the car, still holding the money. When she stood on the street, she stuffed the bills into her cleavage and walked quickly away, unable, even under the circumstances, to keep an inviting sway out of her hips. Jake watched her hurry around a corner and disappear into the night.

He still felt on the verge of heaving. He opened his door and stumbled out, leaned on the car, breathing deeply of the cold night air. Looking down, he realized he was still flapping in the breeze. He put it back in his pants, catching hair in the zipper and whistling through his teeth at the pain.

He vomited, splattering what was surely everything he'd eaten in the past two weeks all over the sidewalk. The convulsions were so violent he half expected to see his viscera lying there as well.

At least the hiccups had subsided. He turned around, feeling utterly drained, and leaned back against the car to stare up at the night. The moon, almost full, looked down on him.

Only one or two stars were visible through the glare of the streetlights. He had been in the Valley the night of the Northridge quake, and after the shaking had subsided he remembered looking up and being stunned by the starry panoply, visible to Angelenos in all its glory due to the power failures. The stars were still up there, he knew. Somehow the thought made him feel a little better.

His head and gut were a bit more steady now. He got back in the car and began to drive, turning west on Melrose. The streets were all but deserted at this hour, the trendy boutiques and ultra-hip restaurants dark and quiet. City of night, he thought, remembering Jim Morrison droning the words in an old Doors song. "We're all vampires," he said out loud. We all suck.

He turned north on Laurel Canyon, following the narrow, twisty street to Lookout Mountain Drive, and from there to the little cul-de-sac where he lived. By the time he parked the car, the eastern horizon was beginning to show the faintest pink taste of dawn. Jake stumbled inside and managed to pull the futon out and get out of his clothes before collapsing on it. His last thought, before he toppled into the welcoming dark, was that tomorrow was Halloween.

CHAPTER 35

Thursday, October 31

Sarah unlocked her office and deposited her purse and brief-case in the chair by her desk. She glanced at the phone, saw the blinking red light indicating voice mail and punched the "play" button. The tape rewound with a chipmunk chatter of high-speed voices in reverse, loud in the quiet room.

The first message was from Matt, asking if she could take Brandon for an extra day the weekend following Halloween, as he had to attend a seminar on the special needs of movie stars' children. Sarah felt conflicting emotions at this: grati-tude at being able to be with her son one more day, and an-noyance at Matt for what she felt was the cavalier way he was taking his parental responsibilities. It was no real contest, however—let Matt hot tub with the glitterati all he wanted, if it meant she could spend more time with Brandon.

The next message was from Latham, asking for a copy of a post-mort report on a DUI from last week. Sarah made a note of the request and then pushed the "erase" button, feeling more than a little upset that neither of the two messages had been from Jake. She had not heard from him since he had stormed out of her office. He had not been in the best of moods then, and there was no reason to assume things had gotten any better.

She was worried about him, she admitted to herself. And that meant she cared about him. It might not have taken a detective to figure that out—after all, she had slept with him, and she was not in the habit of going to bed with casual acquaintances—not since college, anyway—but it was nevertheless something Sarah had studiously avoided admitting to herself until this minute. She wasn't at all sure if she was ready for another man in her life; at this point she wasn't even ready for a pet in her life. Besides, she told herself, the last person she should get involved with was a cop. And the last cop she should get involved with was Jake Hull.

All that, she admitted, was true—but it didn't change matters. Like it or not, she had feelings for Jake Hull, feelings that could very easily mushroom into love, and at some point very soon both of them were going to have to deal with that.

Or maybe not, she thought, if he's dropped off the face of the earth. . . .

Sarah glanced at the wall clock: nine-twenty. She hesitated, then picked up the phone. So she ran the risk of waking him up—let him arrest me, she thought. She realized that, although she'd only called him once over the past week, she remembered his phone number—another bad sign.

The phone rang several times before the machine picked up. Jake's voice, weary and disinterested, instructed her to leave a message. "Jake? Are you there? It's Sarah. Please pick up if you're home." She waited a minute, and was about to say something else when the machine, evidently voice-activated, hung up on her. "Shit," she muttered at the dial tone, cradling the receiver a bit harder than necessary.

Sarah stared at the morning sunlight slanting through the

blinds for a moment, then sighed and picked up the phone again. She dialed his division office, feeling obscurely relieved that she had to look that number up in her Rolodex. Stoughton answered and said that Jake hadn't been in.

I certainly can pick 'em, she said to herself. First Matt and now Jake; neither of them prime candidates for the Robert Redford Mr. Sensitivity Award.

But she would be lying to herself if she did not admit that her thoughts had been turning constantly to Jake Hull since the night they had made love. It was a fitting euphemism in this case, because he had been surprisingly tender and aware of her, stroking and petting her and seemingly in no particular hurry to get to what most men considered to be the reason sex was invented. He had seemed like a completely different person there in her bed with the lights out; even more so than the time she had seen him at Griffith Park with his boy. He had said little, but there had been a quiet gratitude in the way he held her and kissed her, and he had been almost hesitant to enter her, as though he could not believe that the opportunity had been given to him.

All in all, it had been an experience she would gladly repeat, assuming he ever gave her the chance again. Which, at this point, it didn't look like he was going to do.

Sarah shook her head and sat down before the snowdrift of paperwork on her desk. He would either call her or not. She had given him the chance; she could do no more. Time to put him out of her mind and get to work.

Dan Stratton had to admit he had seldom enjoyed working as much as he had last night.

Cruising Hollywood Boulevard on his shift, he thought about it. It had been a pleasant surprise running into Tace Daggett at the Joke Joint. He had stayed until two A.M., talking with her and Franklin Conner and enjoying their company very much. Conner had been full of old-world style charm, and it had been a treat to talk with someone whose movies he had enjoyed as a kid and still enjoyed today, but it had been Tace who had captivated him. She had been witty, charming and, in a leather motorcycle jacket, boots, tight jeans and a red tank top, impossible to look away from.

No question about it, there had been major pheromone action going on, at least on his end. And the best thing about it was that he had a legitimate reason to call her again—she had told him something that might pertain to the Night Hunter case.

It wasn't a breakthrough kind of a clue, but he'd take what he could get. She had seen some guy in the audience giving Alstadler a funny kind of eye while he was performing.

"Mid-thirties, I'd say," she had told him. "Looked like he'd pushed some iron in his time, though since he was wearing this big loose coat it was hard to tell." Dan had asked some more questions about his appearance and she had been very definite in her answers: the guy was medium height, blond-haired and "intense." She remembered him so well because of his interest in Alstadler. She couldn't say for sure if it was the same man who had knocked her down in his escape from Alstadler's bungalow, however.

A slim lead, true enough, but more than he and Jake had had up to this point. The problem, of course, was that they were no longer on the case, and Jake seemed determined to wallow in a trough of self-pity about it. Well, let him—if one wanted to get brutally honest about it, it wasn't Dan Stratton who had pulled the trigger on the druggie. He'd gotten reprimanded by I.A., but Jake was looked upon as the instigator of that particular fiasco. Which meant that if Dan could come up with something that might break the Night Hunter case, he still had a good shot at a promotion because of it.

The thing to do now was pyramid out from the Joke Joint, see if anyone else had seen the guy Tace had mentioned. The trail wasn't terribly cold yet. He would also question Alstadler's neighbors, see if any of them had noticed the guy hanging about the decedent's place.

And if all this investigation brought him into contact with Tace Daggett again, why, that was just an extra added benefit of police work.

It had been some time since Dan had had anything that could even remotely be called a relationship. He had learned fairly early on that cops and stable partnerships with the opposite sex did not mix well. This was particularly true when, as a rookie, he had let the job consume his entire life. Police work was as fascinating as it was frustrating, and his preoccupation with it had eventually detonated his live-in situation with Sherry, a woman he had been with for over two years. He had been sorry to see it go, though, truth to tell, he had been getting somewhat tired of her endless stories about her parents' experience in Chicago in '68 against "Daley's pigs."

It was true that Tace did not seem at first glance—or even repeated glances, which she certainly warranted—the kind of woman who would be interested in a cop. Still, she had evidenced no sign of the knee-jerk suspicion and wariness with which most people viewed the police; had seemed interested, in fact, in his line of work. She had not gushed over him, either, the way some civilians did. She seemed to treat what he did as a job, the same way telling jokes was her way of making a living.

It was this attitude that made Dan think that maybe she might not puke on his shoes if he asked her out on a date. It was certainly worth a try.

"After all," he said out loud, as he steered the unit down Highland toward Sunset, "if she says no, I can always shoot her."

Franklin Conner nestled into the Nautilus upper body machine, cinching the Velcro strap tight around his waist. He seized the overhead bar and pulled it down over his chest, exhaling as he did so. Repeating the action five more times, he then released the bar and sat in the chair, staring at his reflection in the mirrored wall before him. It occurred to him that, strapped as he was into the high-tech workout device, he looked like an astronaut in some kind of training module. "An ancient astronaut," he said under his breath as he reached for the bar to do his second set.

He was tired this morning, having been up rather late the night before. The conversation he had with Tace Daggett and Dan Stratton had been one of the most enjoyable he could recall in recent years. It had been rather a thrill to have been included, however tangentially, in the investigation of a murder case that was making headlines even in jaded L.A.

He had pretty much given up on the idea of somehow milking the superficial similarities between the movie he had been in and this case for publicity. He had some vague hope of landing a part because of it—stranger things had happened, after all—but even Marty had felt it was too long a shot to pursue. Besides, he had been offered another voice-over gig—this one in a commercial for a new automotive import—this morning. It was more work in a shorter period than he had had in several years. At this rate he might soon find himself in the miraculous—and luxurious—position of having money in the bank.

Conner moved on to the next machine in his routine, the biceps curls. Feeling pleased with himself and life in general, he added an extra plate to the weight stack. He thought he might go back to the Joke Joint at some point in the next few days and see if he could catch Tace's act again. He had few friends among the younger generation—in fact, outside of a biweekly poker night with some other B-picture relics at the Motion Picture Retirement Home out in Woodland Hills, he really had no friends at all. It would be nice to get to know Tace better, although he was under no illusions about how far it would go.

Still, he mused, as he looked at himself in the mirror again, you never could tell. He was certainly not bad-looking, if she went for a more mature sort of man. He had had a few short-term relationships since his wife had passed on, but nothing serious. He wondered now what his reaction would be if something serious came along. He certainly wouldn't mind being given the opportunity to find out. . . .

CHAPTER 36

Thursday, October 31

Jake Hull awoke just before ten with a mouth that tasted like the floor of a baboon's cage and a headache that could split rocks. He lay there for a few minutes, unable to move, full of amazement that anyone could hurt this much and still live.

At least his ulcer was giving him no grief at the moment, or maybe the pain lines had simply become overloaded and nothing more could get through. Eventually he managed to stagger to the bathroom, where he was faced with the choice of downing four or five aspirin or relieving his full-to-bursting bladder. Fortunately the bathroom was small enough that he could accomplish both almost simultaneously. Those tasks accomplished, he collapsed once more on the futon, thanking whatever indifferent gods there were that he had remembered to pull the blinds last night. You know you're in bad shape, he thought, when the blinking red light on the phone machine hurts your eyes. He had a vague, dream-like memory of it ringing earlier.

Jake lay there praying for the aspirin to take effect, wishing vaguely that there was some service he could call that would come in and brush his teeth for him. He felt a distant urge to see who had called him, but nothing pressing enough to risk widening the fissure in his head by moving. What did it matter who had called, anyway? It was undoubtedly more bad news of some kind or other—either from work or from his ex-wife. Those were the only two realities in his life at this point, neither of which he cared to have anything to do with at the moment.

Another possibility occurred to Jake as he watched the dim red pulsing of poisoned blood behind his eyelids. It might have been Sarah who called him. He found it difficult to imagine why she would, considering what an asshole he had made of himself the last time he saw her, but if nothing else had become abundantly clear to him in the course of his life, the fact that women were strange and incomprehensible creatures surely had. Though of late Jake could find very little to like about himself, evidently Sarah had discovered something in him that made his company desirable.

He tried to ignore the thought, tried to burrow back down inside himself and sleep some more to escape the full-body malaise and give his system time to flush some of the toxins out, but, even with his eyes closed, he knew that little red light was blinking insistently. Finally, with a groan of defeat, he rolled over and groped with one hand, managing to press the "play" button without having to lift his head from the safety of the pillow.

"Jake? Are you there? It's Sarah. Please pick up if you're home."

So she *had* called. Even more amazing, she sounded worried, concerned for him. The tone of her voice made it almost possible to believe that she would welcome a call back.

Jake pulled another pillow over him, sandwiching his head

between two thick layers of cotton and linen, and thought about it. There was no question but that he liked Sarah—he just couldn't fathom why she should return the emotion. From his point of view he had nothing going for himself—on the downhill side of forty, an aging, ineffectual homicide dick who had once had delusions of helping to stop the decline and downfall of civilization, and who had long ago realized that he would be lucky not to be crushed under it when it collapsed. While he didn't think she had gone to bed with him out of pity, he wasn't sure if he had been so memorable in the sack as to warrant a return engagement. That's what they'll put on my tombstone, Jake thought glumly: "Not particularly memorable."

What had he accomplished in his life, after all? He had some solved cases to his credit, true. If asked, he could probably point to people who would agree that their lives were better because he had done his job. But how much did that really matter? If most people who lived there had any idea what a jungle Los Angeles really was, they would barricade themselves in their homes and not even come out for food. And that went for just about any major American city, Jake knew. He had looked into the heart of darkness for too long to believe that there was any light, any redemption, possible.

There are so few of us trying to make any difference, he thought. So few, with lives so brief, that there's no real chance of turning things around. He remembered Stratton saying once that what cops needed on the street was not just more Kevlar or better guns, but tanks and invulnerable robot bodies. Not to mention Double-O-Seven's license to kill. *Then* maybe they could start making a difference.

Unfinished business. Tom's line echoed in his mind, as it had over and over again since the shooting months before.

He was letting his thoughts wander, he realized. The topic was Sarah. Should he call her back or not?

There was no question but that he wanted to. But—and it was hard to admit, even hiding deep in the forested depths of

Laurel Canyon with a pillow over his head——he was afraid to. He'd already seen one relationship that he'd poured his heart and soul into turn to shit——what if it happened again? He wasn't sure if anyone could take that kind of pain twice.

But what was the alternative? In that same deep dark level of honesty Jake knew that if he let this opportunity with Sarah slip by, he would truly be on a greased slide to hell with no way to stop himself. For more years than he cared to think about there had only been the work, and now it was looking more and more like he wouldn't even have that. Perhaps it was wrong to define oneself through one's job or one's marriage, but he didn't know how else to do it. And he was——admit it—— terrified of seeing the remnants of his identity scattering to the winds, with no way to prevent it.

But what if it *didn't* work? He moaned out loud, the sound muffled by the pillow.

At that point there came a knock on the door.

The sound was so surprising that Jake jerked upright, the sudden movement sending a white-hot shaft of pain spearing through his head. He fought down an urge to throw up and squinted toward the door. Through the curtain that covered the windowed upper half, he could see a silhouette he recognized.

Sarah.

His surprise nearly made him forget how lousy he felt. She had come looking for him!

Jake lurched to his feet and managed to open the door a crack, squinting at the sunlight. Sarah peered at him with concern. "Jake? What's wrong? I tried to call you. . . ."

He felt suddenly ashamed that she should come all the way to his house to check on him, thinking that something was seriously amiss, when all he was doing was recovering from a hangover. He must have drunk quite a bit last night; he vaguely remembered throwing up, but even that hadn't cleared his system sufficiently. He also dimly recalled the hooker in his car, but his mind shied away from the details.

"It's nothing," he mumbled. "I was just about to call you. . . ."

"Are you going to let me in?"

"Uh . . ."

She pushed the door open and came in as he staggered back and sat down awkwardly in a chair. She looked at him and said, "I think you could use some coffee." As she headed for the kitchenette, the belated realization that he was naked broke through his mental fog. He groped for a nearby pillow and dropped it into his lap while listening to her opening cabinets and rattling utensils. The only thing he could think of to ask was, "How'd you know where I live?"

"You're the detective," she said, running water into the coffee pot. "You tell me."

He didn't bother to answer—his home address was easily available to anyone he worked with. He wasn't quite up yet to asking why she'd come.

She brought him a cup of black coffee; he inhaled the steam rising off it and felt blood vessels in his head opening like floodgates. He sipped it, wincing at the heat but welcoming the warmth it spread within him. As he did so, Sarah sat down cross-legged on the open futon and watched him.

The coffee was helping, but slowly. "I feel like hammered shit," he said.

"You don't look much better." He was expecting a lecture from her, but instead she merely said, "Nothing's new on the case, if you were wondering."

He waved a hand in dismissal. "I don't care. It's somebody else's problem now."

Sarah looked at him searchingly. "That's good to hear."

He rubbed his face with the back of one hand. "So, why'd you come by?"

Sarah said, "Come on, Jake. This is bullshit—you know it and I know it. Okay, you got drunk, maybe even got laid, I don't know—no one's holding that against you. After what happened, you deserved a bender. But it's over now, and it's time to be an adult again."

He avoided her eyes. "I don't need a lecture."

Sarah stood up, her lips pressed into a grim line. "I'm starting to think that what you need is a swift kick in the butt. I came over here because I thought you might need me. If you'd rather sit there and feel sorry for yourself, fine—but don't expect me to hand you hankies. I've been down this road before, and I don't like the scenery."

She had the door open when he said, "Wait."

For a moment, he thought she was going to leave anyway. Then she sighed, closed the door and turned to look at him. "Okay—I'm waiting."

Jake chewed his lower lip, uncertain what to say, only sure of one thing—that he didn't want her to walk out the door. "Look, I'm—glad you're here. Really."

She went to him, squatted by the chair and looked into his eyes. "I've never understood this about cops. They, of all people, should know that the world's not fair. And yet they all act like it's this big cosmic injustice when things don't go their way."

Jake forced himself to meet her gaze. Sarah smiled. "Look, Jake, this wouldn't be a difficult choice for most guys. You can either get yourself together and start a relationship with a healthy, intelligent, good-looking woman, or you can crawl into a bottle and pull the cork in after you. What's it going to be?"

She was right, of course. He was still afraid, but damned if he was going to admit that to her. He stood up, pulled a pair of briefs from the chest of drawers by the bed and put them on, managing to stay upright through the operation.

"I'd hate to see what your liver looks like," she said. "You sure you don't want to sleep this off?"

"I could use a complete blood transfusion," Jake said as he pulled on a sweater. "Any vampire who tries to drain me tonight is in trouble."

He sat down and started to put on his socks, then stopped, staring at the wall.

"Jake?" Sarah's voice was half amused, half concerned. "Don't you dare stroke out on me. . . ."

He looked at her. "This is the first and probably the last time you'll hear me say this," he said, "but maybe I'm wrong."

"Meaning?"

"Meaning maybe Magus isn't 'Van Helsing,'" he said. "But he's definitely a vampire."

CHAPTER 37

Thursday, October 31

Tace pulled up to the guard's kiosk at Universal, told him her name and was directed to park in the North Lot. The guard gave her a map showing where Jerry Todd's office was. She checked her watch—five minutes to eleven, which was when they had agreed to meet.

She had never been on a movie studio lot before, and was somewhat surprised by how ordinary it looked. It consisted mostly of office buildings and the huge, hangar-like sound-stages. The little encapsulated worlds of streets and buildings that could make a film seem to be set in Paris or New York or the Old West without ever leaving the studio were nowhere to be seen. She remembered being fascinated, as a child, with movies about movies—*Singin' in the Rain, Sunset Boulevard* and so forth. In them the studios were always swarming with extras in various costumes: Indians in warpaint, pirates, aliens wearing silvery form-fitting costumes and so forth. Tace saw nothing like that here; just stagehands with toolbelts hanging low on their hips and lots of suits.

Well, they made more movies back then, she told herself as she followed the map to a nest of small bungalows nestled against the dry brown hills.

A tram full of tourists eased past her and several cameras went off like flak bursts in her direction, evidently on the assumption that she had to be someone famous. Not just yet, but soon, Tace mentally promised them as she found the bungalow number circled on the map.

Todd's production office was surprisingly small. A secretary sat at a desk of blond wood, typing on a computer. Tace gave her name and the secretary, who was as blonde as the desk, announced her in a cool crisp voice.

Almost immediately the inner door opened and Todd came out. He seemed delighted to see her, complimenting her on the way she looked and ushering her into his office. The room was small, full of light from the windows and decorated in a Southwestern motif. A bleached cow skull hung on one wall; framed posters from movies Tace had never heard of dominated the others. Todd steered her toward a pastel couch and sat down in a director's chair that faced it.

He got right down to business. "The studio just greenlighted this," he said. "It's going to be a comedy based on Henry James's 'The Innocents.'"

Tace nodded, struggling to see how the concept would work. "You mean 'The Turn Of the Screw'?"

He grinned and pointed a finger at her. "Very good. Just wanted to see if you'd catch that. We're calling it 'Ghostsitter.' It'll be a contemporary comedy about a nanny brought in to a house to take care of a little boy who happens to be a ghost."

Tace felt stunned. Was she being offered the starring role in this movie? Things like this just didn't happen, not in real life, not since Lana Turner had worn that tight sweater at Schwabs's. . . .

Todd moved from the director's chair to sit beside her on the couch. "Naturally," he continued, "we're going after a name for the lead—Whoopi's expressed interest. But I'm thinking you for the maid—it's not a big part, but she's got a cocky, smart-ass attitude that you could have fun with. It's the kind of role people would notice you in—it could start you on a career track. What do you say?"

Tace gave a short laugh of disbelief. "What do I say? I say *yes*! Where do I sign?"

"Do you have an agent?"

She shook her head. Todd waved a hand in dismissal. "No problem, I can recommend a few. We start shooting in three weeks."

He moved closer to her then, and grinned at her as he put his hand on hers. "Welcome to show business," he said. "We're going to have fun."

Tace felt a small worm of discomfort begin to stir deep within her. She smiled back and tried to pull her hand away, but he seized her fingers and held on. His face was only a few inches away from hers now; he was staring at her. His voice had a husky rasp now as he said, "You're beautiful, you know that?"

Then he was on top of her, pushing her back against the couch cushions, one hand finding her breast with the accuracy of a heat-seeking missile, his mouth covering hers.

Tace was frozen with shock for a moment; then instinct took over. She brought her knee up, not catching him right where it would do the most good, but still clipping his hip bone a good solid blow with her kneecap that sent a blaze of pain up her own thigh. The force of it was sufficient to knock him off the couch. Todd sprawled between the mesquite wood coffee table and the couch as Tace scrambled to her feet.

"You sleazy motherfucker," she said, grabbing her purse and backing toward the door.

Todd pulled himself to a sitting position, face crimson. "I'm sorry," he said. "Look, I got carried away—"

"You should be carried away in a body bag, asshole!" Tace yanked open the door and ran through the reception area, startling the cool blonde secretary. Then she was out in the dry October air again, almost running past the soundstages toward the parking lot, wiping her lips roughly with the back of her hand to rid them of the feel of Todd's kiss.

I guess this means I don't get the part, she thought.

She didn't care. Even though this was part of the Hollywood legend as well, she didn't want to get into pictures this way. Maybe this was the way it was done, and maybe she was blowing her chance at stardom—but at least that's *all* I'm blowing, she told herself.

She got in her car, pulled out of the parking lot with a screech of tires and turned north on Lankershim Boulevard. She drove, letting the rhythm of shifting and stopping for lights calm her somewhat. She was in the area of North Hollywood called NoHo, which was trying desperately to be a hip artists' community and failing miserably. The buildings she passed were a strange mixture of taco stands, auto repair shops, acting studios and little theaters.

Eventually she pulled to a stop next to the Academy Plaza, a grouping of pink rococo buildings with a giant sculpture of an Emmy in a fountain. She got out of the car, walked into the courtyard and sat down next to an iron statue of Jack Benny. The look of mild shock on his face seemed to express sympathy.

Tace drew in a deep breath and felt herself shudder involuntarily. She felt furious, shaken and chagrined at the same time. She wanted a film career, of course—what young standup comic in Los Angeles didn't? And for a brief moment it had seemed like it was really going to happen, just the way she had always hoped it would. And then to have it all come down to the fact that some scumbag had a hard-on for her. . . .

She had let her guard slip, that had been the problem. She had let herself get sucked into the celluloid fantasy, had forgotten the truth—that miracles like what she had thought this

was just don't happen in the real world. Tace stood, walked
back to the Mustang. She saw a sign for a pay phone at a
newsstand across the street and braved the boulevard's traffic to reach it.

However, once at the phone with a quarter poised at the
slot, Tace hesitated. She had intended to call Davis, to tell him
that he'd been right about this whole sleazy situation. But the
thought of talking to him made her feel slightly uncomfortable. The tension between them that had started when Todd
made his offer had not evaporated. It was almost as if Davis
did not feel entirely comfortable with her reaching a certain
level of success. She could not stand the thought of hearing
his "I told you so"—not that he would ever actually say it, of
course. He had too much class for that. But she knew the
thought would be there, spoken or not.

Tace stared at the phone for a moment, then dropped the
quarter in. She dug a business card from her purse and dialed
the number on it.

Dan was just getting ready to go back out on his shift when
the call came. He picked up the phone. "Stratton."

"Dan, hi. Tace Daggett."

He felt a grin begin to spread over his face and turned
quickly toward the wall so no one else would see it. "Uh, hi,"
he said. "What's, um . . . what's going on?" Smooth.

"I was wondering if I could buy you a cup of coffee or
something," she said. He could hear the tension in her voice
and knew immediately that something unpleasant had happened to her. "I—wanted your advice."

"Absolutely. Where are you?"

They decided to meet at Johnny Rockets on Melrose. Stratton hung up and headed for his car, thinking, Thank you,
Jesus. He was fairly certain from her tone of voice that whatever had happened to her was not serious in a life-threaten-
ing way.

But whatever it was, she had called him.

The Night Hunter investigation could wait. It might be a stretch to call this a date, but that's what he was calling it.

They sat in a booth near the back, where the nonstop Phil Spector hit parade from the jukebox was not quite so loud. Dan listened while Tace explained what had happened to her.

"So I'd appreciate it if you could shoot him and then throw him in jail," she finished.

Dan sipped his coffee. "Hey, you want to make a complaint, I'll be happy to haul his sorry ass in. Even if we can't make it stick, I can make his life a living hell for a while. Lose his paperwork, bus him from this jail to that. . . . L.A. County's a labyrinth, take his lawyer *days* to find him. Drop him in a holding tank with some guys who'll stretch his asshole for him, let him know how it feels."

Tace looked at him, realized he was serious. Realized it was within her power to cut Todd some serious payback. This man sitting across from her at the table was casually offering to inflict the tortures of the damned on the douche bag who had just tried to rape her. She toyed with the idea a few seconds, enjoying the sense of power, the taste of incipient revenge. Then she shook her head. "No. If we were talking actual rape here, I'd say do it, the whole *Midnight Express* route. But it didn't go that far, thank God."

Dan looked at her, his gaze level. "Your choice. But a lot of pricks like him get away with this kind of shit because women say, 'Ah, let's just forget it.' I'm not saying we let the guys inside use him for a Ginsu commercial. I *am* saying we put the fear of God into him, maybe make him think twice before he pulls this again with somebody else. But I can't do jackshit without a complaint."

The waitress brought them hamburgers and fries. Dan up-ended a bottle of catsup over his plate as Tace considered his words.

"Let me think about it," she said finally. She took a bite out of her burger, realized abruptly that she had no appetite and pushed the plate away.

Dan tried not to watch her too much while he ate. She was amazing to look at—heads had turned when they had entered the restaurant. It was the first time he had ever walked into a place with a woman to whom other men gave the eye. He supposed it was not particularly liberated of him to feel glad about this, but he couldn't help it. He was proud to be seen with her.

The story she had told him about the movie producer enraged him. Dan promised himself privately that, even if Tace decided not to press charges, he would do something to be an instrument of this dickwad's karma. There were all kinds of ways to zing him for this. He didn't have to resort to anything as obvious as busting Todd. He had a computer and a modem and he knew the most effective ways to use them. As a cop, he had access to all kinds of databases, including the D.M.V., T.R.W., the Social Security Administration and others. He could make Todd's financial life a living hell. He could fuck up his credit rating, have his Lexus or Range Rover or whatever kind of yuppiemobile the shitbag drove repossessed. . . . Just thinking about the possibilities made Dan smile. He was not normally a vindictive person, but just now he felt very protective toward Tace Daggett, and woe betide anyone who caused her grief.

"You going to eat those fries?" he asked her.

CHAPTER 38

Thursday, October 31

It was dusk when Jake and Sarah parked in front of Magus's
house. The Porsche was in the driveway, he noticed, which
probably meant the Satanist was home. Jake wasn't sure if he
was glad or sorry.

Magus himself opened the door—Jake assumed it was the
butler's day off. The Satanist reacted in surprise and shock at
the sight of the detective.

"May we come in? Thanks," Jake said, shoving the door
open and propelling Magus back into the entryway.

"You can't do this!" Magus sputtered in anger. "This—this
is—"

"Breaking and entry," Jake said. "And this—" he continued, grabbing Magus, spinning him around and pinning his
wrist in a come-along, "—is aggravated assault and battery."
Magus cried out in pain as Jake put a little more pressure than

was strictly necessary into it. "You could probably make a trespass charge stick, too," he added.

He moved Magus down the hall and into the latter's bookcase-lined study. The room was quiet, save for the faint sound of a clock ticking somewhere, and dimly lit. It smelled of old leather and a faint hint of the same incense Jake had noticed on his last visit to Magus's house. Several massive books that looked very old were lying on the desk. Jake made mental notes of some of the titles: *The Book of the Dun Cow* and *The Mabinogion.*

"Sit," he said, pushing Magus into a chair. As he released his arm, he reached for Magus's neck and tore the gauze bandage off. Magus hissed in pain as the adhesive tape came free of his skin. His hand flew toward his neck in an attempt at concealment; then, apparently realizing the futility of such a move, he let it drop to the desk.

Clearly visible on his neck was a puncture wound. Scabs and healed scars indicated previous lacerations in the same area.

Jake looked at Sarah. "He's a blood fetishist."

Sarah looked at the wounds and nodded slowly. "Hematophagy," she murmured.

Jake said to Magus, "That's one of the little treats you have for your 'flock,' right? What do you do, bite them and bugger them at the same time? Probably the only way you can really get off."

He had heard about people with Magus's fixation: living vampires, men and women who derived intense erotic satisfaction from drinking blood. There were even auto-vampires, those who had learned by careful experimentation how to puncture the jugular or the carotid and let the jetting lifeessence fill their own mouths.

Magus was pale, but he had apparently regained his composure. "What my companions and I do in the privacy of this house is no one's business but ours," he said coldly. "I care for these boys; they are well-fed and protected. Ask any one of them if they do not prefer living with me to living on the street."

"Yeah," Jake said. "Why don't we ask that poor bastard I had to put down in the warehouse? He seemed pretty happy with the way things were here, didn't he?"

Magus seemed about to reply to that, but apparently thought better of it. "You still haven't said what you want here," he said instead.

"Maybe you're not the guy who staked out Tate and Al-stadler," Jake said, "but I think you know more about it than you've told me. So let's have it."

Magus looked down at the desk. His hand trembled as he closed one of the books and pushed it to one side. After a moment, he sighed and said, "Are you familiar with the Celts?"

"I'm familiar with the Celtics, though I'm not a big hockey fan."

Magus gave him a strained smile. "The Celts were an ancient people, quite widespread over Europe and the British Isles at the height of their power, which was before the rise of the Roman Empire. Not much is known about them today; they revered the spoken word and the art of memory, and so left little written history.

"Their religion was polytheistic and animistic." Magus apparently noticed the look of impatience on Jake's face and continued hastily, "That is to say, they worshipped many different gods, some of which were deified animals, such as the raven, the stag and the bull. One of these was the triple goddess known as the Morrigan, who could be a single entity or a triad, as the need required. Two of the component deities, Badb and Macha, symbolized war and death, but the third, Danu, was the mother goddess, the bringer of life. The Morrigan thus symbolized dying, death and rebirth.

"They entrusted their religious teachings to a sect of priest-poets called druids. These were—"

"Magus," Jake interrupted, "I'm assuming that this history

lesson has *something* to do with the two guys who got staked. So cut to the chase."

Sweat was beginning to bead on the Satanist's upper lip. "This is *necessary* history, Detective." He leaned forward in the leather chair and massaged his temples.

"When you first told me about Tate's manner of death, it stirred a memory in me; some vague recollection of a similar method of killing that I had come across in my readings over the years. I'm not talking about the popular myth of how to slay a vampire; this was something quite apart from that.

"Fortunately, my library of the occult is extensive. I searched for that reference and eventually found it.

"It seems that around the fourth century B.C., a druid, whose name is lost in antiquity, claimed that the Morrigan had granted him a path to eternal life. This involved the sacrifice of several victims every year around the time of Samhain, the celebration of Summer's End, also known as the Feast of the Dead." Magus paused, then added, "This holiday was usurped by the Christian religion as All Saint's Day—November the first. We celebrate the day before, Halloween, as the time in which all things unholy are allowed to revel.

"Keep in mind that this story was only written down centuries after it supposedly happened by a Roman historian. As I said, the Celts preserved their legends and traditions orally, not in writing. As a result, the particulars are vague. But apparently the method of obtaining eternal life involves driving an ash wood stake—the ash being a sacred tree to the druids— through the sacrificial victim's heart after appropriate rituals had been performed. The victim's life force then flows through the stake and revitalizes the killer."

Jake stepped forward and leaned over Magus's desk; Sarah put a restraining hand on his arm, but the detective shrugged it off. "Are you telling me," he asked, "that the guy we're looking for is some thousand-year-old warlock?"

Magus did not draw back from Jake's intensity. "I am saying that the aspects of the case as you've explained them to me fit this ceremony to an uncanny degree. I think you will agree with that." He paused, then added, "And if it is true, Detective, your killer would be considerably older than a mere thousand years. Closer to twenty-five hundred, give or take a century."

Jake looked at Sarah. He could tell by her expression that she didn't believe it, and didn't expect him to believe it.

He thought of the stake in his hand, the thrilling jolt, like warm lightning, it had delivered. He didn't know what to think.

Sarah said, "There was a clove of garlic in both victims' mouths. What about that?"

"Garlic has long been known as a cleansing herb, considered to have purifying powers. It is because of this that vampires supposedly consider it anathema. Evidently, it is placed in the mouth as part of the purification ritual, to help sanctify or sterilize the life force."

Jake eyed the Satanist for a long moment. It was impossible to tell if Magus was yanking his chain or not, but all his experience with assorted dirtbags over the years had given him a fair sense of when someone was being serious. And Magus seemed to be quite serious.

"It does all seem to tie together," Sarah said. When Jake glanced at her, she added hastily, "I'm not saying our boy really is some kind of druid immortal. But if he's playing out this ceremony for who knows what reason, we might be able to anticipate his next move."

"Unfortunately, I can tell you little more about the specifics of the ritual," Magus said. "Except that his next victim will in all probability be tonight, on Halloween—the eve of Samhain, the Feast of the Dead. And it will be someone young, since the life force he craves is stronger in the young.

"Beyond that, I can't even speculate who he will kill next. But I think that, if you do not catch him before he kills again, you won't catch him at all. The Samhain sacrifice is the final one, and he will then be satiated for another year. During that time he will in all probability move on to another city or even another country—which is no doubt what he has been doing for centuries." Magus paused and added, "Assuming, of course, that he really *is* an immortal." He smiled slightly. He seemed more in control of himself now, more the sly and manipulative personality that Jake remembered.

Before Jake could reply to that, Sarah asked hastily, "Is there anything else we should know about this character—assuming, which I'm not for a New York second, that all this might be possible? I mean, does he have to hide in a coffin during the day, like a vampire, or . . . ?"

"Or can he only be killed by certain methods, such as silver or a stake?" Magus continued. "Is he supernaturally strong, able to influence animals, or any of the other powers attributed to warlocks, vampires and other creatures of the night?" He shrugged. "The legend is noncommittal on these points. I would assume that he is an ordinary man in terms of physical strength and needs—that he must eat, rest, and that he fears all the same things that mortal men fear, save death by old age. The ceremony of the stake, inasmuch as I could determine, only grants *potential* immortality. Although if he has lived this long, I would speculate that he is resistant to disease."

Magus found and held Jake's gaze with his own. "I think, Detective, that you are linked somehow with this killer, this vampire priest, this Night Hunter. You and he share the same dark nature. It is your destiny to face him, to come to grips with him, to see your own soul reflected in his eyes."

Jake felt a cold finger trace the length of his spine at Magus's words. Could the Satanist somehow know of the zap he had received from the stake in the evidence locker? He suppressed an involuntary shiver. "More head games," he said. "I'm sick of them, Magus. I'm sick of *you*." He turned and started for the door. Sarah followed him.

Magus called after them: "One more thing, Detective. Perhaps the most important thing."

Jake looked back toward Magus.

"According to the legend, the state of immortality was transferable. Though our druid can be killed by anything that can dispatch you or me, if one were to drive an ash wood stake through *his* heart, the unnaturally prolonged life force would be shifted, like electricity through a conducting wire, to the killer. Of course, the new immortal must then continue to prolong his or her life by the same means as before."

Well," Sarah said, as they drove down the winding road a few minutes later, "this certainly puts a new wrinkle on things."

"You're not going to tell me you believe one word of that shit, are you?"

"Well, I'm not going to tell you that I think there's some two-thousand-year-old druid running around Los Angeles sucking people's life force through stakes," Sarah replied. "But I certainly agree that 'Van Helsing' might have co-opted this story for his own twisted reasons. Unfortunately, I don't see how it will help find the sicko before he plants another tent pole in somebody."

"If he is following this script," Jake mused, "then after tonight he might crawl back into the woodwork without popping any more civilians. Which means we might never find him."

"That's not acceptable," Sarah said.

"Then we've only got a few hours. If we don't find him before the night's over, some poor bastard's going to get something in his trick-or-treat bag that's a hell of a lot worse than razor blades in a candy bar."

CHAPTER 39

Thursday, October 31

He watched the young woman performing on the stage, laughing along with the rest of the audience at her statements. He appreciated humor, and her observations of life were genuinely amusing. That was another misconception people had about the undead; that they had no sense of humor. On the contrary, the ability to laugh was a survival trait—it helped one adapt with the changing times.

He was living proof of that.

She would do very well as the final sacrifice. He had watched her surreptitiously for several days now, and there was no doubt in his mind. Her life essence would replenish his own and, together with that which he had taken from the others, keep him young and vital for another year. It was not by any means a steep price to pay for immortality—certainly better than drinking blood every night and never having a glimpse of the sun. Over the centuries, his victims had been easy to hide—and for the last few decades the task had been growing steadily easier. True, crime detection methods had become more sophisticated—he chuckled to himself as he thought about the raised eyebrows that a specimen of his DNA would cause at a police lab—but the increasing population and declining respect for human life more than made up for that.

He joined in the applause when she finished and thanked the audience. He watched her leave the stage and the room, then settled back to sip his drink. He would take this woman's life force and be gone before the police could begin to track him down. Perhaps he might even enjoy her fear a little before he drained her; this he had done before, many times. The Goddess had made no stipulation that the sacrifice be unsullied in that way.

Sometimes he still felt a sense of astonishment and disbelief at his own life. He, alone, as far as he knew, had achieved what every member of the human race had desired since the dawn of time—immortality, a lifespan measured not in mere years or decades, but in centuries and millennia. It was amazing how the knowledge that one could potentially live forever affected one's outlook. He remembered going through a period of intense paranoia in the late fourteenth century, becoming a recluse and never leaving his villa in Italy save to find and dispatch the requisite number of victims a year. He had been convinced that he had run out of the luck that had kept accidental death at bay all those years, and that to venture outside the gates was to court disaster. Eventually, of course, he had to move on, to re-establish a new identity and a new life in order to keep the locals from becoming suspicious, and by doing that he had resolved his fear. If you live long enough, you can get past anything.

It was not easy being immortal. There had been times when he had wanted to die, when it had seemed so much easier to simply give up the struggle than to keep on going. Looking back on it now, he really did not know how he had made it through the first millennium. In the last few hundred years, however, and particularly since the beginning of this century, the pace of progress had been moving faster and faster, and that in itself was sufficient to keep his interest. For the first thousand years, life had changed very little, and he had been beset with ennui. He had wandered the world, taking enormous risks in exploration and war just to find new reasons to keep going. But these days he felt more fascinated by life than he had in centuries. It was definitely a watershed time for the human race—his unique perspective allowed him to see that clearly. If mankind survived, it was entirely possible that he might live to visit other worlds.

Though he still remembered his origins, there were large gaps in his memory—dozens of decades that were lost to him now. He did not know if the memories were still there, just waiting some obscure stimuli to be made available again, or if he was reaching the limits of his brain's memory capacity. Oddly enough, the prospect of forgetting more and more as he went on did not depress him—on the contrary, it seemed a gift of renewal. Since the time he spent several years in a Chinese monastery in the tenth century, he had tried to cultivate living in the moment. It was a tactic that served an immortal well.

Tonight he would complete the ceremony once more—and then he would move on, leave Los Angeles for other climes. Perhaps Paris, he mused. . . . He had not been there since the early eighteen hundreds. . . .

Jake swallowed his bite of pizza, stared at Sarah and said, "You can't be serious."

The look of astonishment on his face was almost enough to make her laugh—she took a sip of her Coke to prevent this. "All I said was, 'What if it's true?'"

After a moment, Jake replied, "What if it is? What if the

moon's made out of green cheese? Means all those moon rocks must stink up the museums pretty bad."

"Look, I'm certainly not saying it *is* true. But if we accept Magus's theory, then we have to assume 'Van Helsing' believes in his own immortality."

Jake shook his head. "I don't know why I let you talk me into this. It's not even my case anymore."

"Yes, it is," Sarah said softly. "You know that as well as I do, Jake."

Jake looked at her steadily for a moment, then nodded slowly. "I can't tell the other guys," he said. "They'd think I'm crazy."

Sarah studied the bubbles in her Coke for a moment, then looked up at Jake. "You're the detective—think of something."

Jake leaned back against the red upholstery of the diner's booth and frowned. "There's no such thing as a truly random killer. Every murder spree's got a pattern to it—the trick is finding it. To do that, you've got to get inside the killer's head—think like him."

"Doesn't sound like a pleasant experience."

"It's not—but it's usually the only way to anticipate what he'll do next." He was quiet for a moment, thinking. Sarah watched the shifting patterns of concentration in his face. The prevailing opinion among cops she had talked to was that Jake Hull was a damn good detective when he got his head out of his ass long enough to take a good look around.

She hoped they were right.

"Okay," Jake said, "let's say this guy is immortal. Or let's say he *thinks* he's immortal. Somebody who's lived for centuries. . . . It must be really hard keeping up with the changes in the world." He gave a snort of dry laughter. "Hell, I'm only forty-two, and I feel like a fucking dinosaur. Imagine how this asshole must feel."

"Okay . . . so?"

Jake took another bite. "So," he continued with his mouth

full, "he'll do everything he can to keep up. Stay on top of things, follow the trends. You live for hundreds of years, I'd think you'd have to work hard to keep your interest up."

Sarah drained the last of her Coke and pushed the glass aside. "So where does this take us?"

Jake thought about it. "Nobody's found any connection between the first two guys he whacked. Jimmy Ray was a street hustler and drug runner; Craig Alstadler was an aspiring comedian and actor. I guess there are those who'd say they weren't all that different, but—"

"Maybe 'Van Helsing' did just pick them out of a crowd. If so, that's a dead end."

They were quiet for a moment. From behind the counter came a loud sizzling noise as the short-order cook poured oil on the griddle. The sharp smell of hot oil tickled Sarah's nostrils.

Jake said, "Ol' Jimmy was moving dope. Just small time: grass, coke, anything to make a few bucks. Nobody's been able to trace his connection yet."

The waiter brought the bill. Jake looked at it and pulled out his wallet. He fished inside it, extracted a five and two ones. He stared at the bills, face reddening slightly.

Sarah reached across the table and picked up the tab. "This one's on me, Jake," she said softly. He did not look at her as he nodded acknowledgment.

Outside, the sun was nearing the horizon, beginning to redden like a huge Unocal ball. The wind was starting to blow again, a cold, dry desert breeze that made Sarah shiver and zip up her windbreaker. Jake looked across the street at an apartment building that had orange and black crepe paper strung across the windows. "Halloween on Hollywood Boulevard. Ever seen it?"

"Oh, yeah. Not something I care to repeat."

Jake started for his car. "C'mon. If Magus is right and 'Van Helsing' is going to do it again tonight, we've only got a few hours."

"You really think we can break this case in a few hours?"

He started the car and pulled away from the curb. His face looked more resigned than she had ever seen it. "Not really," he said. "But what the hell—it's something to do. I've blown my career anyway—might as well fuck up my pension, too."

CHAPTER 40

Thursday, October 31

The sun was touching the horizon as Dan Stratton drove west on Willoughby. Already young trick-or-treaters, some with their parents, some not, were out working the bungalows and seedy apartment buildings of the area. After dark, the real freak show would begin. Halloween in Hollywood was a holiday that every cop in the division dreaded. Every eight-wheel freak whose sanity was none too stable at the best of times would have gone sailing far over the edge into lunatic darkness before this night was over.

Dan remembered an episode he had heard about last year in which a whacko wearing a gorilla suit had jumped on some hapless citizen's car and caused the poor bastard to hit a lamppost. The citizen had suffered a broken rib and some lost teeth in the crash, and the gorilla guy had vanished into a crowd of costumed onlookers. You'd think some asshole in a monkey suit would be easy to follow, Dan thought. But not in this town, and especially not on Halloween.

There were plenty of other incidents that went down on this particular night, most of them a lot more serious. Gangs like the Hollywood Rats and the Goblins seemed to view it as a time to conduct no-holds-barred gang warfare; the hospital emergency rooms were always a lot more crowded on Halloween. Centuries ago the night was supposed to be the year's last big hurrah of all the world's demons, fiends and devils, and here at least that still seemed to be true.

He turned right on Vine and headed up toward Hollywood. The wind was beginning to pick up as the evening came on; he could see the palm trees swaying and bits of trash paper whipping through the air. Stratton had a feeling this was going to be a real problem night. It was nothing he could put his finger on; just a sense of uneasiness about the coming dark. Probably on some level he expected "Van Helsing" to fling another stake in the general direction of someone's pectorals. God knew that Halloween was the perfect night for some looney tune to go vampire hunting. . . .

He turned right again on Hollywood, cruising east for a few blocks. So far, things looked reasonably quiet. Then, just past the Aztec, he saw a few gangbangers gathered on the sidewalk in front of a boarded-up electronics store. As he drove closer, Dan could see one of them push the other. Like kids in a schoolyard, he thought. The difference was that these kids probably hadn't been in a schoolyard in years, and were more familiar with how to field-strip an AK-47 than with playground etiquette.

He sounded a brief burst on the growler, stopping the fight. The youths did not even look around before running, their baggy oversized clothes flapping ludicrously. In a matter of seconds they and their companions had vanished into the shadows.

He didn't bother to pursue them—that was pointless, since they probably knew a hundred places to go to ground in a single block. With any luck, he had broken up the confrontation at least temporarily, and given them a few more weeks or months of life before one or the other or both wound up prone on a bloodstained sidewalk or riddled with bullets in a gang sled over some other inconsequential dispute. None of these kids expected to live past twenty-five.

The sun was down and the first stars were coming out. A car full of costumed teenagers sped past in the other direction, heavy-duty speakers producing a nearly subsonic, bone-rattling bass that Dopplered quickly past. Dan shook his head.

It was going to be a hell of a night.

Halloween was one of the times when Tace felt most alive. This was when the city was at its most surreal, when a fascinating parade of the fringe element filled the streets. She was looking forward to hitting the clubs tonight. The thought of being a possible victim of the Night Hunter had receded into the dim far reaches of improbability; she was too young and too cocky to take seriously the idea of her own death.

First, however, there was something unpleasant that had to be done; she had to talk to Davis. Odd to think of that as uncomfortable, but there it was. She had never really confronted him with her feelings about the whole Jerry Todd fiasco. It was true that he had been a hundred percent right, but she still felt that he could have expressed his reservations more diplomatically. She hoped he would listen and not be defensive when she told him this.

Complicating the matter was the fact that she wanted to see Dan Stratton again. This was definitely not something she could have predicted. The idea of someone like her being even vaguely romantically interested in a cop was about as believable as the Ayatollah joining the Salman Rushdie book-of-the-month club. But again—there it was. Dan was cute in a winsome, slightly hangdog way; he had a sense of humor and wit that could at least attempt to keep up with her own, and he did not seem judgmental. Only time would tell if any or all of these appearances were deceiving—but in the meantime, it seemed worthwhile to see him again.

Probably not tonight, however—she knew that Halloween was a real four-alarm fire for his kind. She hoped he would give her a call in the next few days. If he didn't, then she'd call him—hell, these were the nineties.

She shrugged into her leather jacket and locked the door behind her. She strolled the half-block to where she'd parked her Mustang, passing on her way several laughing, costumed children running down the sidewalk. The wind, she noticed, was beginning to blow pretty seriously. She grinned.

It was going to be a wild night.

CHAPTER 41

Thursday, October 31

Franklin Conner peered out his window at the wind-whipped twilight and debated the wisdom of the course he was considering. Tonight of all nights was definitely a time to stay indoors. On Halloween, he usually kept all the lights out except one in his bedroom, to discourage trick-or-treaters and any other, more sinister types who might use the night's tradition as an excuse for robbery. He had done this for the past seven or eight years.

So why in God's name was he considering venturing out on the street tonight?

Part of it was because he still felt slightly uneasy here. Of course, that had been entirely due to his own overactive imagination—he knew he was much safer inside than outside. But he still started at sudden sounds, such as the water heater's flame roaring to life or the refrigerator kicking on.

He was thinking about walking over to the Joke Joint on

Sunset in hopes that Tace might be there. He had not been able to stop thinking about her since he met her. Conner knew he was being foolish—he was old enough to be her father, very nearly old enough to be her grandfather—but no amount of intellectualizing could quell the irrational hope that she might find him appealing as well. After all, young women were much more likely to be interested in older men than the reverse.

He sighed. It was a sad state the world had gotten to when an old man was too afraid to walk the five or six blocks needed to possibly strike up a relationship with a beautiful young woman. He looked about the apartment, finding it suddenly confining. Damn it, he had a right to walk the streets as much as anyone else. He did not want to spend the remainder of his life in hiding from the world just because he was old.

Fired by a sudden resolution, Conner called the cab company he was in the habit of using. When the car arrived, he put on his Twilight Zone jacket, zipped it up and unlocked the door. He hesitated, then turned to a small table and pulled open its drawer. Inside was a small .22-caliber pistol; he'd bought it years ago when there had been a rash of muggings near the Y. Odd that he hadn't thought about it the other night. He checked to make sure it was loaded, then slipped it into the pocket of his jacket. Its weight felt comforting.

He devoutly hoped he wouldn't have to use it, but better safe than sorry. Armed and trying not to feel foolish, Franklin Conner opened the door and started down the stairs on his mission of love.

The wind was howling like a chorus of damned souls by the time Jake and Sarah entered Phoenix House once more, looking for the elusive Ziplock. Simon Rhys met with them. The man was friendly enough; either he didn't know that Jake had killed Angel or understood why it had been necessary. Jake doubted the latter reason was the case.

"Zip hasn't come around much since he hooked up with that pederast Magus," Simon Rhys told them. "It's a damned shame. I wish he'd do something against the law so you could bust him."

Jake glanced at Sarah. Neither of them had known that Ziplock was one of Magus's boy toys. It looked like another trip back to the Satanist's lair was in order.

"We know he was running dope for somebody around here," the detective said to Rhys. "Do you have any idea who his connection was?"

"I'm sorry, I don't," Rhys said. "They guard those aspects of their lives very closely."

I think we'll know a lot more when we find Ziplock," Jake said as they crossed Hollywood and Franklin and headed up North Beachwood. It was almost full night now, and the maze of winding streets and avenues leading up to Magus's place had taken on a mysterious, even sinister air.

They parked in front and started toward the door. As they started up the steps, Jake heard a door slam somewhere around the side of the building, the sound almost carried away by the wind. Could be nothing, he thought; another house, the wind. . . .

He took a quick right angle, crossing the lawn and peering around the edge of the house. He was just in time to see a teen-aged boy climbing over a tall fence that protected the rear property. Robbery was not his motive, since he was climbing out of the yard rather than into it. As he balanced for an instant on top of the wall, a motion-sensitive security light installed under the mansion's eaves switched on, illuminating him mercilessly. Jake could plainly see the marijuana leaf tattoo on the skinny kid's arm. Then the kid leaped down and took off running across a neighbor's lawn and down the street.

"Stop!" Jake shouted, but he knew it was hopeless; Ziplock was already barely a shadow lost among shadows ahead.

Still, he started to pursue. After all, the street ended in a cul-de-sac . . . maybe he would get lucky. It was about time. . . .

As he ran up the dark street, he heard Sarah calling his name. A moment later, she caught up with him, even though he was running flat out and already beginning to puff with exertion. Probably she's one of those five-miles-a-day people, he thought. No doubt could run the L.A. marathon without breaking a sweat. . . .

"Where're we going?" she asked. He pointed up ahead at Zip's fleeing figure. "Wherever . . . he's going," he managed to get out. "Must've . . . seen us coming . . . panicked." He had no breath for any more speculation. He had thought that he had recovered fully from his bender of the previous night, but now he felt like if he ran another fifty yards, his lungs would implode.

He hoped that Ziplock was indeed rabbiting. Hell, for all he knew, the boy could be the bait to lead them into the hills where black-robed devil-worshippers would slaughter them and bury them in shallow graves. Nothing connected with this mess would surprise him anymore.

The cul-de-sac was illuminated only by porch lights and security lamps. Ziplock ran into the darkness between two houses and another pair of high-intensity bulbs flashed on, spotlighting him as he started to climb the steep hill beyond. A moment later, Jake and Sarah had left civilization behind and were wading through the sage and chaparral as well.

"Freeze!" Jake shouted, firing a couple of rounds into the night sky in the hope of scaring the boy into submission. The wind masked his voice, and possibly even the sounds of the shots as well; in any event, judging from the sounds of the other's passage through the brush which the dry gusts carried back to him, Ziplock had not been impressed. Jake pushed on through the darkness and the dry, scratchy vegetation, Sarah right behind him. He tried not to think about rattlesnakes, or about the possibility of Ziplock having a gun. The boy had the high ground, after all. Their only advantage was the darkness.

Don't worry about it, he told himself as he wheezed and labored for breath. You'll probably have a goddamn heart attack before he gets a chance to shoot. He had thought running down the street was bad, but climbing toward the summit of Mount Lee with the wind battering down was sheer torture. Nevertheless, they reached the crest of the steep hillside only moments after their quarry.

A fire road ran along the top of the ridge, leading up to the "D" in the gigantic sign. The sign was not illuminated, but from this angle the letters stood out starkly against the night sky. A historical monument, Jake remembered. It had been rebuilt back in 1978, and still looked pretty good almost twenty years later. He recalled when they had torn down the old sign that had been there since the twenties in order to raise the new one; for several days, the mountainside had seemed naked, the entire area weirdly bereft of its identity.

Ziplock seemed to be making for the sign. Jake knew that leaping from the tops of the huge letters was a favored form of suicide, just as a swan dive off the Golden Gate in San Francisco had a perverse attraction. He hoped this was not Ziplock's intention. Let me find out what I need to know first; then I'll carry the little prick up on top of one and toss him off myself, if that's what he wants.

Zip dodged between the third "O" and the "D" and disappeared into the blackness beyond. Jake and Sarah followed, the former feeling like his heart was going to burst at any moment. When they reached the flat white metal of the letters, Jake stopped and spent a few moments trying to get his pulse rate back down into the low hundreds.

"Stay here," he managed to gasp to Sarah. "No telling . . . what this asshole . . . might do."

The wind howled. The city lights sparkled below them like a galaxy flung to Earth. Jake pulled his .38 and a speedloader from a coat pocket to do a tactical reload; no way he was going any further without a full piece. He popped the chamber, ejecting the live rounds and the empties, and slid the tips of the loader's bullets in, working by touch in the darkness. He twisted the release and the spring action drove the six slugs into the chamber, which he then snapped back in place. The whole action had taken less than five seconds. Muscle memory.

Then, gun in hand, he moved into the darkness behind the sign.

The backs of the letters were braced by huge metal struts. A few feet further up the hill was a chain-link fence protecting a service road. Perhaps Zip had hoped to reach it.

The wind was vibrating the metal sheets on the poles, producing a keening sound like the cry of a banshee. Jake moved cautiously eastward past the second "O" and into the shadow of the "W." It was blacker than a pimp's heart; the only way he would find Zip was by tripping over him.

A momentary lull in the wind caused the metallic screeching to die down. Jake leaned against the center pole supporting the "W." He was about to move on when he felt a tickling on his neck and the backs of his hands, like a dry rain. For a moment, he was perplexed, then realized what it had to be: dirt and rust fragments settling down in the briefly still air.

Jake looked up. Directly above him, clinging to one of the cross struts and silhouetted against the sky, was Ziplock's huddled form.

CHAPTER 42

Thursday, October 31

Ziplock was quite surprised to learn that Jake had no intention of arresting him. Magus had told him that the detective would make sure he was thrown into the most dangerous holding cell the city had to offer. The Satanist had tried to convince him to hide in the labyrinthine maze of the house, but Zip had panicked and decided to run for it.

Jake held him by his shirtfront as the wind buffeted them, seemingly strong enough to pick them up and toss them in the general direction of Los Feliz. "I just want to know one thing," the detective shouted over the gale. "Who was your connection? Tell me that and you can walk."

"S-Sands," Ziplock said, his eyes wide and dark. "Davis Sands."

Jake rolled his eyes heavenward. "Fuck me," he muttered in God's general direction. He released Zip and started back down the fire road without so much as a backward glance. Sarah hurried to keep up.

"What is it?" she shouted over the pounding gusts.

"Asshole he's talking about deals meth and crack. Vice has been looking to bust him for months. A lot of his customers hang out at the Phoenix House. I should've made the connection myself."

"They found dope in Alstadler's house," Sarah said. "Do you think—?"

"That Sands is 'Van Helsing'? At this point I don't know what to think," Jake said as they left the hillside for the asphalt circle of the cul-de-sac.

"Why not call the other detectives in on it? They might have something you don't."

Jake did not answer. Of course that's what he should do, he knew. Hotdogging a case like this, one he wasn't even officially involved with anymore, could earn him at best the bad will of the other detectives in the unit, at worst some heavy-duty disciplinary action. He knew it was stupid. Tombstone courage. But it had gone beyond choice now; for better or worse he had to see it through. He felt like he was operating on automatic, like moving through Hogan's Alley at the situation simulation range, firing at the targets that popped up, not thinking, just reacting. . . .

They had reached the car by now. He was about to open the door when he stopped suddenly and looked at Sarah across the sedan's roof. "Muscle memory," he murmured, half to himself.

Sarah looked at him. "What?"

"Muscle memory. It's why they make rookies practice those arrest-and-control handholds over and over. To perfect the technique, make it so familiar it's automatic."

"Okay," she said. "What's that got to do with—?"

"Think about it," Jake said as they got into the car. "If you've lived a couple thousand years, wouldn't *everything* you do be burned in that way? No matter what it was, you'd do it like a pro—hell, you could win awards for brushing your teeth." He glanced at her. "You're the expert on how the body works; does that make sense?"

"Who knows? It sounds reasonable, if you could keep your reflexes and muscle tone for two thousand years. Or maybe you'd wind up like the old Mel Brooks routine. The only way to know for sure would be to live that long."

Jake didn't reply as he started down the street. If he was right—if this whole crazy notion that they were looking for an immortal was right—then "Van Helsing" would be a formidable opponent. And here he was going after him on his own.

He decided to make one concession to sanity. Dan Stratton was out on patrol tonight; it wouldn't take him long to rendezvous with Jake as backup, just in case anything happened. And he owed Dan that much. He still wasn't expecting anything to go down tonight, but if it did, Stratton should be in on it. He picked up the radio handset and thumbed the button.

Dan made it to Phoenix House within ten minutes of getting the call. He could see Jake's car parked in a red zone, and parked his own unit a few spaces further down. He had almost decided not to meet Jake; no doubt the detective just wanted to talk some more about Magus. But there was still a chance that Jake had really come up with something that might be useful. Dan felt he owed Jake one more chance.

Jake was sitting in the car with Sarah Allen, the M.E. Dan felt an eyebrow raise before he could clamp down on it, but neither of them acknowledged his surprise.

"Thought you were off this case," he said to Jake by way of greeting.

"What can I say? It's more than a job, it's a goddamn way of life." Jake quickly explained the possible connection between Phoenix House, Sands and the Night Hunter's victims.

"So you think 'Van Helsing' trolls this place for his vics," Dan said. "Okay, now what?"

"Word is that Sands has been hanging out over at a comedy club on Sunset called the Joke Joint. What say we drop by, work the room a little? If nothing else, we might get a few laughs."

CHAPTER 43

Thursday, October 31

Conner sat at a table near the back of the main room and sipped a glass of white wine, trying to relax. In the short ride between his apartment and the club, he had seen several young teenagers in glowing skeleton costumes hurl bricks through a dry-cleaning establishment, and had been nearly knocked down by a devil pursuing an angel, both on bicycles riding full-tilt down the sidewalk. He was beginning to think that coming here wasn't the smartest thing he'd done in his life. But now that he was here, he told himself, he might as well stay for the show.

He saw no sign of Tace, however. Another woman was on-stage discussing her sex life in embarrassing, albeit humorous, detail. Conner felt disappointed and vaguely foolish for coming here. It was a pathetic role he was playing, that of a horny, lonely old man hoping that a woman not even half his age would find him attractive.

He glanced about the room and noticed the policeman he had met here before talking to one of the waiters. The man was in uniform now. Another man and a woman stood with him. Conner debated going over and saying hello, but decided against it. He realized he really wasn't having a good time here; it was noisy and crowded and not particularly entertaining. He decided that he would finish his drink and leave.

It was then that he saw Tace.

The woman he had chosen was here; sitting at a table alone, nursing a drink, obviously waiting for someone. It was tempting to approach her, but he knew from centuries of experience that such an action was not the best way to stalk his prey. Better to approach her when she was alone. It might be that he would not have time to enjoy her before draining her, but that was acceptable as well. Certainly he had not lacked for sexual encounters over the centuries, both women and men. That sort of release was always available. What he needed from her now was not her body, but her soul.

He could still be patient. As long as the stake was driven before the moon set, his life would be renewed once more. If she met someone and went home with him, he would simply kill her companion as well as her. Then he would vanish; there was nothing to keep him in Los Angeles after the final sacrifice had been accomplished. Over the course of several hundred years he had amassed a fortune in investments, the interest on which was now enough to let him live comfortably. He could come and go throughout the world as he pleased.

He ordered another drink and returned his attention to the woman on the stage. She was crude and vulgar, but still occasionally amusing.

Tace was waiting for Davis to show up, and as the evening wore on she was becoming more and more certain that he wasn't going to. She wasn't sure how she felt about that. One part of her said, in righteous indignation, that if he couldn't even bother to keep a date, then to hell with him. Another part was slightly worried; it was unlike him. He had been very attentive and caring during their affair. Tace realized she was thinking of their relationship in the past tense, and that made her feel even worse.

She didn't want to just let it fizzle out; she'd ended way too many romances that way. If it was indeed over, then they both needed some kind of closure. But they could only have that, she knew, if both were willing.

Tace looked at her watch. She'd give him five more minutes. . . .

Sarah followed Jake as the three of them moved through the crowd. The room was maybe five hundred square feet, she estimated, and crowded with tables and customers. She watched Jake as the latter eyeballed the room. She knew he had come to look at this case as something far more than just another red ink listing on the board, and that worried her. She had always heard that one of Jake's greatest attributes was his pit bull tenaciousness on cases, but this one had gone far beyond that. This was a vendetta.

She had realized sometime earlier in the night that there was no question anymore of whether or not she was going to fall for Jake Hull. It had already happened, in a big way. Which made her even more concerned about his future.

Her thoughts were interrupted when she saw a pleased expression on Dan Stratton's face. He was looking across the room at an attractive woman who looked to be in her midtwenties, sitting alone at a table. He started across the room toward her, only to see her rise and head for the far exit before he got halfway there. Dan called out "Tace!" which Sarah assumed was her name, but a loud burst of audience laughter drowned him out. The woman, Tace, disappeared through the curtained exit door.

A moment later, someone else left by the same door: a

blond man wearing a full-length coat. Sarah watched him go, finding his movements oddly mesmerizing, like watching a dancer on a stage. She turned to Jake, only to see him staring intently at the man also. He nodded slightly, as though finding a suspicion confirmed. Then he started quickly through the crowd toward Dan. The cop reacted in surprise as Jake grabbed his arm and pulled him along behind, shoving people roughly aside to cross the rest of the room. Sarah hurried to follow.

Conner had just left the building when he heard the scream. It echoed up the length of the narrow alley that led to the club's rear parking lot. Oddly enough, the first emotion he felt was anger—he had been certain there would be trouble this night, and he had been right. He thought for a moment of ignoring it, but he couldn't do that. He ran down the alley, fumbling in his pocket for his gun.

In the parking lot he saw Tace struggling with a man wearing a long, duster-style coat that whipped like a flag in the wind. The man had clapped a hand over Tace's mouth and twisted one of her arms behind her. He was dragging her toward a late-model Lexus.

"Let go of her!" Conner shouted. He had the gun in his hand now, but he knew he couldn't shoot as long as the man held Tace. The man looked toward him when he shouted, and the shock of recognition froze the actor for a moment.

Tace's abductor released her mouth long enough to reach under his coat. Tace screamed again as the man withdrew something long and silver that glittered in the high-intensity light on the rear of the building. He whipped his hand forward and Conner felt a sudden cold pain in his chest.

Abruptly his legs lost their strength. A silent roaring sensation filled his head, and he couldn't seem to grasp what had happened. He heard the sound of a shot; it seemed far away, but he felt the gun in his hand recoil. Then he collapsed, feeling no pain as he hit the asphalt on his back. He couldn't seem to get his breath. He saw the man shoving Tace into the car, but the action seemed to be taking place at the far end of a rapidly lengthening dark tunnel.

Oh, I know what this is, Conner thought with a strange calm as the black mouth of the tunnel rushed forward to engulf him. God knows I've played enough of these.

It was a death scene.

CHAPTER 44

Thursday, October 31

Jake, Sarah and Dan heard the screams just as they pushed open the exit door. They rushed from the rear entrance to the club in time to see what looked like a Lexus or other high-level foreign car screech out of sight through the alley, narrowly missing the body of an older man who was lying on his back near the alley's entrance. Jake pulled his .38 and fired four quick shots, trying to hit the rear tires. No good. The car was gone too quickly for him to read the license plate.

"Help him!" he cried to Sarah, pointing to the old guy, whom they could now see was lying on his back with the hilt of a throwing knife protruding from his chest. As she hurried over to him, Jake and Dan ran down the alley to Jake's car.

Jake cranked the ignition, which protested for a moment and then caught. They could see the Lexus, several cars ahead. "Call it in," Jake said as they headed away from the curb.

Dan did so, requesting backup in terse, clipped tones. A few blocks ahead Sunset Boulevard was narrowed down to two lanes by the orange road cones of a Caltrans crew. The Lexus turned north on La Brea, moving fast but not driving recklessly. He's a cool one, Jake thought. Doesn't want to attract attention.

Of course he's cool, something in the back of his mind whispered. He's over two thousand years old. He knows what he's doing. . . .

Jake brushed the thought aside, concentrating on driving. He flipped on the siren as Dan slipped the magnetic misery light onto the roof of the car and said, "I *knew* there'd be a goddamn car chase." He popped the clip on his Glock and made sure it was full while Jake tried to maneuver closer to the Lexus. "Motherfucker's got Tace," Dan said, his face grim in the passing lights. "I know it."

"Doesn't matter who he's got," Jake replied. "He's going down."

Dan asked, "Do we know who he is?"

"Yeah," Jake said. "That guy at Phoenix House—Rhys."

"Not that I'm arguing with you, but—why him?"

"It's a long story, and you wouldn't believe most of it anyway. If I hadn't been so obsessed with busting Magus, I might've figured it out when you told me about that martial arts style with that old English name."

"Shit," Dan said. "I didn't think you even heard me."

The Lexus reached Hollywood Boulevard and was slowed there by the heavy holiday traffic. Jake followed, the light and siren clearing traffic only a little, since there wasn't much room for anyone to pull over. They were one lane over and several cars behind the Lexus. The sidewalks were thronged with laughing and yelling people in all manner of costumes and disguises. The car in the next lane over from Jake's appeared to be driven by a rotting corpse, with several more zombies in the backseat passing a joint. In front of Frederick's of Hollywood someone wearing a Spider-Man outfit was performing gymnastic feats, backflips and handstands, while a crowd applauded and dropped coins in a webbed basket.

The Lexus tried to switch lanes abruptly, was clipped on the right rear fender by a low rider, and shot up over the curb in front of the Aztec Theater, knocking over a fire hydrant. A fountain of water rose, the wind sending it sheeting across several lanes of traffic. It drenched some costumed celebrants on the sidewalk, who danced in the spray, laughing.

Jake pulled over and he and Dan tumbled out of the car, guns drawn. They started toward the Lexus, which could be seen dimly through the geyser. They moved cautiously, the water soaking them, plastering their hair. A few street people, some dressed like witches, ghosts and other creatures of the night, approached curiously. Dan waved them back as he and Jake drew closer through the spray to the Lexus.

It was empty.

Dan pointed up the broad steps of the theater, where the plywood covering one of the huge doors had been pulled loose, revealing a narrow black opening. "In there," he shouted over the roar of the broken hydrant. "Only place he could've gone."

Shit, Jake thought. No way. "Wait for backup," he yelled.

"Fuck that. What if he does Tace before we get to him?"

And he will, Jake realized grimly. Either they went in alone and did their best to stop him, or they went in later with backup and found Rhys long gone, leaving behind a chick on a stick. There was no other way to play it.

They moved up the stairs toward the theater's entrance.

CHAPTER 45

Thursday, October 31

The Aztec had been built back in the twenties, during the heyday of movie palace construction. Intended by Marathon Studios as their answer to Grauman's Chinese and the Egyptian, the huge structure was designed to look loosely like an ancient Central American ziggurat, with a stepped pyramid roof and statues of feathered priests and priestesses crowning the opulent cinema showcase. At the apex of the pyramid was a flat sacrificial altar, and for a time, when Marathon was ruthlessly housecleaning its management tiers during the forties, *Daily Variety* had run a column naming the latest mogul to have his or her heart metaphorically cut out on the sacrificial platform atop the Aztec.

Dan had read all this in a history of Hollywood's heyday years. The book had included pictures of the Aztec at the height of its glory, showing crowds of people in evening dress assembled in the massive lobby, with a huge chandelier shedding light over them all. Even in the black-and-white photos, a sense of the rich colors and hues came through.

It looked nothing like that now.

The lobby was lit by the moon shining through a bank of high windows, broken long ago by vandals' bricks. Dan could dimly see the intricate frieze work that covered the ceiling, the peeling wallpaper over the huge and dusty concession stand. Cyclopean columns rose at intervals from the floor, their surfaces carved with elaborate mosaics of ancient Indian cities. Over the three entrances to the auditorium was mounted a huge bas-relief of the feathered serpent Quetzalcóatl. Even filmed with the dust of ages, the serpent's jeweled eyes seemed to glitter balefully in the moonlight.

The place reeked of stale urine and feces. Trash was piled in mounds in the corners; empty fast-food cartons and broken glass crunched under their shoes. He and Jake moved warily through the semi-darkness, the dust disturbed by their passage rising like forlorn ghosts in the silvery shafts of moonlight.

Jake put a hand on his arm, stopping him, and pointed to the floor. Black drops of blood shone there, leading toward the far left auditorium entrance. Somehow either Rhys or Tace had been wounded.

Up until this point, the adrenaline rush had been sufficient to keep Dan from feeling fear. Now, however, it came rolling in on him like a black tide. This motherfucker was hiding somewhere in the sooty darkness, no question, his eyes already adjusted, watching them come. He could have a gun, could already be lining them up. . . .

Dan wriggled his fingers slightly to get a firmer grip on the Glock. He tried to will himself to be calm, to focus. Outside, the wind howled faintly, mournfully. This place felt rife with the discontented spirits of the city's past . . . it seemed to embody everything that was wrong now with Hollywood, the one-time glamour and sheen that had faded and shredded away to reveal the nacreous rotting core. It was, at this point, very easy to believe that "Van Helsing" had known something they had not—that the bloodsucking undead really did lurk in the shadowed alleys of this city of lights, that one of them waited even now for them in the black heart of this rococo film mausoleum. . . .

Dan swallowed, his throat painfully dry, as he and Jake moved toward the left arched opening to the cavernous auditorium, which was as black as the door to Tartarus. Jesus, he thought. Sweet Jesus, let me live through this. . . .

He crouched on the crumbling tile in front of the first row of seats, leaning over the unconscious woman. Careful pressure on the nerve in her neck had caused her to pass out when he had put her in his car; it was a technique he had learned centuries ago in the Orient.

He had underestimated the policemen's ability to track him; that they, and that foolish old man, had shown up in the parking lot had been the biggest surprise he had had in decades. That, and being wounded by the old man's gun, which he had fired even as the knife blade had entered his chest. He felt under his coat, found the shirt soaked with blood. His healing powers were greater than that of mortals, but it would still take a few days for this wound to recuperate. And he did not have a few days. It was possible that he did not have even a few minutes. After all these centuries, he was abruptly running out of time.

He refused to panic. With all that was going on out on the street, there was no way they would find him in here in time to stop the final sacrifice. He would complete the ceremony quickly and vanish into the night. In a matter of hours, he could be at the airport. . . .

Feeling for her face in the darkness, he slipped the purifying bulb of garlic between her lips, then ripped open her shirt. Her spirit was now prepared; in another moment it would nourish his own. He had two ash wood stakes left, strapped to the inside of his coat. He pulled one free, along with the mallet, but his haste and the wound combined to make him do something he had not done in centuries; he fumbled and dropped the mallet. It clattered loudly on the floor.

An instant later, two voices shouted *"Freeze!"* in unison. A moment later, the beam of a high-powered flashlight swept the breadth of the auditorium, finding his crouched form.

He reacted with an instinct honed from centuries of survival. He rose, hurling as he did so the last knife in the direction of the flashlight beam and diving for cover in front of the first row of seats. He was rewarded an instant later by a cry of pain and the extinguishing of the light, but then he heard several gunshots echo in response.

There was no way to complete the sacrifice now. Had he come to the end of his long existence? There was no time to ponder the question; if he did not escape these policemen, the answer was certainly yes.

He quickly crawled the length of the row to the next aisle, then gathered himself and leaped to his feet. He ran toward the moldering curtains that still hung on either side of the screen. Another shot came, and he heard the bullet smack into the wall inches from his head. Then he was behind the curtains.

There was a narrow passage here which led behind the screen. His questing hands found a ladder bolted to the wall at the corridor's end, and he began to climb. He had no idea where the rungs led to, nor at the moment did he care. All the energy of his mind and body was focused on only one thing—survival. He had lived for centuries; it could not all end now. . . .

Jake saw the knife blade strike Dan high in the chest. The flashlight fell, shattering, plunging the auditorium into darkness once more.

Dan fell to his knees. Jake crouched beside him. "Bad?"

"Go, *go!*" Dan whispered through clenched teeth. "Get the cocksucker!"

Jake turned and started down the aisle, feeling his way in the dark, his gun held close to his body. There were only two shots left. The darkness was like it had been in the warehouse: thick, cloying, almost smothering.

He heard the rapid clatter of feet somewhere ahead of him—Rhys was rabbiting. Jake moved faster through the darkness, feeling his way with his free hand.

He nearly stumbled over the woman's body in the dark; he crouched down beside the soft mass his foot had struck and ran his hand over her still form. Her shirt had been ripped, and the bare skin beneath it was still warm to the touch. He found her neck, pressed two fingers against the artery and was reassured by a strong, steady beat. Jake stood and moved on.

The curtains were still moving slightly when his outstretched hand found them. He pushed them aside, found the corridor and kept going.

When he found the ladder at the dead end, he began to climb.

CHAPTER 46

Thursday, October 31

Tace awoke with a headache so strong that she had to control an urge to retch. This sensation wasn't helped by a strong taste of garlic. The fist of fear that slammed into her a moment later when she realized she was somewhere in unknown darkness didn't do her much good either.

She rolled over, spitting out a clove of garlic, trying to remember what had happened, how she had gotten to wherever this was. Then memory flooded back and she suppressed a whimper of terror.

The man in the parking lot—he had grabbed her, dragged her to his car. It had happened so fast that she had been frozen with disbelief and fear. She remembered someone yelling for him to let go of her. . . .

Oh, God. Conner. Her attacker had either killed or badly wounded the old actor, had hit him with a knife from clear across the parking lot. But Conner had managed to wound the

man who kidnapped her; she remembered his body jerking
with the impact of the bullet as he shoved her into the car.
Then there had been the pressure of his thumb against her
neck, and that was all. Until now.

But where was he? Tace listened, trying to still the beating
of her heart, which seemed to be pounding as loud as jungle
drums. The silence about her was as thick and frightening as
the darkness. She could hear nothing. She could feel cold air
on her chest—her blouse had been ripped or cut. She moved
her hands cautiously over the dusty floor, trying to feel any
clues that might help her decide where she was. Her left hand
struck something that rolled away with a clatter, and she
gasped. Then she cautiously felt for it—she seemed to be
lying on a floor of tile or linoleum—and her fingers closed
about a wooden shaft almost as thick as her forearm. She
traced its length, found that it narrowed to a sharp point.

She felt another wave of nausea and fear overcome her.
Anyone with two brain cells to rub together could deduce
from this who had kidnapped her, who might be returning any
minute to give her the old Transylvanian cure for heartburn.
In fact, he could be right next to her, waiting for some sick
reason of his own to grab her and pull her down and drive the
stake into her. . . .

Tace choked down a sob of terror and tried to get to her feet,
but vertigo and nausea caused her to stumble. She fell against
some form of metal chair, bruising herself. Another moment
of tactile exploration convinced her that she was crouched
next to a row of theater or movie seats. They hadn't been used
in quite some time, if the dust that tickled her nostrils was any
indication.

Tace started to crawl on her hands and knees, using the
seats to guide her, holding onto the stake as a possible weapon,
although in her condition she knew she had about as much
chance of winning a fight with a psychotic murderer as a but-
terfly had of hefting a barbell. In a moment she had reached
one of the aisles, and she began to make her way up the in-

cline. Any moment she expected to feel the Night Hunter grab her, wrench her around and plunge a stake into her heart. . . .

Tace clenched her teeth and kept crawling. It seemed that she labored for an eternity in the silent and dusty darkness, her skin crawling with anticipation of that heavy hand falling on her. . . .

After what could have been minutes or hours, she realized that there was someone in the darkness ahead of her. She wasn't sure by what subtle sense she had divined this, but she was able to confirm it by listening intently. She could hear rapid, shallow breathing from the blackness. Was it someone who could help her?

Or was it *him*?

Tace pulled herself to her knees, the stake clenched firmly in one hand. Whoever it was, he sounded like he could use some help himself; she could hear small groans of pain mixed with the rapid breaths. Her assailant had been wounded; maybe he had crawled away in an escape attempt. She moved forward slowly, one hand outstretched, and a moment later her fingers touched a leg lying prone on the floor.

She heard a sharp gasp, and then a voice that shook slightly said, "Don't try it, asshole. I got a gun pointed right at you."

Tace nearly fainted with relief, just like some heroine in a dime novel. "Dan? Oh, Jesus, Dan! It's me, Tace!"

A sound that was half gasp, half sob was her reply. She hurled the stake away, heard it go clattering off in the darkness as she lunged forward to embrace him. He arched in pain and cried out as she did so, however, and she quickly scrambled back off of him.

"What's wrong?"

"Left . . . shoulder. . . ."

Tace felt over him quickly, found his chest and the knife blade protruding from it, felt the sticky welter of blood surrounding it. For a wrenching moment, she thought he was completely covered in blood, but then realized that his face and uniform were wet with water. Even so, she once again felt her last meal trying to abandon ship. She had to turn away and take several deep breaths to calm down.

"Can you walk?" she whispered.

". . . think so. . . ."

She managed to make it to her feet and stay there this time, and helped him to his. Leaning on each other and the rows of seats, they staggered together up the inclined aisle toward the gray rectangle that marked the exit.

They emerged from the auditorium into the lobby in time to see several cops entering cautiously from the outside. As if controlled by one mind, all the guns swung toward them, then lowered as the cops recognized one of the two walking wounded as their own.

A moment later, the paramedics were attending to both of them. Tace, strapped to a gurney, saw a woman bending over Dan while a paramedic applied Vaseline and gauze pads to his wound. "Where is he, Dan?" she heard the woman ask anxiously. "Where's Jake?"

Dan whispered, "He went after 'Van Helsing.'"

Then Tace was wheeled toward the waiting ambulance, but not before she saw the look of stricken worry on the other woman's face.

CHAPTER 47

Thursday, October 31

Jake Hull climbed for what seemed an endless time through the darkness. Occasionally he broke through filmy barriers of cobwebs, tasting their cold, dust-laden strands. The rungs of the ladder were pitted with rust, and his fingers soon grew sore from gripping them. The darkness ahead, below and around him was absolute. It seemed that he had been climbing for hours, that the building had somehow telescoped up to a size rivaling that of the Library Tower. His sodden clothes weighed him down; at one point he stopped and managed to divest himself of his waterlogged sports coat, letting it fall. His neck and shoulders hummed with tension. He had thought the chase through the hills to the Hollywood sign had been bad, but this was a thousand times worse.

There was no way to know whether Rhys was waiting for him somewhere above, maybe crouching on some sort of platform next to the ladder, poised to kick him free of his grip and send him falling to the floor far below. Every time he reached for a new rung, he expected something like that to happen.

And then, after what seemed like a climb that reached from the depths of hell, his questing fingers suddenly encountered a flat metal surface above him.

Jake hugged the ladder, his muscles trembling. His breathing came in gasps. After a moment, he reached up with one hand and pushed on the trapdoor. It creaked open, and the moonlight that shone through was bright enough to momentarily dazzle him.

He pushed the trapdoor back, letting it fall with a metallic clang, and scrambled out as quickly as he could, drawing his .38 as he did so. He was on the roof near the apex of the pyramid, standing on one of the broad steps of the ziggurat. The wind tore at him, screaming in his ears, slicing through the thin wet shirt with invisible cold knives. From up here he could see almost the entire neon jungle that was Hollywood, its designer colors pulsing hot against the night.

Rhys was nowhere to be seen.

He could be hiding on one of the other sides of the pyramid, Jake thought. He begin climbing cautiously up the steps toward the apex, his gun cocked and ready. From there he should be able to see an attack coming from any of the four sides.

Of course, he told himself, from there he would be particularly vulnerable to a knife attack as well. Rhys had already proven himself pretty handy with a blade. But Jake doubted that his aim would be helped any by the wind—it was blowing so hard up here that it was difficult to keep his footing. A thrown knife might—he hoped—be blown off course.

He started up the few remaining steps toward the altar. He didn't even stop to think about how fucking weird all this was. It was too dangerous for even the gallows humor of a cop.

The moon, bright in the clear air, lit up this side of the pyramid like a spotlight. The other side was as dark as the pit. That was where Rhys had to be hiding.

Jake moved cautiously toward the altar, gun at the ready. The sacrificial block of stone rose nearly chest-high before him. The designers had been thorough—there was even a shallow basin in the top of it to catch the blood from the victim's wounds.

Jake put out a hand to keep his balance as a particularly strong gust struck. Heart hammering in his chest, he stepped around the square stone, which was about three feet on a side.

Rhys was not behind it.

Something, some subtle sense, warned him. Jake turned, had just enough time to realize that Rhys had moved down the back side of the ziggurat and circled around to come up behind him. The blunt end of the stake, wielded like a club, struck the gun from his hand. It sailed off the roof and into the night.

Jake staggered back against the altar, his right hand numb from the impact, barely managing to avoid the next blow, which smashed into the stone beside his head. He caught a glimpse of Rhys's face, his eyes emotionless save for the desire to kill. The man's coat whipped in the wind like a vampire's cloak.

Jake managed to get an elbow up as his attacker struck again. He blocked the stake's blow, though his arm rang with pain. He pushed himself forward, causing Rhys to stagger back down a couple of steps.

Over Rhys's shoulder, he could see the bright light of a police helicopter approaching. By the time they arrived, however, this fight would be over—one way or the other.

Even with the wound slowing him down, Rhys was practically unstoppable. Jake rolled to one side as the immortal struck again and lashed backward with a fist, catching Rhys in the solar plexus. Rhys grunted, a pained explosion of breath. He dropped the stake; it landed in the altar's blood basin.

Jake tried to grab it, but Rhys was too fast. He grabbed the detective by the jacket, bent him backward over the altar. Jake managed to get a knee up between them and thrust out with all the strength he had left. Rhys toppled back, lost his balance and fell, rolling down several steps. He came immediately to his feet and charged back up the steps toward Jake.

Jake was still sprawled half across the altar. His right hand groped for and found the stake lying in the basin behind him.

As Rhys leaped for him, he pushed himself off the altar, whipping the stake forward. The sharpened point plunged through Rhys's coat, through his shirt, through his ribs—straight into his heart.

Rhys's mouth and eyes went wide in astonishment and horror. Something screamed—either Rhys or the wind, Jake was not sure. Blood, black in the moonlight, bubbled up around the stake and gushed from Rhys's mouth, soaking the front of Jake's shirt.

But Rhys did not die.

His eyes still blazed with life and a hatred cold as the stars. His hands moved up, slowly, jerkily, the fingers twitching as they reached for Jake's throat. Horrified, Jake seized the stake, now slippery with blood, in both hands, pushing away from him this thing that refused to die. Rhys strained forward, impaling himself further in his efforts to reach Jake. His fingers touched the detective's neck, wrapped themselves around it, began to squeeze. . . .

The cold silver moonlight began to fade in Jake's vision, replaced by a pulsing darkness; the whistling howl of the wind was drowned by the pounding of blood in his head, and he . . . was . . .

Falling. . . .

CHAPTER 48

Thursday, October 31

Business was brisk in the ER of Hollywood General during the final hours of Halloween, a fact that surprised none of the staff. After tending to a gunshot victim, one of the MDs had a free moment to meet two paramedics gurneying a patient through the sliding doors. "Let's hear it," he said, pacing the gurney as it rolled down the white corridor lined with sufferers.

"Twenty-four-year-old white male stabbed in the upper left quad," one of them said hurriedly. "Got a patch over a sucking chest wound about three centimeters long. BP is ninety over sixty, pulse one-twenty. Respiration shallow and labored."

The doctor looked down at the victim, saw the uniform that marked him as a cop. The man was still conscious, his eyes panicky above the oxygen mask.

"Relax," he told him. "We're professionals; trust us." He

looked up at the two nurses who had come to flank him as they moved and spoke briskly. "Jessie, Karen, we got a traumatic pneumothorax, possible hemothorax here. I want a chest tube, surgical kit, get a portable X-ray prepped."

"Can do," Karen said, veering away on her mission.

"Type and crossmatch three units, keep NS going TKO," he said to Jessie as they wheeled the cop into an exam bay. He fitted the stethoscope's plugs to his ears and started listening to his patient's breathing and heart. Good news there, he thought; no indication of blood filling the chest or of cardiac tamponade. "You won't need surgery," he told the cop. "Patch you up, you'll be back in the doughnut shop by next week."

An intern and more nurses moved in to patch the wound and reinflate the lung as the MD moved on to the next crisis. Within five minutes the cop with the knife wound had faded completely from his mind.

It was a busy night.

Dan Stratton lay propped up in the uncomfortable hospital bed, hidden from the room's other patient by the plastic curtain, trying to find a way to breathe that didn't make him feel like he had broken glass in his lungs. The saline solution from the IV drip was cold where it entered his arm, his chest hurt like a motherfucker and, all in all, it wasn't a Halloween he was going to remember fondly.

The time he had lain there in the old theater, hearing the sickening bubbling sound his blood made with each breath he fought for, had been the most terrifying moments of his life. He had been certain he was going to bleed to death there, alone in the dark. It had been an eternity of silent dread before Tace found him.

He wondered what had happened to Jake Hull.

The door opened and Tace Daggett poked her head in. Dan felt a surge of joy and gratitude so intense that the room seemed momentarily to sway.

She grinned and came to sit beside the bed, her leather jacket, T-shirt and jeans making her look like a drawing in black ink against the white walls and floor. "Hey, hero," she said softly.

Dan had to speak slowly, but he found to his relief that he could get the words out. "Excuse me? I thought *you* saved *me*. Much as I'd like to remember it the other way. . . ."

"Go ahead—I won't tell anyone." Tace looked down at him and Dan saw a softness in her eyes and expression that contrasted oddly with the spiked hair and silver jacket zippers. He hoped he wasn't giving her a sappy look in return. On second thought, he hoped he was.

"Did you hear anything about Jake?" he asked after a moment of warm silence.

"The guy who went in with you?" Tace shook her head. "But then, you were the only one I asked about." She let her gaze pass over the monitors and equipment beside the bed, then gave him a coy look. "Hey, I've never done it in a hospital bed. How about it? C'mon, it'll be just like the end of *Love Story*."

Dan laughed, then cut it short when someone revved up a chainsaw behind his ribs. "Sorry, 'fraid I'll have to pass," he said, coughing. After a minute, he asked, "Rain check?"

Tace smiled again, then leaned over and kissed him, lightly and tenderly, but with passion behind it. "Oh, you bet, officer."

"I have to warn you—the LAPD advises strongly against its people becoming involved with civilians attached to cases. Never works out. They've done studies. It's usually just an intense physical relationship that only lasts a few weeks."

Her smile had become a grin. "What's your point?"

Dan chuckled, then yawned. He was starting to feel very sleepy; whether it was something they had given him or just the fatigue and shock catching up, he didn't know, but he could feel himself starting down that greased slide to slumberland. "Be here when I wake up?" he mumbled as his eyes closed.

"Depend on it."

Maybe, Dan thought as he sank into the friendly dark, just maybe it wasn't such a bad night after all.

When Sarah walked into Jake's room, the detective was staring out the window at the night sky. She saw him turn his gaze toward the door, register who it was and then turn back to gazing at the stars.

Thinking about it afterward, she realized that she had known right then. It had just taken her those last few moments to admit it.

She sat down in the chair beside the bed, wishing the guardrails didn't make it impossible to sit beside him on the mattress. She could see the red welts Rhys's fingers had left on his neck. She reached for his hand, but stopped before her fingers touched his.

"They say you'll be fine," she told him. "You weren't unconscious for more than a few minutes." Her words sounded flat and hollow in the sterile air.

Jake nodded. "I know." He still wasn't looking at her.

"You got him," she said. "It's what you wanted. 'Van Helsing' is dead, Jake. I would've thought you'd be a little more upbeat."

He looked at her then, and his face was that of a stranger. "I'm sorry. I guess there's still a lot on my mind. One battle won, but the war goes on, right?"

"Right," Sarah said. "Right."

Silence rushed to fill the room like air into a vacuum. He was looking out the window again. She felt she would have more rapport with a cadaver on a slab than she did right now with Jake Hull.

A hundred questions fought to be the first out of her mouth. *Why are you shutting me out? What happened up on that roof? Is it something I did? Is it something we can fix?* She asked none of them. Instead, she simply said, "Look—call me when you're feeling better, okay?" It sounded much more like pleading than she had hoped it would.

Jake looked at her again, and now Sarah knew for certain. She stood and walked out of the room, not looking back.

Fucking son of a bitch, she thought. And then: At least I didn't cry.

She walked rapidly down the carpeted hallway, through the lobby, past the brightly lit twenty-four hour pharmacy and out into the night.

Not even a good-bye. Not even a goddamn good-bye. . . .

Now she felt tears starting, and shook her head angrily, clamped down on them. No way she was going to cry over this. No fucking way. At least, not now.

The papers and the news services wouldn't report this one, Sarah realized with bitter irony, but she was the last victim of the Night Hunter. She had just gotten the final stake through the heart.

She walked across the parking lot toward her car. The winds had stopped, and there was a change in the air that at first she didn't recognize: the distant scent of rain. In the moonlight, she could see a cloud front coming in from the Pacific.

The sound of her car alarm disarming was startlingly loud in the still air. Then, before she could open the door and get in, she heard another electronic beep: her pager. She looked down at the number on the read-out, knowing what it was. Somewhere on the streets of Los Angeles, another death awaited her ministrations.

Sarah leaned against the Jeep's door. Her cellular phone was in her purse; in a moment, she would answer the call. But this death, and the ones that would follow, could wait. Something had just died within her as well, and it deserved mourning.

EPILOGUE

Friday, November 1

He looked out the hospital window at the stars.

They seemed to speak to him with silent voices, to confirm what he suspected as truth.

He thought back to those last few moments on the roof of the Aztec Theater. He could still feel that implacable grip trying to crush his throat, even as Rhys's blood poured over the stake, coating his hands. Jake had almost passed out when he saw the murderous intensity in the immortal's eyes vanish as though extinguished by the wind. Then Rhys had slumped forward bonelessly, the sudden dead weight of his body almost tearing the stake free from Jake's hands.

And then Jake had felt again the strange shock he had experienced when he had touched the stake in the evidence locker, only this time it was a hundred times more intense. It felt like an electrical surge, like a warm liquid wave, like nothing describable in any human language. It seemed to flow through the stake and up his arms, suffusing his entire body. A sensation so powerful and exquisite that he could not tell if it were pleasure or pain filled him momentarily. Then it was over, and he had watched Rhys's limp body sag down the steps. Jake released the stake and slumped back against the altar, the basin of which had filled with Rhys's blood, shining like a puddle of darkness.

It was then that he had passed out.

He had revived to see a concerned paramedic leaning over him. The police helicopter he had seen earlier now wheeled overhead, its spotlight providing merciless illumination. Jake had looked for Rhys's corpse, half expecting to see a withered desiccated form lying at his feet, the wind stripping the bones of powdery flesh even as he watched. But the body that sprawled there had been indistinguishable from countless other bodies he had witnessed in the course of his work.

Now, lying in the hospital bed, he realized abruptly that his ulcer was not hurting. He had been aware of it on a low, almost unconscious level ever since he and Dan and Sarah had arrived at the comedy club. But now the pain was gone, and somehow he knew it would not be back.

Jake remembered the last thing that Magus had said about the spell that had kept the Celtic wizard alive for over two thousand years. He knew that by all rights he should be feeling like day-old dogshit, given what he'd been through. But he didn't.

As a matter of fact, he felt pretty damn good.

Unfinished business. That was what Tom Nivens had called the hundreds of unsolved cases that piled up, month after month, in this city of angels and demons. Victims left unavenged, criminals left unpunished, justice left unserved because of the one thing every good cop needed that was always in too short a supply.

Time.

A shame about Sarah. He had been fond of her, perhaps

even had been starting to love her. But he had a different perspective on things now. It was for the best, really.

Jake got out of the bed and tore the hospital gown free from his body. They wanted to keep him there for another day to make sure he was all right, but he knew that wouldn't be necessary.

He thought about Darlene and Max, still defenseless against a savage world. There was still little he could do to change the danger they faced day by day, but over the long haul he could make a difference—not just to his wife and son, but to thousands of people. Interesting how taking the long view changed one's priorities. Jake knew he would not be following Max home from school anymore. He had larger responsibilities now.

He would have to learn the rituals that purified and empowered the stakes. That would be difficult, but not impossible. The knowledge was out there somewhere. It wasn't like he was in a hurry.

He glanced out the open window, noticing the fire escape landing that provided access to the alley below.

Unfinished business. . . .

As he dressed, Jake Hull reflected that in all probability he would be asked to resign from the LAPD, even though he had brought the Night Hunter case to a close. That was all right with him. He didn't need the authority of a badge anymore.

All he needed was time.

And a good supply of ash wood stakes.